HEIDI HEILIG

A KINGDOM FOR A STAGE

Greenwillow Books, *an Imprint of* HarperCollins*Publishers*

Content notes: Mental illness (bipolar), blood use in magic, gun violence, war, colonialism, racism, descriptions of dead bodies, mention of reproductive coercion, mentions of torture, mention of suicide

A Kingdom for a Stage
Text copyright © 2019 by Heidi Heilig
Map illustrations copyright © 2019 by Maxime Plasse
Music for "Wings," "Help Me, Brother," and "Till We Meet Again" copyright © 2019 by Mike Pettry; lyrics copyright © 2019 by Heidi Heilig. Reprinted by permission of the authors.

www.epicreads.com

The text of this book is set in Minion Pro. Book design by Sylvie Le Floc'h

Library of Congress Control Number: 2019946965

ISBN 9780062651976 (hardback)

19 20 21 22 23 PC/LSCH 10 9 8 7 6 5 4 3 2 1

First Edition

 Greenwillow Books

To the rebels

CAST OF CHARACTERS

The Chantray Family

Jetta Chantray. *A shadow player and nécromancien.*

Akra Chantray. *Her brother, once a capitaine, now a deserter from the armée.*

Samrin Chantray. *Her adoptive father, whose stage career ended when the Aquitan questioneurs cut off his tongue.*

Meliss Chantray. *Her mother, a flautist and drummer.*

The Chakrans

The Tiger. *The ruthless and mysterious leader of the rebellion.*

The Boy King. *Raik Alendra, the only known survivor of La Victoire, and heir to the throne of Chakrana.*

Leo Rath. *A mixed-race violinist, half brother to Xavier and Theodora Legarde.*

Cheeky Toi. *A showgirl who took refuge with the rebels after the fight at Luda.*

Tia LaLarge. *A singer and impersonator who fled Luda with Cheeky.*

Mei Rath. *Leo's mother, a chanteuse and Julian Legarde's mistress before she died.*

Le Trépas. *The nécromancien who fought the Aquitans, using the souls of his own people.*

The Aquitans

General Xavier Legarde. *The new young leader of the Aquitan armée in Chakrana.*

Theodora Legarde. *Feted as the most beautiful woman in Chakrana, she is also the armée's scientist, and was engaged to the Boy King.*

Lieutenant Armand Pique. *Given a desk job after leading retaliatory attacks against Chakran villagers, he is the most experienced officer left in Chakrana.*

Antoine "Le Fou." *The mad emperor of Aquitan.*

ACT 1

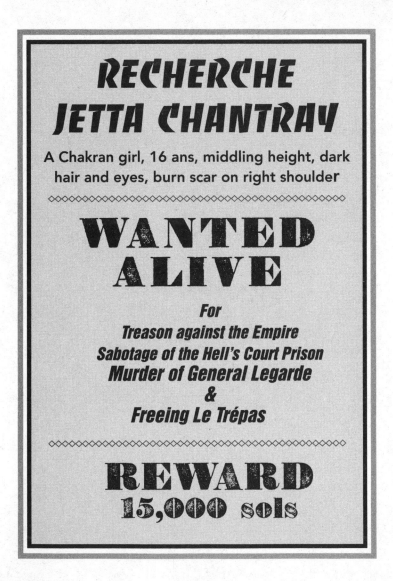

To Jetta of the Ros Nai

We accept your offer. Your skills will be
of great value to the rebellion.
Wait where you are.

||||

CHAPTER ONE

I used to dream of seeing my name on posters all over Nokhor Khat. But those dreams included words like CELEBRATED SHADOW PLAYER and SOLD-OUT PERFORMANCE, rather than WANTED ALIVE.

The flyers are papered all over the city—including the gates, where the armée guards search everyone going in or out for a scar like mine. Papa used to say there was no such thing as bad publicity, but I haven't told him our family name is on a recherche. Though there is a bitter sort of pride in being more infamous than the leader of the rebellion himself. The armée offers just ten thousand sols for the Tiger.

Of course, the rebel leader is only wanted for treason, sabotage, and murder. Freeing Le Trépas was easily worse than all three combined. It's the one crime I'm accused of that I hadn't meant to commit. Despite my malheur, not even I am so insane.

"What are you waiting for?"

I startle at my brother's harsh whisper, looking down at the message I've scribbled on the blank back of the recherche. I have asked much the same question in my note to the Tiger. It's been more than three weeks since I received his letter, and I've grown tired of waiting. Carefully I fold the recherche into the shape of a bird, ready to fly at my bidding. But when Akra holds out his hand, I shake my head. "I still have to put a soul inside."

I speak softly, not wanting to disturb Papa as he sleeps in the dank corner of our little lean-to; he is still healing from General Legarde's torture. But Akra has no trouble hearing me. His lip twists—a smile or a grimace? It's hard to tell with the scar that stitches up his chin. One of many, though none so ugly as the angry knot at the base of his throat. Such a small thing—no bigger than a bullet. But the sight of it is a constant reminder of the way he died—and the way I brought him back. "There must be something dead nearby," he says.

My brother makes a vague gesture around the small room, though he cannot see the little vana buzzing in circles in the air—the souls of mosquitoes—or the arvana of the mice that crawl through our meager provisions. At least I don't think he can. My own brush with death had been the catalyst for my abilities to see spirits, but Akra is reticent to talk about what happened to him at Hell's Court. To be honest, so am I.

The memories haunt me: treason, sabotage, murder. But the recherche doesn't list my worst crime: stopping my brother's spirit on its way to the next life and tucking it back into his broken body. Sometimes I count us lucky that his wounds healed . . . that his heart still beats . . . that he lives again. But then I see the haunted look in his hollow eyes.

"No birds, though," I say aloud. It isn't even a lie. "But it won't take me long to find one. Don't worry, Akra. I'll come right back."

"I'll come with you," he says, standing at the same time I do.

We hesitate before the doorway, half bent under the low roof of the shack. I narrow my eyes, but he doesn't back down. "Why?" I ask.

Now he looks away, glancing out through the crack between the curtain and the doorframe. My palms start to sweat in the silence. Does he know what I'm planning? Akra is leery of the rebels, and they don't like him much either. My brother had been a capitaine in the Aquitan armée until quite recently; his desertion only painted him a traitor to both sides. Even though joining the rebellion is our best chance to escape the city and reunite with Maman, I doubt he'll approve of my plan to get the Tiger's attention. Which is why I need to go alone.

"There's something in the air tonight," he says at last, and I hold my breath on my sigh of relief. "I have a bad feeling, Jetta."

"Come on, Akra." I scoff to mask my own nerves. "You know I'm the most dangerous thing in the slums."

"Not if Le Trépas is out there too."

The name chills me; I do my best to suppress a shiver. In the corner, Papa stirs in his sleep. "If he is, there's nothing either of us can do about it. And what if Papa wakes up and needs help with something?"

"I thought you said we were coming right back."

I fold my arms, but my brother folds his. The words dance on the tip of my tongue: *Stay here.* An order. I bite them back. I may have given him life, but my brother is not just another fantouche for me to control.

"Please," I say instead. "I just need to get some fresh air. Some space. I'm going crazy in here."

The word hangs between us. *Crazy.* Will it work? Akra narrows his eyes, weighing the threat of Le Trépas against the lurking presence of my malheur. At last he steps back with a half bow, gesturing toward the curtain. As I reach for the tattered cloth that hangs over the doorway, Papa stirs again.

"Jetta?"

I turn back, my heart squeezing at the sound of Papa's voice. He doesn't speak these days—at least, not while he's wide-awake. He's too ashamed of the way the words slur and melt in his mouth, of the cloth he has to hold near his chin to catch the saliva. I hadn't heard him say my name in weeks. Not since Legarde's questioneurs cut out his tongue.

Treason. Sabotage. Murder. When the litany makes an endless refrain in my head, I tell myself that General Legarde deserved what he got.

Kneeling beside Papa, I touch his shoulder, trying to ignore the sunken skin under his collarbones. He used to be a barrel-chested man. "Yes?"

Reaching up to grasp my hand, his three fingers slip into mine. His eyes flutter open and he smiles, and that, at least, has not changed. But he doesn't say anything else. I stroke his forehead—blessedly cool—and he closes his eyes again. Still, I can't help but smile back. He said my name. That's progress, right?

I can feel minutes passing, like ants crawling down my arm. Escape is important—the rebellion is important. But not as important as the people I love. So I wait till Papa's breathing grows deep and even before I release his hand. Then I duck under the curtain, avoiding Akra's stare, hoping I haven't delayed too long.

To the leader of the rebellion,

    It has been three weeks.

    You may be content to wait, but I am not.

    Keep an eye on the next supply ship from Aquitan.

I will expect your prompt thanks in person.

Jetta Chantray

CHAPTER TWO

Picking my way toward the meeting place, I run the creases of the letter through my fingers. Bold words for something still undone, but confidence has always been one of the hallmarks of my malheur. My hand falls to the fold of my belt, where the glass bottle makes a rounded shape under the tattered silk. The feel of it comforts me, though there's nothing left inside. Last week I'd gone to half doses, trying to stretch the remaining drops, but they ran out two days ago, with no way to get more. It's too bad. After a month of the treatment, I had only just begun to discover who I might be beneath the pall of my madness.

I wish I'd had a chance to show Leo.

Quickly I push the stray thought out of my head. Leo had fled when he'd seen the worst of me—or of my malheur. No sense in wishing him back for the best. Especially since that had been a limited engagement.

Better to focus on the plan. It's simple enough—isn't it? The supply ships from Aquitan come every few weeks, carrying victuals or uniforms, guns or reinforcements. The last one came just after Hell's Court fell, so another must be on its way. It's easy enough to ensoul a few stones with the souls of turtles and send them to smash the ship's wooden hull. All I need to know is when it will arrive. Souls tire eventually, and they can't wait in the bay forever.

I stick to the shadows, ducking my head against the drizzle. I used to love the rain: the smell of it, the rhythm, the rush and percussion of a song that played the whole rainy season. But that was back in Lak Na, under the snug grass thatch of the cottage I grew up in. Here, in the slapdash colony of sheds and shelters propped precariously along the muddy riverbank, the weather is much harder to enjoy. The dampness is pervasive—the streets run with mud and muck even when the sky is clear, and the breeze from the nearby bay cannot overcome the smell of the waste and sweat of hundreds of refugees.

But despite the thickness of the air, the filthy street glitters gold with the light of the souls. Vana, and arvana too, like drops of flame: the souls of rats, still scurrying in corners as they did in life. Even a few birds perched on the edges of the huts—the ghosts of gulls, looking for trash. They gleam like paper lanterns, like fallen stars. I slip the pin from the hem of my belt, pricking my finger and calling to the nearest gull. As she spreads her wide wings, I marvel . . . not at the eager way she dives into the new flesh of the folded page. But at how bold I've grown, to use forbidden magic on the open stage of the street. Of course, between the armée's curfew and the fear of Le Trépas, I have no audience so late at night.

The letter flutters in my hand as the gull gets used to her new body. Should I send the message now, while the dark can hide her journey out of the city? No, best to wait till the show is over to take a bow. I tuck the letter in my belt, beside the elixir, as I reach the crossroads where I'd arranged to meet the fouilleur. Nothing special—only the intersection of two crooked alleys in the slum. Just like any other, aside from the four parallel ruts dug into the mud of the street.

The sign of the Tiger. I've seen it more and more these

days—slashed into hems or scratched onto walls. I doubt that even half of the people who draw it are committed to the rebellion, but it belies a growing sentiment—if not for the Tiger, then at least against the Aquitans.

But where is the fouilleur? I grimace at the sky; it is already starting to blush. Has he come and gone, leaving the symbol behind to let me know he'd been there?

No—as I wait, he slips soundlessly from the shadows, and I am surprised all over again by how small he is. No older than ten, and short for his age, he reminds me of a rose finch: tiny and sharp-eyed and ready to fly away on a breath. "Good morning," he says, with a wry glance at the lightening sky.

"Is it so late?" I duck my head in a little bow, an apology, and gesture down at myself: bedraggled hair, stained sarong, muddy feet. "I was getting my beauty rest."

He snorts—the closest I've ever seen to a laugh from the boy. Then he holds out his hand. "As long as I get my breakfast."

I drop a few étoiles into his palm, taken from our own small stash. Not that I begrudge the boy his coins. The fouilleurs spend their time finding things to sell and people who can buy, and neither is easy in the slums—especially when what is being brokered is armée information.

But when the coins disappear into his dirty belt, he turns down the path. "Come with me."

I balk at the command. "For what?"

"For the shipping schedule," he says, as though the answer was obvious.

"You can't just tell me?"

"I don't know it," he says. "But I know someone who does."

Wetting my lips, I hesitate—this wasn't the deal. But he already has my coins, and unless I want to hunker down with a spyglass for a long wait, I need to know when the ship is coming. "Who is it?" I say at last, but the boy's eyes glitter.

"No names," he says. His eyes flick to the shawl that covers the scar on my shoulder. "Unless you want to tell me yours first."

I resist the urge to check that my shawl hasn't slipped. Has he guessed who I am? Akra and I had come to the slums for the anonymity—everyone here must be cautious. Though most of the residents claim to be fleeing the crossfire between the armée and the rebellion in the jungle, I'm certain some of the prisoners who escaped Hell's Court have found their way here. Not to mention the Chakran men growing out their short hair and hiding their pale bare feet with mud—men like my brother, who deserted the armée. But no matter where the residents have come from, we have one thing in common: a hatred of the Aquitans.

Even if the boy knew who I was, he wouldn't tell them. Not least because they'd never give a Chakran that kind of reward money.

"No need," I say at last. "Show me the way."

The fouilleur turns, leading me down the twisting streets, mud and worse squelching beneath our feet. The shantytown runs almost to the dock, where boats full of sugar or sapphires used to trade berths almost daily with armée ships full of supplies and soldiers. But the traffic has slowed to a trickle ever since the fire that ended my own bid to escape to Aquitan.

And here, listing on the riverbank amid the ramshackle hovels, is the charred hulk of the boat that would have carried me across the sea. It is battered and burned and stripped of all its finery, but lacquer still gleams on the proud red scales of the dragon head at the prow of *Le Rêve*. The sight of it shames me. I had pushed past a hundred other refugees to climb aboard, none of them less desperate or worthy—only less lucky.

Or so it had seemed at the time.

Now the sad remains of the wreck are caught up in a stand of mangroves, gently rising and falling with the tide. The people in the slums claim it is haunted, but the only soul I see nearby is the fat, lazy spirit of a crocodile on the bank. Still, the rumor leaves the cove deserted: the foullieur and I are alone.

"Where?" I say, scanning the streets for someone waiting in the shadows.

But the boy jerks his chin at the ship. "In there."

Squinting at the broken boat, it takes me another moment to realize that the dim light gleaming from a hole in the hull is not the flickering flame of a spirit, but the clear steady glow of a lamp. I give the boy one last look, but he's already starting back into the slums. The tide is out, so I step from the muddy bank into the fetid bilge. Here, rounded ballast stones rise like skulls out of the murky water. The lamplight shines from a trapdoor above. As I climb the ladder, I feel it—the premonition Akra mentioned. A sense of impending doom. Suddenly I don't feel dangerous at all.

Then a hand reaches down through the hatch, ready to take my own, and by the gesture alone, I know who is waiting above. The curve of his fingers seems meant for the slender neck of a violin.

A wild thought—I can still turn and run. Back to the lean-to, to Akra and Papa, to the safe anonymity of the slum. But then his face appears in the frame of the hatch, and his lips move, and though I can read my name on them, all I hear Leo saying is "Au revoir."

Le Petit Phare

*Nokhor Khat * Jeudi le 15 Octobre 1874 **   *Prix deux étoiles*

THE SEARCH CONTINUES FOR THE BOY KING

Raik Alendra, the only remaining heir to the throne of Chakrana, is still missing. Reports claim the rebel kidnapping was a plot to prevent his marriage to his beloved fiancée, renowned beauty Theodora Legarde, in the hopes of destabilizing the strong union between Aquitan and Chakrana. But rumors hint that the Tiger covets the throne himself. Some fear the rebel leader has already disposed of the rightful king, while others claim he is being held against his will in appalling conditions deep in the jungle. . . .

continued

LE TRÉPAS STILL AT LARGE

The mad monk who once sought control of all Chakrana remains on the loose after rebel forces freed him last month. In the wake of General Legarde's murder, his son, Xavier Legarde, has stepped forward to protect the country from his father's old foe. But this time, Le Trépas is not working alone. Rumors speak of another nécromancien at large, and his revenants—the corpses of the dead, revived—have been spotted lurking in the jungle.

REBELS ROUTED IN LA SUCRIER

Equipped with superior numbers and weaponry, armée forces routed a rebel stronghold near the town of Sekat. The guerilla fighters are unsuited to facing a head-on challenge, and quick work was made of the enemy by our brave soldiers. However, the armée remains on the alert against the Tiger's sabotage, and all citizens—Chakran and Aquitan alike—are asked to stay vigilant.

CHAPTER
THREE

I hadn't seen Leo since that night at Hell's Court—at least, not outside my dreams. But now, face-to-face with the boy who fled from me, I wish it had been Le Trépas instead. He at least could not judge my many crimes. I take a breath, steadying my voice. "What are you doing here?"

Leo peers down at me through the open hatch, his face framed by the dark halo of his hair. Is he paler than he was a month ago? Perhaps it's just a trick of the light—or the Aquitan side of his mixed heritage. What does he see, looking at me? I already know: bedraggled hair, stained sarong, muddy feet. "I should never have left in the first place," he says.

His words take my breath away. How many times had I told him so in the weeks since he'd left, in the silence of my own mind? But coming from him, they sound hollow. "Why did you?" I ask, hoping that his answer will surprise me.

It doesn't. "After what happened in Hell's Court—"

I raise my hand to cut him off—the reminder itself is too painful for both of us. Treason. Sabotage. Murder. Just because General Legarde deserved what he got didn't mean that Leo deserved to watch me do it. "I shouldn't blame you for being afraid of me," I say at last, more for myself than for him. "I know what I am. What I've done. And so do you."

Leo hesitates, his hand still hovering in the open hatch. "I was afraid," he says softly. "But not of you."

I do not take his hand. "What's worse than me?"

"Everything that isn't." His answer is immediate, but unconvincing.

"You ran, Leo."

"Au revoir means 'Till we meet again.' Not goodbye." I take a step down the ladder, but his hand darts out to catch my wrist. "I needed time!" he adds quickly. The heat of his skin sears mine. "I've lost so many people I . . . I care for.

I thought it might be easier if I left first this time. I was wrong."

I stare up into his haunted eyes. What spirits does he see? His father, the general, dead by my hand? Or his maman with her malheur, dead by her own? Even Eve, one of the girls at his old theater, lost in the fight that erupted after we left Luda. "I would never have abandoned you, Leo."

"Not on purpose," he says. "But in war, anything can happen. Please come up."

I hesitate on the ladder. "Give me one good reason."

Leo bites his lip, considering. "How about four?"

Confused, I cock my head, but he curls his thumb against his palm, making claws of his four fingers and drawing them gently from my elbow to my wrist. My breath catches in my throat as understanding dawns. "The Tiger sent you?"

Leo pulls his hand back. "He did."

"Then he's just as cruel as they say," I mutter. I know I shouldn't blame Leo for leaving, but I do anyway.

Even so, I reach for the next rung and climb up through the hatch. The belly of the ship was made for storage; Leo's lantern rests on the remains of a wooden crate. There are many such boxes scattered across the deck, most pried open by scavengers, others smashed to kindling. Detritus litters the floor, and glass glitters in the low light. Gingerly, I step off the ladder, careful of my bare toes, but Leo sheds his linen jacket and spreads it on the splintered deck.

Giving him a look, I tread on it with my muddy feet. "You took your time."

"It isn't easy figuring out how to get you where you need to go." Leo's voice carries a hint of reproach as he reaches for a satchel set beside the lamp. "Especially with the recherche."

"Fair enough." I watch as he digs through the bag, pulling out a bundle of canvas and a pair of leather gloves. "What are those for?"

"A disguise," he says, handing over the gloves. They are soft as velvet, finely stitched. Raising an eyebrow, I slip them on. I have never owned a pair of gloves, and a set so exquisite is not meant for working hands. Nor for Chakran weather.

"What am I disguised as?" I ask, flexing my fingers, marveling at the leatherwork. "Someone with money?"

"People stare at the rich," Leo says, holding out the bundle of canvas. "But everyone avoids looking at a madwoman."

From anyone else, the word would sting. But in Leo's

mouth, it is not an insult. "Some disguise," I say wryly. But when I shake out the bundle, the blood drains from my face. "What is this?"

"A carcan," he says. There is an apology in his eyes. "A straitjacket."

"A *what*?" My voice rises an octave as I stare at the thing: long sleeves, leather straps.

"It will hide the scar on your shoulder," he says quickly. "Anyone who sees us will think you're just another run-of-the-mill criminal on the way to the prison ship. Trust me, Jetta, please." He takes my hand again, cutting short the protests building in my throat.

I meet his eyes . . . they are so earnest. Leo *had* abandoned me—but he had come back. Perhaps that is the part that's most important. And I have to admit, it seems like a good plan. Slowly I slip one arm into the canvas sleeve, followed by the other, crossing my arms over my belly so he can close the dangling straps behind me. "What about Papa and Akra?" I say over my shoulder. "Do you have carcans for them too?"

Leo finishes with the buckles before he answers. Then, very gently, he wraps his fingers around my wrist and squeezes gently through the canvas. "Jetta," he says carefully, his voice pitched to carry. "Your papa died of his wounds weeks ago."

The words take a moment to make sense. "What?"

"And your brother fled the city," Leo says, squeezing my wrist again. "To avoid being shot as a deserter."

"What are you talking about?" I wrench my arm out of his grip. My shoulders flex—almost involuntarily—straining against the carcan. For the first time in weeks, I feel insane. "My family would never abandon me like you did."

"It's the elixir, isn't it?" he says sadly. "You must be out by now."

For a moment I falter, as though the deck has given way beneath me. I have hallucinated before, though never anything so elaborate. But something about Leo's expression gives me pause—a flick of his eyes, almost imperceptible. And why had he squeezed my wrist? I frown, but before I can say more, another sound brings me up short. Quieter than Leo's voice, but almost as familiar: the soft snick of a cocked gun. My heart sinks as I turn to face the soldier creeping up behind me.

As he steps from the shadows behind the broken crates, I recognize this man too. Leo's half-brother—the general's older son, Xavier, the only son Legarde acknowledged as his own. He's thinner than he was back in Luda, like a well-loved knife, whetted daily. There is something different about his stance as well, as though his right leg is even stiffer than his spine. But his face is familiar twice over; he looks so much like his father—especially holding the gun. My fists clench inside the carcan, the leather gloves creaking. It wasn't the Tiger who sent Leo after all. "Capitaine Legarde," I say through my teeth.

"General, now." On one shoulder, new epaulets gleam. "I was recently promoted."

Unbidden, guilt wells up; I hide it with a scoff. "Did you come to thank me?"

Rage flashes quick as lightning in his ghost-blue eyes—for a moment, I see my death in them. But he only takes a deep breath, raising his fingertips to the gold medallion at his throat: the symbol of the Aquitan god. "I came to save you," he says. "To save all of us in this godforsaken country. Turn around."

He gestures with the gun, and I hesitate. Would I rather be shot in the back than see the bullet coming? My heart hammers against the canvas of the carcan as Leo tugs sharply at the buckles at the small of my back. "She's secure,

Xavi," he says. "You can put your gun away."

Xavier ignores him, but I can't. "How could you?" I say through my teeth, but Xavier is the one who replies.

"Leonin finally decided that blood is thicker than water," he says. "Turn around."

I tense my back at the command, unwilling to comply, but Leo takes my shoulders gently, spinning me to look him in the eye. Behind me, Xavier checks the straps himself. "We only want to ask you some questions," Leo says quietly.

Panic rises in my throat like bile at the memory of Papa's broken bones, his stumped tongue. "I've seen what the armée's questioneurs can do."

"The questioneurs have been reassigned," he says quickly.

"Then who?"

"You're meant to answer questions, not ask them." Xavier tucks his gun in his belt and slides his hands along my waist. Trapped as I am by the carcan, his touch makes me want to scream, to lash out. But with Xavier distracted, Leo's lips move again.

"*Trust me.*"

I narrow my eyes, but before I can respond, the general's hand stops at the curve of the bottle. "A weapon?"

"It's only my elixir." Cringing, I curl away from him, trying to protect the flask. It may be empty, but I want it anyway.

"Ah yes." The general's voice is carefully quiet. "The drink you killed my father for."

"That's not what happened—"

He cuts me off by yanking the straps of the jacket. "I hear it's supposed to keep you sane," he says, his hand worming up under the hem and dipping into the fold of my belt. "Easier to keep you in the carcan, though."

Rage flares in my chest as Xavier's fingers close over the neck of the bottle. I slam my head backward, connecting with his face. Pain bursts on the back of my skull. The general swears, reeling, pulling the bottle out of my belt. The recherche comes with it—my plans for sabotage, ensouled with forbidden magic. I bite off a curse. "Fly!"

At my command, the letter lifts into the air, but Xavier is quick enough to snatch it in his fist. "What's this?"

"It's nothing!"

The young general spits blood onto the deck as he watches the message flutter frantically in his grasp. "Is it so little to you?" he says, half in awe, half appalled. "This crime against God and nature?"

I shift on my feet, glancing at the medallion he wears. "I don't know your Aquitan god."

"Maybe you will someday." Xavier smiles; there is blood on his teeth. "He rose from the dead too, did you know that? But his flesh was uncorrupted. Whatever you do in Chakrana, it has more to do with hell than heaven." The general spits again, stuffing the fantouche into his pocket. The bottle he tosses over his shoulder, as though it means nothing. It shatters in the corner, just another handful of broken glass. Then he jerks his chin toward the hatch. "Allez."

I glare at the general through the dark curtain of my hair. My heart flutters like the soul of a bird; sweat makes the leather of the gloves tighten around my fingers. But I can still feel the soft pressure of Leo's hand on my wrist . . . hear the echo of his unspoken words. *Trust me.*

Despite everything, I still do.

So I clench my jaw and take a deep breath through my nose. Then I toss my hair out of my face as best I can. "Are you carrying me down the ladder, General? Or are you going to lie down in the bilge and pad my landing?"

"I'll carry you," Leo says before the general can respond. "Xavi, can you put out the lantern? The slums are a tinderbox." He scoops me up, slinging me over his shoulder; I fold there like a costume, the carcan drawing tight. "Your elbows," he complains as he starts down.

"Your plan," I reply through my teeth.

Leo only grunts as he hauls me outside, where the surface of the water shines pink and silver as the sun reaches toward the dawn. The souls of minnows scatter before us as he wades toward the shore. Leo sets me down on the muddy bank so we can both catch our breath. I glance at him, hoping for an explanation, but he only turns toward the ship as his brother climbs through the hole in the hull. The general's gun is back in his hand.

As Xavier splashes his way toward us, movement catches my eye down the bank: a dark shape, crouching in the reeds. Sudden relief floods in when I recognize my brother—he hasn't fled the city after all. But my heart skips a beat when I see the silvery light reflecting from the machete in his hands.

"Don't!" The word slips out before I can bite it back. The general whirls at my shout, searching the shadows, but Akra stays hidden, unmoving—no. Unable to move. My stomach churns. I had promised him I wouldn't treat him like a puppet. That I wouldn't give him orders. But better a broken promise than another bullet. After all, Akra is a deserter. His recherche says to shoot on sight.

"What did you see?" Xavier's gun is still high as he scans the dark water.

"Just a shadow," I lie. Deliberately, I turn away from where Akra lurks and trudge up the bank, the Legarde brothers trailing behind me. Best to let Akra know where I'm going, though. "Where are you taking me?" I say, louder than I have to.

Will it be the barracks at the fort? The prison ship in the harbor? But Xavier's answer brings bile to my throat. "Hell's Court."

My dear nephew Xavier Legarde,

Words cannot convey to you the depths of my condolences. Your father's death was a heavy blow to all of us. Alas, it was also a blow to the war effort.

Sentiment at home has turned against the occupation of Chakrana. The fight has dragged on for decades. With the rebellion only growing, the Aquitan people fear there is no end in sight. Just last week, a riot broke out and a conscription officer was shot. The papers have gone so far as to print an anonymous essay claiming that the rumors of nécromancy are true—and that if reinforcements are needed, they should be recruited from the dead!

Instead of sending men, we shall focus our efforts on your sister's work. Your father's last letter to me included a schematic for the machine she invented—the one he claimed took flight. Rumor has run wild with that too, and the populace is agog with the possibilities. And though my own scientists tell me her calculations are impossible, I have every faith in her. And in you, of course. I am certain that together you will be able to strike a blow decisive enough to change public opinion. Indeed, you must, for in the wake of the general's death, you are now in charge.

I know you are young, but your father always hoped you would take his place when he retired. You have prepared for this all your life, and you have my full confidence.

Your uncle,

Antoine Le Fou

Roi des Aquitains

CHAPTER FOUR

"**H**ell's Court?" Treason . . . sabotage . . . murder. The carcan seems to tighten as my breath comes fast and shallow. The scent of blood fills my nose—a hallucination, or a memory? "I'm not going back there."

"It's not the same as when you left," Leo says. Is he trying to reassure me? "My sister has taken the space for her work."

"Your sister?"

The general misreads my question. "The armée scientist."

"I know." I take another deep breath, and another, until all I can smell is rain and mud. The identity of the armée scientist had become something of an open secret since her marriage to the Boy King had been indefinitely delayed. The papers praise every new invention, but these, at least, are not mere propaganda. In the last month, I've seen the repeating rifles she designed slung over every soldier's shoulder as they patrol the streets of Nokhor Khat. The slums shake and rattle with the boom of shells launched into the bay as the armée tests the new artillerie at the fort. And of course, there was the half-built flying machine I'd stolen from her workshop—thankfully I'd sent the rest of them up in flames before she could give the armée a prototype that worked without a soul inside.

But Theodora's genius is not limited to the making of war. The elixir I'd been taking to treat my malheur was her invention too.

Might there be more where that came from?

I glance at Leo, but with Xavier standing between us, his face is carefully neutral. Is controlling my malheur more important to him than helping the rebellion?

Xavier pushes me forward again. "You must also know that Theodora's former workshop was destroyed."

"I do." Another crime for my recherche. "But what does she want with me?"

"I've told you," Xavier replies. "Questions."

His answer is less than helpful, but as I walk, I make my own guesses. It will be the same question all audiences have after seeing one of my shadow plays, where my fantouches seem to dance without stick or string: how do you do it? Unfortunately, the usual lies will not work. Theodora had already seen behind the curtain. Will she ask me to ensoul a new flying machine? I'm almost sure of it. Though she might change her mind when she realizes my fantouches follow my orders alone.

The thought brings a bitter sort of satisfaction. The feeling fades quickly as we approach the temple and the street turns familiar in the way of a childhood nightmare. How I wish that night was only a dream! Xavier claims my powers are a crime against god and nature, but Hell's Court was the first time I had felt that way. Dread coils in my stomach like a snake. I doubt the King of Death will look kindly on my return to a temple I so nearly destroyed. Then again, the god himself might have fled long ago, when Le Trépas desecrated the holy place.

I wish I could flee too. But I have little chance as Xavier and Leo march me down the street. The black arch of the entry is guarded by four soldiers, all of them Aquitan. Is it because the armée does not trust Chakran soldiers after my brother's defection? Or because a local soldat would rather defect than linger so close to this cursed place? The white men salute their general, dragging aside the hastily erected bamboo arm that sags across the wide road. It takes all my will to walk past them, but the dark temple that looms in my nightmares is not the one at the end of the path.

When I fled Hell's Court, the granite walls of the prison had been tumbling down around me: pillars cracking like rotten teeth, and the old stone god crumbling under the strength of the soul trapped inside it. In the weeks since, the rubble has been cleared and a new roof erected: a scaffold of bamboo, covered in canvas dyed armée green. And instead of the dim flickering light of torches, the clear gleam of electricity makes the massive tent glow in the gray murk of the rainy dawn.

There are more Aquitan guards stationed at the entry, though they step aside at the general's gesture. The interior of the prison—no, the workshop—is even more changed. The smell of filth and unwashed bodies has been seared away by the oily scent of chemicals; instead of the cries of prisoners, the soft hum of a generator fills the air. Scattered across the floor of the sanctuary like offerings to the old god are piles of crates: munitions, guns, fuel. But in the middle of it all, there is an empty space, as impossible to ignore as a missing tooth. The god himself—or rather, the stone idol—is gone.

Once, the statue stood as tall as the roof of the temple: a paean to the King of Death, and to the people who worshipped him enough to carve such a massive offering from granite. Now, all that remains is the platform on which it stood. Where are the pieces? Has Legarde's soul gone with them? Was his spirit carted away with the gravel and tossed into a pothole on a crooked street? Or did the stone I trapped him in crumble into dust so fine that he was able to escape—to go on to his next life, or his jealous God, or wherever Aquitan souls go? I doubt I'll ever know.

But, thinking of Papa, I hope Legarde is just as trapped as I now am.

I am so busy comparing my memory of Hell's Court to the new reality that it takes me a moment to notice what hasn't changed: the souls—or rather, the lack of them. Temples usually glow brightly with spirits, all come to wait for their rebirth. Here, the only light comes from the glass bulbs. Not a single vana drifts through the air. When I was last in this place, I thought it was Le Trépas's presence that scared them away. Does his effect still linger, even after his escape? Was the man so evil that his repellence seeped into the stone?

Will souls eventually fear me in the same way?

The lack of souls only adds to my discomfort. Even Leo seems subdued, but Xavier doesn't falter. Of course not—he believes in another god. Unflinching, he marches me to the altar. It takes me a moment to recognize it, for the carved black stone is half hidden by a huge wooden trunk beside it, and both are covered with a veritable wealth of paper and books. Sitting before the makeshift desk is a familiar figure. Is she up early, or late? But despite the hour, and the drab canvas coveralls that hide the curve of her famed belly, Theodora Legarde is still stunning.

La Fleur, they call her: the most beautiful woman in Chakrana. And they would have called her queen, if the Boy King hadn't fled. Her red lips are pursed in concentration; the electric light gleams gold in her blond curls. The dimples of her plump wrists flash as she taps a pen against the paper. As we approach, she glances up from her work to my face— no, to the carcan. My cheeks flush.

"So they found you after all," she says. A wry smile reveals her white teeth. "Welcome to my new workshop. Try not to destroy it."

Does she think she can shame me? I raise my chin, ignoring the disparity in our dress. "Try not to deserve it."

Her eyes widen. Then, to my surprise, she laughs. "I suppose the thatch was a mistake with all the fuel I kept about," she says, as though I am impugning the design of her last workshop rather than the war machines she'd been building inside it. She pats the altar with one manicured hand. "Stone is more durable. Then again," she adds, cocking her head. "I never needed all that fuel, did I?"

Her look is pointed, and I understand her meaning. But I'm not about to make it easy. "How should I know? I'm not a scientist."

"No," Xavier says. I can feel his stare like a boot on the back of my neck as he holds up the note I'd ensouled. "You're a nécromancien."

The word echoes in the sanctuary. Weeks ago, the accusation would have made me shudder, but there's no denying it. Not when he holds the evidence in his hand. "Sounds like you should update my recherche."

The general takes a quick breath, but before he can respond, Leo interjects. "That would have been a good way to get you shot on sight," he says. "You're wanted alive, no matter how Xavier glares."

"It's natural for your people to associate nécromancy with Le Trépas and his atrocities," the general says, cutting Leo a look. "But we want to give you a chance to prove better than your blood."

My eyebrows shoot up. "Interesting idea, General *Legarde*."

Xavier opens his mouth to respond, but Theodora puts a hand on his arm—the gentlest warning. "Say what you will about our father," she says softly, holding my gaze. "But he saved this country from yours."

"That man is not my father." My response is immediate, though her words send me reeling. It's a hollow claim to them. I know it is. How can they understand what it means to have a father who chose you? My heart squeezes—is Papa awake by now? Has Akra told him what happened?

Xavier smirks, but Theodora lets it go. "Then you should have no problem helping our cause," she says.

"You mean stealing the throne," I say. "That was your father's intention, anyway."

"With the Boy King missing and Le Trépas in the shadows, we're less concerned with stealing the throne than protecting it," she says.

Leo makes a face. "And with the rebel forces growing, we need all the help we can get."

The general barks at him. "Leonin!"

"Desolée, Xavi," he says quickly. "I'm sorry. But it's true."

"It's classified!"

"Bien, of course. Desolée." Leo lowers his eyes, though I don't for a moment think he's ashamed. The rebel forces growing . . . the armée is on shakier footing than the newspapers suggest. That must be why I'm here—no. That must be why Xavier and Theodora want me here.

What about Leo?

When I glance at him, he's looking back at me, but I can't exactly ask him now. Instead, I give the general my most infuriating smile. "You want me help you guard the throne with the magic your own father suppressed? I'm sorry," I say, not sorry at all. "But the old ways are forbidden."

"Would you prefer Le Trépas bring them back?" Xavier steps closer, and the look on his face wipes the smile from my own. "When your priests fought your princes for power, it was your people who suffered. People like your mother. Or all your half-brothers and half-sisters, born and buried and raised as evil things. That is what my father suppressed."

"The suffering didn't stop when Legarde took power," I say, trying to keep my voice from shaking. "The armée has killed far more Chakrans than Le Trépas ever did. Give me some of your war machines, if you like. Just keep in mind that what I create, I control."

Xavier glances at Theodora; what is the look that passes between them? Leo frowns too. "I told you it wasn't so easy," he says, but Xavier grimaces.

"War is never easy, Leonin."

"Neither is discovery," Theodora says quietly—the silk to Xavier's steel. "Fighting is not the only way to help protect the country, Jetta. I've studied what I can about nécromancy. Not just the interviews or the old reports. But the songs and the legends about the old ways. You probably know quite a few of those," she adds with a little smile. "Considering you were also a shadow player. But you have something I don't have."

"What is that?"

"Practical experience." The answer comes from Xavier. "And that's what counts, with the enemy."

I cock my head, trying to understand. "You want me to teach you about nécromancy?"

"As much as you know. After all, knowledge is power." Theodora gestures at the papers spread on the altar. Armée interviews and old reports . . . the knowledge the Aquitans had kept from my own people.

"It is," I say, staring at the papers. If La Fleur has been studying nécromancy, it's possible she knows more than I do. The thought is galling. But is this my chance to learn?

My heart quickens. Is *that* why Leo brought me? After all, the rebellion will make best use of my skills if I know the extent of them. Deliberately, I avoid looking at him; out of the corner of my eye, I can tell he's doing the same. "I'll help you," I say slowly, as though I'm still considering it. Best not too seem too eager. "If you help me."

To my surprise, Xavier laughs. "You need a bribe to protect your country? The more time I spend with you people, the more I understand the cliché of Chakran avarice."

Is Leo gritting his teeth as hard as I am? Only half as hard, perhaps. Before either of us can protest, La Fleur holds up her hand. "What is it you want, Jetta?"

"The elixir," I say.

"Is that all?" she replies. "I was going to make that a prerequisite of your staying. Where did I put that flask?"

"A prerequisite?" The thought hurts—as though I cannot be trusted any other way. But how can I protest, standing here in the ruins of my last outburst?

"I know the bottle you got from my father had a month's

worth. . . ." La Fleur rummages through the papers on her desk. The pages shift like mudslides. At last she unearths a curved metal bottle. The flask gleams dully in the light from the electric bulbs—the shine is gone in more ways than one. "This bottle contains about half that much, though I'm happy to refill it as we go. Your last dose must have been a week ago, is that right?"

"Only a couple of days." When she raises an eyebrow, I elaborate. "When I ran low, I started taking smaller doses."

"That might have saved you the worst of it," she says. "Still, while you're here, be sure you don't miss any."

Even in the humid cocoon of the carcan, her words chill me. "What do you mean, the worst of it?"

"My father didn't tell you?" She lifts a brow. "The immediate effects of stopping the treatment can be worse than never starting it in the first place."

The words take a moment to sink in, but when they do, they drop all the way down, through my gut, to my knees, leaving them weak. "Effects?"

"The mania worsens for a while. The melancholy too. My uncle stopped his treatment once, thinking he was cured. Two weeks later, the servants caught him trying to hang himself." At her words, Leo tenses. His sister notices, softening her tone. "It won't take more than a few days for the elixir to build up in your blood. But in the meantime, tell me if you have any concerning thoughts."

Is that pity on her face? Anger rises like bile. Would I have started the treatment if I'd known? I don't know, I don't know. This complicates matters—surely I'm not going to stay at Hell's Court forever. But what will happen when it comes time to leave? It isn't only nécromancy I'll need to learn about while I'm here. Is the formula for the elixir somewhere in Theodora's pile of papers?

A soft voice interrupts my thoughts, making all of us turn. "Pardon me, Miss Theodora."

"Camreon!" She straightens up, blinking rapidly at the worker—another Chakran, I'm pleased to see. He has stepped so softly in his armée boots that I hadn't noticed him coming. Or is it his deferential posture that let him sneak up on us? He bobs his head at Theodora, almost obsequious, and my initial joy twists into disgust. But of course any Chakran still employed by the armée would need to keep his head down. Especially in this cursed place.

"I'm sorry to interrupt," he murmurs, bowing even lower than respect would dictate. Then he waves a hand toward the archway, where two soldiers look on. "But you and the general are expected at the palace soon."

"Already?" Theodora hesitates, as though she wants to argue, but Xavier nods.

"The advisers will be eager for an update, no?"

"You have good news to share," Leo says. Then he plucks the flask out of Theodora's hand. "In the meantime, I'll get Jetta settled into her room."

"Her room?" The general laughs, without humor. "You must mean her cell. You had the right idea about the prison ship—"

"She's not a prisoner, Xavier."

"She's not a guest, either!"

"That what it's like in the armée, ness pas?" Leo's smile is brief; I recognize the look in his eye. He's talking fast now, trying to broker his deal. "She should stay here, with the rest of the corps of engineers. Makes it easier for Theodora to work, considering her schedule."

"Leonin . . ." Xavier takes a breath, but now I know my role.

"Stay here? In Hell's Court?" I put a tremor in my voice. "No. Take me to the prison ship instead."

"I don't think a ship full of dying men is the best place for a nécromancien," Leo says pointedly. "There's a bed made up for you on the west hall. Have you slept at all recently? I won't even ask if you've bathed."

Though his touch is gentle when he pushes me forward, I stumble as though he had shoved me—the general deserves a show. "If I'd known you were coming, I could have prepared," I say over my shoulder.

"With a nicer dress?" Leo smirks.

"With a better hiding place."

Leo opens his mouth to retort, but Xavier interrupts. "Arret! Wait."

It's barely imperceptible—the way Leo stiffens. I too hide my disappointment. We have nearly reached the relative privacy of the hall, and there are a hundred questions trapped under my tongue. I bite them back as Xavier approaches. The smile Leo gives him is casual. "Don't you have somewhere more important to be?"

"There is nothing more important than being my brother's keeper," Xavier replies. "I know you have our father's weakness for a pretty face."

"Ah yes." Leo's smile remains, but I know him well enough to see the tension of his jaw. "Too bad I never inherited my mother's love for men in uniform."

"I hope the girl doesn't mind soldiers," Xavier says,

jerking his chin at me. "There will be two stationed outside her door. Why don't you go, Leonin? I can handle her myself."

"Bien," Leo says, as if it doesn't matter, though the smile is more of a grimace now. And indeed, the two men who had been waiting at the archway have joined us in the hall at the general's gesture. Leo only passes Xavier the bottle of elixir and makes a little bow. "Au revoir."

The words echo in my memory—as does his defense. Not goodbye. *Until we meet again.*

I follow Xavier through Hell's Court in prickly silence.

It was the east side of the temple that had borne the brunt of the destruction; here in the west, the rooms that line the passageway are mostly intact. Originally, they had been monks' chambers, but after La Victoire, when the temple was converted to a prison, they had been used as offices for guards and questioneurs. Now they house Theodora's various workers: engineers, chemists, machinists. All of them Aquitan, aside from the one I'd seen earlier. But that's no surprise, here in Hell's Court.

Most of the heavy teak doors are still shut this early, but a few stand ajar. In them, I catch glimpses of clean beds, drafting tables, even books. One of the occupants, seated at a desk, catches my gaze, staring back with frank curiosity. His blue eyes make me shudder.

Midway down the hall, we find it: an empty room. Unlived in. But it seems cozy at first glance. There is a soft bed on a low stone platform, a gauzy mosquito net, a little table with a pitcher of water and a washcloth—even a lamp and a book of armée matches. Best of all, some fresh clothing: a set of green coveralls of the sort La Fleur was wearing. Simple things, but a luxury after weeks in the slum—I am excruciatingly aware of the dust and oil that coat my brow, of the greasy coils of my tangled hair. Still, I hesitate on the threshold. "Can you take the carcan off, please?"

Xavier puts his hand over the buckles at the small of my back. "Get in first."

"In?" I swallow. "To the cell?"

"To the *room* my brother prepared, with so much foresight."

I wet my lips; my mouth is so dry. The last time I'd entered one of these cells, it was as a prisoner. Despite the recent homey touches, the room is still small and square and made of stone, with a window too small to fit through and a teak door thicker than my wrist.

Steeling myself, I take a deep breath, but suddenly the air is thick with the smell of filth and decay; for a brief moment, the silence cracks with the sound of a stranger screaming. Sweat prickles my skin . . . I clench my gloved fists—but my next panicked breath is clear and fresh, and as soon as it started, the screaming had stopped. I glance at the general out of the corner of my eye. By the quizzical look on his face, I can tell the sounds and smells are only in my head.

"The elixir," I say, my voice trembling. "Please."

Grimacing, he unscrews the cap, as though the request is distasteful. Shame blooms in my chest as he holds the bottle to my lips. I drink, but the general's look makes me feel exposed, and I have to fight the urge to spit the treatment back in his face.

I swallow it down with my anger as he puts the cap back on the elixir and sets it down by the pillow. Just where his brother put it the first time—along with the note. Au revoir. He had signed it Leo Rath Legarde—his Chakran mother's last name, and the name he shares with Xavier. Suddenly, doubt pools in my chest. If I'm hallucinating smells and screaming, can I trust the signals I think Leo has been sending? His relationship with his father was complicated at best. Is the truth that the old general's death pushed him back toward his family? "When did Leo come to you?"

"Quiet, cha."

The slur takes me aback. "Do you call your brother the same thing?"

"You're not the only one trying to be better than your blood. Get in," he adds, shoving me into the room, and when I stumble, it is not an act.

But as I catch my footing, my stomach twists. I turn back toward the doorway as the soldiers take up positions on either side of it. When Xavier raises a hand to the slam the door shut, I can't help it. "Leave it open!" My voice is so loud in the enclosed space. I take a breath, trying to slow my heart. "Please."

His blue eyes narrow, and for a moment, I'm sure he'll close it, just to be cruel. But the general lowers his hand to brush the necklace he wears. Is his god a merciful one?

"I'll send someone with a meal," he says. Then he turns crisply on his heel, his footfalls echoing as he walks down the hall, and I am alone but for the soldiers outside and the ghosts in my head.

ACT 1,
SCENE 5

The sanctuary. THEODORA is at her desk, making notes. XAVIER enters, then stops when he sees her, surprised.

XAVIER: I told you to go without me.

THEODORA: The advisers won't talk to me if you aren't there. You know they don't think I can make any real decisions.

The general shakes his head, annoyed.

XAVIER: They'll treat you with more respect when you're queen—

THEODORA: Do you really think so?

XAVIER: Because you'll have the power to dismiss them if they don't.

La Fleur gives a wry smile.

THEODORA: That's true. To be honest, it's the Chakrans I'm more worried about.

XAVIER: Me too. Though possibly for different reasons.

THEODORA tosses down her pen and cracks her knuckles. She stands, falling in beside XAVIER. Side by side, they walk through the sanctuary, down the wide steps and across the plaza.

THEODORA: It all comes down to legitimacy. Without a marriage to the last living heir, my claim to the throne is spurious. The rebels did their best to make Raik's disappearance look like an armée attempt to assassinate him. It doesn't help that our father did in fact want him dead. Now, even if he's still willing to marry, the Tiger can easily claim he was coerced, and the fight would never end. This is why I keep pushing for capital improvements. Roads. Hospitals. Schools—
XAVIER: Save it for the advisers.

The general sighs as they wind through the garden that sprawls between the temple and the palace.

What we really need to end the fight is a decisive blow. Like our uncle said.

La Fleur makes a face.

THEODORA: If you want an armée of walking corpses, we could start right away.

XAVIER's hand goes to the medallion he wears.

XAVIER: None of my men would accept such an abomination. Nor would I. But I have hope that the girl's powers could be different.
THEODORA: You sound unsure.
XAVIER: Of course I am. The things she does are unnatural. But it's possible that God brought her to us for a reason.

THEODORA gives him a wistful smile.

THEODORA: Leo certainly did. Though of course it was a different reason.

XAVIER grimaces.

XAVIER: You act like it's romantic. But she's dangerous, Theodora.

THEODORA: To be honest, I wasn't certain Leo would actually bring her in.

XAVIER gives her a sharp glance.

XAVIER: You don't trust him?
THEODORA: He's our brother, Xavi. Of course I do. But it's like you said. She's a nécromancien. She might have found a way to escape from him.
XAVIER: Our father defeated Le Trépas with a gun.
THEODORA: Leo is capable of many things, but I can't imagine him shooting someone he loves.

XAVIER's lip curls.

XAVIER: I suppose that's why he asked me along.
THEODORA: I thought you went along because you didn't trust him.
XAVIER: Well. Don't you wonder what he was doing in the time between our father's death and the day he showed up at your door?

THEODORA shudders delicately.

THEODORA: Frankly, no. I'm the one who saw him first, remember? I think he must have spent the whole two weeks drinking.

XAVIER: I can't help but feel there's something he's not telling us.

The young general glances back over his shoulder, but the temple has disappeared behind the leafy green of the garden.

Where is he now, anyway?

THEODORA: I sent him to the workshop to pack ammunition.

XAVIER: Is it wise to give him free run of the place?

THEODORA: You may want to act as his keeper, but I'm too busy for that. Besides, we're shorthanded.

XAVIER: That's exactly why you have to be wary of how it looks. Everyone is on edge around cha—around Chakrans these days. Desertion is on the rise, and morale is low enough after the letter from our dear uncle.

THEODORA raises an eyebrow at his tone.

THEODORA: The letter where he pledges you his full confidence?

XAVIER: And nothing else! Read between the lines, Theodora. He didn't put me in charge for the glory. He set me up to fail.

A beat.

THEODORA: You'll prove him wrong.

XAVIER: I'll prove our father right. No matter what it takes.

His voice breaks on the last word. XAVIER stops short, his jaw tight, his hand going to the symbol he wears at his neck. He takes a deep breath, then another, before he speaks again. The words are very soft.

I wish he was still here.

Reaching out, THEODORA puts her own hand on her brother's shoulder.

THEODORA: You have me, Xavi.

He smiles briefly, touching her hand before dropping his own back to his side.

XAVIER: And thank God for that.

They continue through the garden toward the palace. Clouds of white jasmine flutter softly as they pass.

CHAPTER
SIX

Even with the door open, the cell is too small. Or is it only the carcan? I contort my arms, trying to stretch the seams, but if anything, the jacket only feels tighter when I stop. Blood pounds in my ears. I rest for a moment on the edge of the bed before trying again. The longer I wrestle with the garment, the angrier I get. But the carcan is not the worst of it—nor even the cell. After so long spent seeking it, it is the elixir that frustrates me.

How could I dose myself daily without considering what would happen when I stopped? I should have known that nothing the Aquitans offered came without a price.

Then again, I could hardly do worse than I had without the treatment. Treason, sabotage, murder. My brother's soul pulled back into his clammy skin. The memories are a plague. I wrestle with the carcan instead.

Finally I fall back on the thin pillow, breathing hard. My mind is a tangled pile of threads—and the feeling is too familiar. Is the new elixir less potent than the last batch? No . . . it had taken days to start to work the first time around, and I had been at half doses for nearly a week. Besides, my malheur has always been worse during times of turmoil. I laugh, low and bitter. It is a particular weak spot for a rebel, to succumb to upheaval.

I spring to my feet, wishing there was enough room to pace. Hoping for some air, I come to the doorway, but one of the soldiers outside lowers his bayonet to bar my way. "Stay inside!"

For a disconcerting moment, I imagine falling on the gleaming blade; it seems to pull me forward, like a beautiful stranger inviting me to dance. Instead, I retreat back through the door, taking refuge on the bed, my back against the wall. But while my thoughts go in circles, the stone feels like it's closing in. I focus for a while on the basin and the washcloth, but the sight of them is an unbearable torment in the confines of the straitjacket, and my mouth is so dry I can't decide if I'd prefer to wash with the water or drink it.

The smell of smoke creeps in—a hallucination? I cast another accusing glance at the elixir, but the guards are only sharing a cigarette. I am oddly offended. Shouldn't they fear me enough to remain on alert?

Annoyed, I climb, with some difficulty, to stand on the thin mattress—one knee, then the other, to one foot, then the other. My back scrapes against the stone wall as I push myself upward, trying to get a breath of fresh air through the window above the bed. It's too high for me to see anything aside from the blushing gold color of the morning sky, but the smell from the garden is heady: orchids and rain and the faint sweet smell of overripe fruit. I wish more than anything I could be outside in it.

Is Akra? Had he followed me to prowl around the grounds of Hell's Court? Or had he gone back to Papa, to give him hollow reassurances that I'd be back soon? Dare I hope Leo will get word to them? Let them know that I'm safe—at least for now?

I grimace at the next thought: if Leo returned to the slums, my family might already know more about the plan than I do.

But asking myself questions won't bring any new answers, and when the smoke clears, I sink back down, hoping to sleep. Instead I get lost in the carved patterns on the ceiling. The work is exquisite—almost as though the masons had been knitting silk, not carving stone. They show not landscapes or pictures, but words and letters. Old Chakran, though I cannot read it. The language has been forbidden since La Victoire, along with all the old ways. Still, I recognize one symbol among the lovely scrollwork of the language: life.

It repeats so often—how so, in the temple dedicated to the King of Death? What do the carvings say? Are they stories or prayers? Spells or curses? Maman had spent a year in Hell's Court, back before La Victoire. Had she read the writing carved into the walls? Shuddering, I bury my face in the thin pillow. Old songs swirl through my head. Music from shows we've played. In the dark behind my eyes, shadows dance with light: the King and the Maiden. Life and Death, each one side of the other. In all our stories, the King was never evil. How could Le Trépas have become such a monster? Was it his rumored madness that made him do what he'd done? And if so, without the treatment, was I resigned to the same fate? It's only when voices in the hall clear the shadows like a mist that I realize I'd been dreaming.

"General's orders," one of the soldiers is saying. He is talking to someone just out of sight. "No one goes inside."

"I'm not afraid." The reply makes me blink: Leo's voice. "What could she do to me? She's trussed like a goose!"

Struggling to sit upright, I lean to peer around the open door. There he is, holding a tray. It must be the meal Xavier promised. But the guard takes it from him with a pointed look. "The general wants to keep it that way."

"Bien." Leo clenches his jaw under his smile—he can do little more than meet my gaze before the first soldat waves him back down the hall.

The other guard sets the tray down on the stone floor, just inside the door. Aquitan food—some kind of meaty stew . . . a browned bun . . . a hard-boiled egg. I clench my hands in the long canvas sleeves. "How exactly am I supposed to eat?"

Both men ignore me, and I am not yet hungry enough to lower my face to the plate, though I consider it as the hours pass.

The stew congeals. The guards share another cigarette. The sun creeps down the wall in patterns of gold and shadow. How long will I be waiting? It is below the horizon by the time I am led back to the sanctuary.

The walk down the long hall feels something like freedom. I half hope to see Leo at the end of it; another part of me dreads Xavier. But Theodora is the only other person there. She is sitting at the altar she uses as a desk, and it's hard to imagine she hasn't been here all day. Hunched over her work, she looks at home in the heart of the temple. And though the daylight is a memory and the hum and flow of the workshop has ebbed, La Fleur looks up at me expectantly when the guard shows me in, as though the day is only beginning.

"Jetta," she says, closing the book she's been reading and tossing it into the open trunk beside the altar. Then she frowns, her eyes falling again to the carcan. "He didn't release you."

"No."

"Will you kill me if I do?" Theodora searches my face. What does she expect me to say?

"No." The silence stretches. But why would she believe me? I am a nécromancien, after all. Just like Le Trépas. "The legends about . . . about *him* say he was able to kill at a touch, but I only know how to put souls into bodies, and there are no souls here."

She frowns. "What do you mean?"

"They're drawn to temples, but not this one. They must have fled from him, and never came back." My lips twist; a semblance of a smile. "If there were any spirits lurking, I would have escaped much more easily the first time I was here."

"I see." She waves me over, standing as I approach. Her hands go to the buckles at the small of my back; she hesitates for a moment before she starts to loosen the straps. "Leo tells me you're not the monster Xavier thinks," she says then, the metal chiming as she works. "I hope he's right."

So do I, I do not say. I want to ask her what else Leo said about me, but I bite down on that question too. Best not to raise suspicions. At last the sleeves fall and my arms lift, almost involuntarily; for a moment I myself feel ensouled with the spirit of a bird. Then I shrug out of the carcan as fast as I can, tossing it to the floor with more force than necessary. I start to peel off the gloves as well, but La Fleur holds up a hand.

"Leave them," she says. "Please? As a courtesy."

I flex my fingers, but better a concession than the carcan. "Bien," I say, like the Aquitans do, and a little smile flickers at the corners of her red mouth.

"Will you sit?" She takes her own chair and gestures to another beside it, but my eyes are drawn to the dinner tray sitting atop the pile of papers. Coconut curry with roasted duck and fragrant rice. Pickled vegetables. A little pile of shrimp cakes. Real Chakran food, and she's hardly touched it. That's no surprise. When we used to make the circuit, the richer patrons never stooped to eat a curry. What a waste. But my mouth is watering, and La Fleur catches me staring. "Do you want some?"

The offer is tempting, but is this just another tactic? Sharing a meal to gain my trust? Is that why she let me out of the carcan? I press my lips together as I lower myself into the chair. "The general had food sent to my room."

Theodora makes a face. "And yet he didn't bother making sure you could eat it. Then again, if it was armée rations, perhaps that's for the best." She holds out the plate of shrimp cakes. What harm can it do, as long as I don't let it go to my head? Giving in, I take one. To my surprise, La Fleur does too, taking a delicate bite, so careful of her red lips. "Mmm."

I raise an eyebrow. "I would have thought traditional Aquitan food would be more to your taste."

"I've lived in Chakrana as long as I can remember,"

she says with a look. "Besides, the chef is very talented. Go ahead, try it."

I can no longer resist; one turns quickly into two, then three. I'm ravenous—and they're delicious. Meaty and spicy sweet and fried crispy on the edges. Almost as good as Maman's. Maman. The thought of her takes my breath away, and my appetite with it. The bite I am chewing is suddenly hard to swallow, and when Theodora offers the plate again, I shake my head. "Non," I say. "Merci."

Does La Fleur see the pain on my face? This time she does not insist. She only sets the plate aside and reaches into her pocket, pulling out the note I'd written to the Tiger. It flutters limply in her hand. "Bien," she says softly. "Let's talk instead."

I take a deep breath, sitting back in my chair. Maman's instructions are a distant echo: never show, never tell. What would she say to me now? I wish more than anything she was here, even if it was to chide me. "May I have that back?" I hold out my hand, but a smile ghosts across La Fleur's lips.

"I've already read it," she says, passing me the letter. "So has Xavier. Are you still hoping the Tiger will come find you?"

"The Tiger doesn't have my elixir," I remind her, turning

the paper over and over in my hands. It's not even a lie.

"My father did," Theodora says. I tense, waiting for the accusation, but her tone is soft, contemplative. "And yet you rejected his offer."

I blink at her, unsettled. "Leo told you about that?"

She gives me a look. "It doesn't take a genius to guess that negotiations fell through. But the particulars of his offer were here." Theodora taps the trunk beside the altar with one booted foot. The lid is propped open against the stone; peeking inside, my jaw drops.

It is packed with rows of slim leather books—journals, I realize, organized by year. The book she's tossed on the top has a name on the cover: GENERAL JULIAN LEGARDE. "My father kept contemporaneous records during his entire campaign in Chakrana. Nearly twenty years' worth of notes. It's how he compiled his official reports. I've been trying to review them in all my spare time."

Her laugh is hollow; beneath the careful makeup, there are dark circles under her eyes. Is it exhaustion? Overwork? Or something more? For a moment, pity makes a lump in my throat. Twenty years of the general's campaign—of the occupation. How much of it has she read? Her father was a monster too, but perhaps she hadn't known it. Does she know now? "What have you found?"

Her answer disappoints me. "So far, nothing too surprising. The offer he planned to make to you, as I said. The kingdom for the elixir, as long as you followed his commands."

I narrow my eyes; she makes it sound simple. Is she truly so unbothered by her father's offer to me, this girl who had once meant to be queen? "As long as I didn't object to him shooting Leo, you mean?"

Theodora's pale skin goes paler still. She looks once more at the trunk full of journals. "That wasn't part of his records."

"Of course not," I say wryly. "The armée is a master of propaganda."

"Or maybe you're lying," she shoots back. "Leo didn't mention it either."

"You think he wants to admit your father would have shot him to teach me a lesson?"

She frowns, answering my question with one of her own. "Is that the only reason you refused the deal? For Leo?"

"Isn't that good enough?" I raise an eyebrow. She looks away, but not before I see the hurt in her face. "No," I add then, softer now. "I'm not exactly suited to rule."

"I don't think you would have lasted long," Theodora agrees, her voice distant. I can't help but laugh. Pressing my gloved hands together, I half bow in my chair.

"Thank you for your confidence!"

"Not because of you. Or your malheur," she adds quickly. "After all, my uncle has a similar affliction, and he's ruled nearly two decades in Aquitan."

"Then why?"

"My father." She sighs, putting her elbow on the altar and her chin in her hand. "He always resented the fact that his half-brother got the crown and he got a military commission. Not that he wrote that down, either. But his life's work was to see his own children on a throne. Or the children he acknowledged, anyway. Isn't it funny? He was a bastard himself, and yet."

I shift on my chair, not knowing how to respond. "How would giving me the throne help with that?"

"Xavier will marry someday. And wives are even easier to dispose of than husbands," she adds primly. I recoil, but why am I surprised? Legarde had been willing to assassinate the king after the wedding. The general would have had me killed just as readily.

"Did you know?" I ask then, unsure if she will answer. "Did the general tell you the plan was to kill the Boy King after your wedding?"

"Not at the time." Theodora shakes her head, her curls gently bouncing. "Not that I expect you to believe me. But Raik would have been happy as a figurehead, as long as he had money and champagne. And I could have been happy too, with the royal coffers funding my work. My father struck a good bargain . . . if he'd only stuck to it. There is much more of him in Leo than either of them admitted," she adds then, the ghost of a smile crossing her lips.

The thought strikes a spot I hadn't known was tender. How would Leo feel, hearing what Theodora had said? But there was truth in it. The general had maneuvered on the political field just as much as in battle. And Leo was always most comfortable bridging the gap between wanting and getting. Then again, the two of them had their differences: Leo hadn't been willing to shoot his father, even when the general had his own son in his sights. Then I frown. "Raik? Why did he need to bargain with the general? He was the last living prince. The throne was his by right."

"Rights are little more than wishful thinking without the might to enforce them," Theodora replies. Then she waves one manicured hand, as though clearing the words out of the air. Picking up her notebook, she turns to a page marked with a ribbon. "Speaking of which. Tell me what you know about Le Trépas."

"Bien," I say, flexing my fingers in their gloves. But where to start? The first thing that comes to mind is Maman's own fear. Not that she ever mentioned him directly. But I had felt her horror when my own powers had started to manifest—her heartbreak the night I'd learned that Papa was not the man whose blood ran through my veins. Still, it is not my place to share Maman's feelings with La Fleur.

What else, then? The story of La Victoire—but everyone knows it, not least the daughter of the man who starred as the hero. Indeed, Theodora's own research must contain more than I ever knew about the man who sired me. "There isn't much," I say at last. "Superstitions about n'akela, and stories the older children might have made up to scare us. He was like a shadow—we knew the shape of him, but not the features."

Theodora frowns as she takes notes, her golden curls slipping over her eyes. "N'akela?"

"Spirits that want vengeance," I say softly, though there are no souls at all to hear me in Hell's Court. The words summon the memory like a spell: the grit of ash, the smell of blood. The charred remains of a village, and a yawning pit where bodies lie, too pale, too still. And n'akela as blue as her eyes, drifting through the ruins of Dar Som. "The armée made quite a few in their march through Le Verdu."

My accusation is pointed, but Theodora doesn't look up. "Your father did as well, or so I imagine."

I tense. "He's not my father."

"What is he then?" she says distantly, as though talking to herself.

"A monster. Like Xavier says." *Like he thinks I am,* I do not add. I stare at the papers on the altar, tapping the recherche on my thigh until the spirit inside rustles, protesting. "Or don't you agree?"

"Le Trépas himself claimed he was a god reborn, but he seemed human to me." Theodora finishes a line and tucks her hair behind her ear. "Of course, all people are capable of monstrous things."

"Seemed . . . human?" My eyebrows shoot up. "You've met him?"

"I have," she says, and though it shouldn't, the admission stuns me. She must see it in my face. "Do you hope to?"

"No!" I say immediately.

"Why not?"

"Why should I?"

"To ask questions, perhaps."

"What questions?" I look at her askance, but when she doesn't say, they come on their own. *Why?* and *How could you?* are crowded out by *How?* and *Who are you?* Others follow: *Do the dead look the same to you? What do you know that I don't? What can you do that I can't—and how did you learn?* "No," I say firmly, shaking them out of my head. But my eyes are drawn back to the papers on her desk. Do they contain the answers? "But I . . . I want to know about what I can do."

"Ah." Theodora smiles, glancing down at my hands. "So do I."

I follow her gaze to the battered recherche. When had I crushed it? Trying to gather my thoughts, I smooth the paper across my thigh, folding it once more along the creases. Holding it by the center, I let the crude fantouche flap its paper wings. "This is it."

Theodora reaches out, taking the fantouche between her thumb and forefinger. Then, to my surprise, she tosses it up in the air. We both watch it rise, and she grins as it circles above our heads. "It's a good place to start."

How the Gods
Learned to Die

In the days when our ancestors were young, the gods still walked in Chakrana. And while everything else was born, grew old, and died, the gods went on.

The Keeper of Knowledge grew curious first. They went to the King and the Maiden and asked, "Are gods dead or alive?"

The King answered first. "We must be dead, for we never change."

The Maiden disagreed. "We don't rot like bodies, or fade like souls. Certainly we're alive."

"Maybe we're something else," the Keeper mused. They went away to consider it, and thought for a long time. What are life and death and being? The Keeper watched the living in all their forms, and listened to the stories of spirits as they shone and faded. But some time later, the Keeper returned to the King and the Maiden and said "I need to live and die to know more."

Curious, the King agreed to free the Keeper's soul, and the Maiden agreed to put it back in a new body. But without someone to record the Keeper's history, the deity feared all their knowledge would be lost. So the Keeper gathered their worshippers to build a temple to their knowledge, and chip their own stories into stone. Only then was the Keeper ready to die and to live. And when they did, they realized how much they had been missing.

The Keeper shared their stories—of feasting and famine, love and pain, hope and fear and all the things that make up life and death—and the King and the Maiden became curious too. But neither could die and live without the other. So instead, each took half of their own soul and put the pieces into human bodies, to live and die for them.

Some say that splitting their souls made the gods weaker. Others say it made them more understanding. But one day the gods will make their souls whole again, and that is when peace will return to Chakrana.

CHAPTER SEVEN

La Fleur and I begin with the most basic information: the types of souls—vana, arvana, akela, n'akela—the blood offering, the symbol of life. At first it is strangely thrilling; I have never before had the chance to speak so openly about what had been forbidden. But as the night wears on, the questions go deeper. "Why do the souls of birds fly?" she asks.

I answer as I've always believed. "Because it's in their nature."

"Is it?" She looks delighted. "Do dead dogs chase the souls of cats? Do the spirits of fish still live in streams?" At my nod, she grins. "What about the arvana of snakes? Can they poison?"

I frown. "I don't know. I've never checked."

"Why not?"

"Why would I?" I ask. "I was a performer, not an assassin."

She raises an eyebrow, but whatever she's thinking, she makes a note rather than saying it out loud. Then she stares into the middle distance, tapping the pen on the page. Is she wondering about snakes now, as I am? The idea is dizzying—I can see why La Fleur's workshop is so prolific. Can the souls of bees sting? Would the spirit of a chameleon change the color of its own fantouche? The next thought brings me up short: will my own soul feel malheur?

"Can they act against their nature?"

Her question pulls me back to our conversation. "What do you mean?"

She cocks her head, looking up at the fantouche. "Could you give her an order to do something she wouldn't do naturally? Swim, for example?"

"I suppose," I say slowly. "My old fantouches used to perform in shadow plays. But I doubt she'd be much good at swimming."

"But she'd try if you ordered her to."

The question unsettles me; I watch the fantouche, but think of Akra, hiding in the reeds. "Yes."

La Fleur makes another note. "What if you ordered her to follow the commands of someone else?"

I narrow my eyes. "Why would I do something like that?"

"Well." She gives me a helpless gesture with her pen. "You must understand the value of the proposal."

The face I make is bitter. "War machines."

"Any machines! Transport. Manufacture. Automation. But of course the value is limited if there's only one person in command of the mechanism."

"Depends on what you value," I say pointedly. "I for one prefer that my power remain in my own hands."

"So does everyone in power," she says.

I blink at her, taken aback. How can this pale and privileged princess think that I'm the one in power? "There is a difference between being dangerous and being powerful," I say, but she only shrugs.

"There was an interview done with your father—I'm sorry," she corrects herself at my look. "With Le Trépas. In it, he confessed to killing his children. Do you know why?"

"To create disciples," I say immediately. "To force souls to do his bidding."

"That may have been a side effect," she says, making a face. "But he could have killed anyone for that. He told the questioneurs he didn't want his blood to fall into the wrong hands. Do you think he meant someone like you, or someone like me?"

I open my mouth—close it again. "What do you mean by that?"

"I mean, was he trying to prevent other nécromanciens? Or was he trying to limit the sources of blood, so no one else could take it and make their own fantouches?"

"I don't know," I say, drawing back. The curiosity in her eyes is perilously close to hunger. "Why are you asking?"

Theodora hesitates, and for a moment my muscles tense. Does she mean to try it? And if she did, would La Fleur's creatures obey her instead of me? But she only turns back to her notebook. "I suppose it's in my nature to ask questions. To be curious," she says as she writes. "Know your enemy as you know yourself, and you have nothing to fear, they say."

"Know your enemy *and* know yourself," I say; the proverb is a Chakran one. But she only smiles a little.

"And do you?"

I narrow my eyes; the question stings. "I know my enemy, at least."

Her smile falls; she opens her mouth as though to protest, but then thinks better of it. "That still leaves us with one major area of inquiry," she says drily.

"Do you think I'm the same as he is?" The question tumbles out, too quick to stop. I brace myself for the answer, but she only frowns absently.

"As who?"

I grit my teeth. "As the man you keep calling my father."

"Ah." She cocks her head, her curls bouncing. "Isn't that what we're trying to discover? But let me ask you a question. Why do you keep insisting he isn't? Your father, I mean."

My eyebrows go up. How can she ask such a thing? Even if she doesn't understand about Papa, Le Trépas is evil. A murderer. A nécromancien. But my own sins stuff the words back down my throat, for I am a murderer and a nécromancien too. "Because I want to be different than he is," I say at last, and to my surprise, her face softens.

"Now *that* I understand," she says, glancing again at the trunk beside her desk. The admission surprises me, but when she catches my look, she makes a face. "I won't be threatening Leo to make you hand over your blood, if that's what you're wondering about."

I turn away so she will not see the relief in my eyes. Then I hesitate. Is it too obvious to ask? "Where is Leo, anyway?"

By her sly smile, I can tell she doesn't know the real reason I'm asking. Or at least, not the entire reason. "He's staying at an inn by the docks. But he comes by nearly every day."

"To work?"

"Or talk. Or play the violin." Her smile is wistful—the thought tugs at my own heart. It had been so long since I'd heard music. La Fleur stands then, stretching; at the sight, my own body aches. What time is it? "I'm tired of questions," she says then. "Aren't you?"

"It is late," I say, but she only tucks her pen behind her ear and the book under her arm. Then she pulls a ring of keys from under a stack of papers and slips it into one of her many pockets.

"Come on," she says, and I stand, curious.

"Where?"

"To find some souls," she says, as though it was obvious. Then she starts across the sanctuary, beckoning when she realizes I'm not following. So I join her, stepping over the carcan, still discarded on the stone floor.

"Are you sure you trust me not to kill you?"

"You're so insistent that you and Le Trépas are different," La Fleur says with a sidelong look. "Don't disappoint the both of us."

Theodora leads me deeper into Hell's Court, this time down the east hall, still marked by the devastation of my last time here. The tall carved pillars rise proudly, only to end in ruin; between the crumbled top of the wall and the new canvas roof, I can see a sliver of starry sky. The doors are shut to keep out the breeze; the backs of the old cells have collapsed into the garden. In the bright glow of the electric light, I cannot even tell which one had been mine.

Which one had been his?

I do not ask as we pass them by. Soon enough, the hallway opens into what used to be a huge dining room where two hundred monks could eat their daily meals. The scarred wooden tables remain, but they've been pushed to the side to leave a wide-open workshop. Now, the fanciful carvings of the King of Death that adorn the walls look down approvingly on the mechanization of war.

An enormous gun mounted on a cart and fired by a hand crank. A long band of bullets dangles beneath it, waiting to be fed through the machine. There is another weapon on one of the tables, like a rifle with six barrels and a cylinder as big around as a melon. Even a flying machine, akin to the one I had stolen, though sleeker. More graceful.

But there—something I do not recognize. A half-built rig, a bit like a wheelbarrow, though instead of the shaft, it has an arm like a crooked spear, or the beak of a crane. Beside it, another mysterious machine in progress, with rotating blades on the front that look like they could reduce a body to soup.

"A mud plow," Theodora says when she notices my stare. "For rice paddies. That one next to it is an automated planter."

Surprised, I touch the arm of the contraption. Was the metal beak delicate enough to cradle a green shoot? "Does the armée plant much rice?"

"They're Camreon's design," she says, unable to hide the pride in her voice. But where had I heard the name? Theodora sees my confusion. "I think you two met briefly this morning."

"The Chakran boy," I say, thinking back. Was that only today? La Fleur nods, but I still don't quite understand. "These are for agriculture?"

"The rebellion came on in earnest after the last famine,"

she says, as though I could forget the Hungry Year—the year we lost Akra to the armée. "Automation could help prevent another. If we ever have time to finish them."

"The last famine came on because the Aquitans took all the best fields for sugar," I retort. "Not because there was no one to work them."

"Well." Theodora presses her lips together. "After the atrocities in La Verdu, the next one might be. Xavier tells me the fields are empty—the farmers fled. Or killed. Besides . . . it's poetic, isn't it? Swords into plowshares."

I frown, not understanding. "What's that?"

"Oh." She waves a hand as though to clear the air. "Just something one of the prophets said. Our prophets, I mean. It used to be one of Xavier's favorite quotes."

"I thought all you made was weaponry," I mutter.

"Have you already forgotten the elixir?" She gives me a look, and I drop my eyes. But she sighs, turning toward a table where shiny steel combines with leather and polished wood in shapes where the organic meets the mechanical. A cane . . . a brace . . . a graceful sleeve that ends in a carved wooden hand. And beside the table—a chair that glides on rubberized wheels. "These are also my work. Though I suppose if I made fewer weapons, I could make fewer aides à la mobilité. Can you can see my interest in practical applications here? Imagine replacing a missing hand with one manufactured not only in form, but in function."

For a moment, I do imagine it—Papa's twisted legs strengthened with braces that respond to his own commands. Hope rises in me, only to fall. She thinks Papa is dead—at least, that's what Leo implied. I'd have to be a fool to tell her otherwise. Instead, I clench my jaw. "There's a lot of need for them among the refugees."

"I know," she says softly. "The latest supply ship was spotted this afternoon. I'm hoping for enough extra steel for new braces. Someday the fighting will be over, and we'll finally have time to heal."

"We?" The sleeve is still unfinished, but the wood is already painted, pale as Aquitan skin. "Or you?"

"We'll see when the ship comes in," she says. Then she lays the hand back on the table and leads me toward the back wall, where a little doorway has been fitted with an iron grate that opens out into the garden. But in the rear corner of the hall, a squat, square structure catches my eye. It's clearly recently built—likely raised when Theodora set up shop here—and completely out of place, made of Aquitan brick with a steel door studded with rivets.

"What's that?" I say as she draws the set of keys from her pockets.

Theodora pauses, glancing sidelong at me. "We work with chemicals here," she says at last, fitting one of the keys into the gate to the garden. "I've learned it's unwise to leave them lying about."

Her tone is pointed—she must mean kerosene. The door is certainly thick enough to withstand explosives. It's also locked, which makes sense after I'd sent her last workshop up in flames. Is the key on the set she uses to open the gate? After the disaster at *La Rêve,* I know better than to try to make plans when Leo and the Tiger have their own in motion. But it's good information to keep hold of.

Leaving the keys dangling from the lock, I follow Theodora out to the wide stone plaza—a kitchen, once, exposed to the night air. Above, the clouds veil the stars, and the moon is a sickle for reaping. The shadows are deep, but I can make out the long stove against the wall closest to the temple. Leaves are turning to dirt in the corners, and animals have built and abandoned nests in the massive apertures once used for fuel.

On the opposite side, the wild garden grows close, as though reaching for the temple in hope of a blessing. I can see a few bold souls, drifting among the plants, and the fresh air feels like waking from a dream. I hadn't realized how oppressive the workshop was—how ubiquitous the scent of oil and kerosene, how empty without the glow of the dead. I take deep breaths, invigorated. Here, where the spirits draw close, I am in my own territory. "You wanted souls?" I ask softly. "Come with me."

There is a winding path leading toward the Ruby Palace, lit by electric lights strung on poles overhead. I follow it into the garden, with Theodora trailing just behind. If she is afraid of me, she does not show it. "What's the nearest one?"

"There," I say with a nod to the light, half swallowed by a rampant stand of bougainvillea. Living moths flutter around the glass bulb, as do the vana of those who got too close to the heat.

Theodora peers upward. "Where exactly? Can you point?"

Squinting, I glance at the spirits; they flutter erratically, out of reach. So I pick up a stick, using the tip to trace the path of a moth through the air. But when I come too near the bulb, Theodora grabs my wrist.

"Careful," she says as I pull free. "If you smash the glass, the whole circuit will go out."

"What does that mean?"

She makes a face. "It means you should show me a different spirit. Maybe one farther from the light."

"You won't be able to see them either way."

"Please?"

I don't bother protesting. Instead, I use the stick to point into the lush greenery. "There is the soul of an owl asleep in the tree. Mice there . . . and there . . . and there. There is a frog under those leaves, and a bird on that branch. . . ." I falter then. Is that a flash of blue deeper in the garden? I squint into the shadows . . . yes. A n'akela. Vengeful. Waiting. The sight of it chills me. The last one I'd seen had been one of Le Trépas's disciples. Where had this one come from? It keeps its distance, at least. I glance at Theodora, wondering if I should continue. Her brow is furrowed as she peers into the trees, and her expression is so intent that doubt creeps in. "Can you see them?" I ask.

"No." The smile she gives me is rueful; she shakes her head, curls bouncing. "I suppose I wondered if I might see . . . something. A disturbance in the air, or a faint gleam, if I only knew where to look."

"Does it matter so much?"

"To catch a glimpse of something I've never seen

before?" Theodora laughs. "Of course it does." She opens the book, making another note before tucking it into her pocket. Then she looks up at the air—full of drifting sparks of soullight, though I know the only light she can see is the electric gleam of the glass bulb. "What do they look like?"

"Fire." The answer seems inadequate to the yearning in her voice. "The vana are dull, like the embers that float upward when you poke at coals. The arvana . . . they're like the flame itself. Orange and red. The akela are bright gold—the color of afternoon sun."

"Mmm." She watches the sky, as though trying to imagine it. "And n'akela?"

My eyes dart to the shadows in the garden, searching automatically for the hint of sapphire flame. "Blue as your eyes."

"What about my father's soul?" she asks then. The question, spoken so low, is a punch in the gut. I grit my teeth.

"Gold," I say. But guilt is a weight I want to share. "The same color as my brother's."

"I see," she says faintly.

I bristle. "Don't ask a question if you don't want the answer."

"I always want the answer, Jetta. But tell me," she adds, her eyes narrowing. "The official report says your brother survived."

Too late, I realize my mistake. I take a breath, trying to come up with an excuse she will believe, but it has been a long day and I am tired, and La Fleur is much too smart for excuses. "He did."

"But you saw his soul." She stares at me, waiting for a reply that doesn't come. "Le Trépas used to raise the corpses brought to the temple for burial. He turned them into revenants—walking dead. Is that what you did?"

"No!" I suppress a shudder, if not the memory: the dead man in the well. Bright blue eyes in pale bruised skin. The bloated tongue moving as he called me sister. I thank the gods that Akra is different, although I have no idea why. Does La Fleur?

"So he is alive? Jetta. Can you heal the dead?" Her eyes are bright with the thrill of discovery, but as the silence stretches, she clenches her jaw. "If I send the armée to find your brother, I can ask him in person."

"If I take off my gloves, you can find out firsthand." My threat is immediate—does she know it's hollow? I do not know how Le Trépas killed, but I would do whatever it takes to keep my brother safe. Theodora folds her arms; we both glare at each other for a moment. I don't want to hurt her—I don't. Can she tell, or will she try to test the theory?

"It's interesting," she says at last, speaking with careful clarity. "If you truly brought your brother back from the dead, it would be the second difference I've noticed between you and Le Trépas."

My heartbeat quickens at the thought. "What's the first?"

She gives me a look. The silence stretches, but I want to know. Not just for me and Akra. But for the rebellion—or so I tell myself. After all, how can I offer my powers if I don't even know what they are?

"My brother died in the temple," I say at last, and the admission feels like a torn scab. "But I put his soul back and he . . . he's alive. Not a revenant, not a corpse. And not the same as he was, either."

"Let me guess," she says, and the wonder on her face turns my stomach. "He doesn't need to eat or drink or sleep. He obeys your orders, and he can't be killed except by fire."

I blink at her, startled. "How did you know?"

"He's like your fantouches, I'm guessing." She takes out

her notebook again, flipping through as she mutters. "There are legends about this."

"Legends?" My heart quickens. "I've never heard them."

"Written on the temple walls in old Chakran," she says. "I have a translator working on them."

I stare at her journal as she scans the pages, wanting more than anything to rip it from her hands. "What do they say?"

"Quite a bit," she says simply.

The answer infuriates me—I've been too free with my own information. "Will you tell me the other difference, at least?"

Theodora nods, as though accepting my offer in the tacit bargain. "Le Trépas claimed he can't ensoul fabrications. The fantouches you create are something only you can do."

The answer to my question is not half so shocking as the way she'd discovered it. "He . . . he claimed? To who?"

"The questioneurs." The tremor in her voice is almost imperceptible. "They got very little out of him. Torture is a notoriously unreliable way to get information, and Le Trépas was a difficult subject, to say the least. But it seems he broke his silence around the time you entered the city. He asked for you by name. Offered to tell us what we wanted to know if we told him about you."

"Me?" The world seems to tilt under my feet—it is a punishment for breaking Maman's edict. Never show, never tell; you never knew who might be listening. But I knew who it was, didn't I? The dead man in the well. He must have found a way to tell Le Trépas I was near. But . . . "Why?"

"It makes sense, doesn't it? You were his only surviving child. He must have wanted to know what you were like."

"And they told him?"

"There wasn't much to tell," she says, as though that would reassure me. "But what information they had was traded. As you and I did just now. Don't look so horrified." Her blue eyes gleam in the electric lights. "So much was destroyed after La Victoire, with the deaths of the monks and the burning of the scrolls. We're only trying to get some of it back."

I clench my fists; she makes it sound like the scrolls burned themselves. But worse is knowing the old monk has my secrets—even the smallest among them feels like a violation. What does Le Trépas know about me? And how much of his own knowledge had he shared with the armée in return? "What gives you Aquitans the right to have any of it?"

"Not a right. A responsibility." Theodora raises an

eyebrow. "This is my country too, Jetta."

"It might have been, if your fiancé had sided with you instead of his own people!" The retort is cruel, and I want it to be. But La Fleur just looks annoyed.

"Raik was only ever on his own side."

"What's that supposed to mean?"

She takes a breath, as though to respond, but then she passes a hand over her eyes. "We're bickering now. It's late, and we're both tired. Let's get some rest, don't you think?"

Theodora turns back toward the temple, but I hesitate. Out here, in the garden, we are unguarded, alone, and the gloves are a slender barrier. I could have the book in a moment—I could take back all that stolen knowledge. The keys are even in the gate; it wouldn't take long to figure out which one unlocks the closet. I could destroy her workshop, and her along with it.

Could I do it? Could I kill her? La Fleur, the armée scientist, the general's daughter . . . and Leo's sister. Her back is to me—she is weaponless, this maker of war machines. A threat, but not immediately. Not to me.

Folding my hands, I follow her back through the door of the temple. The keys chime like bells as she locks the door behind us.

—Reports of revenants describe them as walking corpses, but Jetta's fantouches appear to act like living things.

—Can she raise men from the dead?

—Are the newspapers so wrong to claim we could resurrect the fallen to fill the armée ranks?

—The Maiden and the King. Is Jetta a nécromancien or something else?

—"What I create, I control."

—Can she command a fantouche to obey someone else?

—Who controls the creature if someone else uses the blood?

ACT 1,

SCENE 8

The slum near the river. It is midnight or later. Rain has made a muddy stream of the crooked street. Through the gray, the wreck of the dragon boat looms over the rows of broken-down shacks. The air is thick with flies—not even the lingering smoke from the many cookfires can keep them away.

AKRA is standing on the riverbank, rain plastering his dark hair to his head. It has gotten longer in the weeks since his desertion, but if you look closely, you can tell he was an officer, once. There is the way he stands, as though ready to be called to attention. There are the calluses on his bare feet, where ill-fitted boots used to pinch.

And of course there are the scars.

He watches the sluggish current for a while—how long has he been out here? Suddenly, AKRA turns his head, though the only sound is the rush of rain and river, and the heavy, oppressive hum of the camp: hundreds of hearts struggling to beat.

AKRA: You've got a lot of nerve coming back to the scene of the crime, you moitié bastard.

LEO (*offstage*): Being a moitié bastard will cultivate nerve.

LEO steps into the scant moonlight on silent feet.

You're up late.

AKRA: Hard to sleep with my sister missing. Speaking of which.

Theatrically, AKRA glances into the shadows behind LEO.

Where's your brother lurking?

LEO: Likely back at the palace. Though it took me some time to shake the soldat he sent to follow me.

AKRA narrows his eyes.

AKRA: He doesn't trust you either? Smart man.

LEO: Especially considering what I'm here to ask.

AKRA: A favor? (*He laughs.*) Don't bother. I wouldn't even forgive you if you asked it.

LEO: It's not for me.

AKRA (*cynically*): For Jetta?

LEO: And the rebellion.

AKRA takes a breath then, suddenly uncertain.

AKRA: What do you mean?

LEO: You must know she wrote to the Tiger. She wanted to help.

AKRA: So you hauled her off to your sister's workshop?

LEO. With a plan in place to get her out again. There's a flying machine in there we need her help to steal, and someone else we need to rescue with it. But it's harder to tell her all that than I thought it would be.

AKRA: Why should I believe a word you say?

LEO: What's the alternative? Sit here and wait for her to come back?

AKRA: I could feed you to the crocodiles to pass the time.

LEO: You didn't take a bullet for me in Hell's Court just to kill me tonight.

AKRA: It wasn't for you.

LEO (*an echo of AKRA's earlier question*): For Jetta?

AKRA: Yes.

LEO: You're more tenderhearted than you seem, Akra.

AKRA: It wasn't because she's foolish enough to care about

you. It was to give her a chance to kill your father. We can both imagine what would happen if she'd fallen into the general's hands. She would have been a pawn at best. A weapon at worst. Just like all of us Chakrans in the armée.

A long silence between them.

LEO: What was it like?
AKRA: Serving under your father?
LEO: Dying at Hell's Court.

AKRA's eyes widen.

AKRA: What makes you say that?
LEO: I was there, Akra. No one loses so much blood and lives. And I've never seen that look on Jetta's face. You died, didn't you?

AKRA hesitates, his jaw working.

AKRA: I did.

He laughs then, but there is no humor in it.

After everything I did in the armée, I knew I'd have to pay in my next life. I just didn't know how much.

LEO: Surely this is better than the alternative.

AKRA: It might have been nice to forget.

LEO: Forget dying?

AKRA: Forget being a Chakran in the armée.

LEO: You could join the rebellion instead.

AKRA: I'm done following orders.

LEO: Except for Jetta's?

AKRA stares at LEO.

AKRA: Jetta isn't here.

LEO: To be honest, it's your other powers we're more interested in. The fact you can't die without walking into fire. Or the way you can talk to her, no matter where she is. Will you give her a message for me?

Another silence. On AKRA's face, bitterness turns to confusion.

AKRA: What are you talking about?

LEO: Haven't you seen her talk to her other fantouches? It's only because their souls are from animals that they can't reply. She needs your help, Akra. We need your help.

AKRA: I may have to listen to her, but I don't have to listen to you.

LEO: Did you want something in exchange? I'm good at making deals. It's what I do best.

AKRA: What could you possibly have to offer me?

LEO takes a deep breath, considering. What does AKRA want?

LEO: The chance to stop the armée. Because until we get both of our targets out of Hell's Court, the armée has the power to make almost anyone a pawn.

A long pause.

AKRA: I'm listening.

CHAPTER NINE

By the time I fall into bed, it is so late it is early. Still, half-formed questions circle like mosquitoes. What had the questioneurs asked Le Trépas? What had he said? What is he like—this man who thought he was a god? Is there anything of him in me? His eyes . . . his build . . . his mind? Is he mad like I am? He must be. Delusions of grandeur are a symptom I've experienced myself.

Sleep, when it comes, is fitful. In my dreams, he is a demon with a tongue like a snake and eyes like a goat and hands like the hooked claws of a bat. But when he opens his mouth, his voice is my brother's, and he is saying my name.

I wake a dozen times, though to judge by the color of the sunlight filtering into my room, it is nearly noon by the time I struggle free of the knotted sheets. With the echo of Akra's voice in my head, the first thing I do is down my daily dose of elixir. It leaves a bitter taste in my mouth, but there is a new tray with breakfast on the little table. Although the tea is already cold, I'm ravenous, so I strip off my gloves and dig in.

It is armée food, as Theodora had warned me: the egg must have been boiled in unsalted water, and what I think is a rice bun turns out to be a roll so crusty it feels like chewing on bark. But although I regret not eating more shrimp cakes last night, this is not much worse than I got in the slums.

As I'm eating, one of the guards knocks awkwardly on the open door. "La Fleur's waiting," he says. "Hurry up."

"Mmhmm," I say, my mouth full of bread. Then I take another bite, chewing slowly. Despite waking late, I am exhausted from dreams and questions, and I want to savor a few more moments of blessed quiet.

When I'm done eating, I run the washcloth over my face, my arms, my feet, trying to take off the grime and the sweat of the last few weeks. Should I change my clothes? The coveralls that Leo had left for me are clean and well made, but I am still hesitant to close the door, even for privacy. Instead, I stand behind it, keeping the heavy teak between me and the soldiers as I step awkwardly into the legs of the trousers, pulling them up along with my sarong so that I remain covered. When I toss my old rags into the corner and emerge from behind the door, the guards look at me askance, but it's no worse than any backstage costume change. And the smell of clean clothes is like heaven. As I slip my bottle of elixir into the pocket, my fingers meet something that crinkles.

A note.

My heart stops, then picks up again, faster than before. Leo had prepared the room for me—why hadn't I searched it earlier? Casually, I turn away from the door, standing once again out of the soldier's line of sight. Drawing out the paper, I unfold it slowly, so it doesn't make a sound. Then I frown. It is not a note, but a flyer, and familiar too. One from the last show we'd meant to do, back in Luda. At the Fêtes des Ombres, before this whole mess began.

When it rustles in my hand, I catch my breath. There is a soul inside it—but which one? There it is on the bottom of the paper, beside the symbol in blood: *hawk*. The page had been torn from the book I'd made—the book of souls

I'd saved. The book I'd left back at the rebel camp. Did Leo have it now?

Eagerly, I flip the sheet over, hoping for a message, but the back is blank. No—there is a drawing there, faintly done, in pencil, as though a mindless doodle. At first I think that someone has sketched the hawk that ensouls the scrap of paper, but on closer inspection, I realize the drawing is meant to be a flying machine. Like the one I'd stolen . . . or the one I'd seen in the workshop last night.

"Jetta? Are you awake yet?"

The voice makes me jump—so close, so familiar. My brother's voice. Could he have crept onto the grounds and found my window? The guards have not moved—did they not hear him? I scramble onto the bed to whisper out the window. "Akra?"

"Jetta!" The response comes right in my ear, and I whirl. But I am alone in the room. Of course I am.

Taking a deep breath, I lower myself back to the bed. Disappointment is a heavy weight on my shoulders. This is not the first time I've hallucinated my brother's voice. The elixir should be helping with that. But hadn't Theodora said it would take a few days to build up in my blood?

"Jetta, can you hear me? Leo came to talk."

I frown. That's the last thing I would have expected my brother to say, especially a hallucination. "Akra?" I murmur, soft enough that even I barely hear it. "Where are you?"

"With Papa, by the river. It doesn't matter—"

"How are you talking to me?"

"I . . ." He hesitates—in the silence, I can practically hear his discomfort. "It's not important right now. Do you have the flyer?"

Startled, I glance at the page in my hand. "Yes, but—"

"Can the soul animate the flying machine in the workshop?"

"Yes, but—"

"We need it by tomorrow night—"

"Is this really you?" I blurt out, too loud.

"Who else would it be?" His voice echoes in my head, but it does not cover the sound of the guards talking outside. I crush the flyer in my fist as one of them bursts into the room.

"Kess kch say?" the soldier says in Aquitan. "What's going on?"

"What does it look like?" I shoot back, gesturing with my free hand to the empty corner of the room. "I'm talking to my brother."

He looks first at the corner, and then at me. His expression is one that I recognize: half pity, half fear—as though madness is catching. It cuts deeper than I expect it to. "La Fleur is still waiting," he says at last.

"When I'm done," I snap, and after a moment, he retreats back into the hall.

Akra's voice comes again, fearful now. "What's happening, lailee?"

The word makes my heart clench: *sister*. It's been so long since he's called me that. Since before Hell's Court . . . if it is in fact him speaking. I want to believe, but isn't that the trick of it? Of course my own mind would suspend disbelief for a play it's putting on. In the quiet, I take a deep breath and whisper. "How can I be sure you aren't just another voice in my head?"

There is a long silence, and despair is a lengthening shadow. I have never challenged a hallucination before. Is the lack of response evidence that I could no longer fool myself? But then, at last, Akra speaks again. "Do you often hear voices, Jetta?"

"Only sometimes." The admission is difficult—new between us. I can almost feel his surprise, like it has a texture in the air. After all, my malheur had only gotten worse once he'd left to join the armée.

"I didn't realize it was so bad," he says.

I shrug, but he cannot see me. "It comes and goes."

"When?" he says, and this time I hesitate. My first hallucination was a song he used to sing, when I knew he wasn't there to sing it. But his wasn't the only voice I'd ever heard. My heart beats faster at the memory: an abandoned temple, a wayward monk. Her question in my head: *What are you?*

I had thought it was a hallucination at the time, but now I'm not so sure.

"It's not important," I say, an echo of his own words. My embarrassment over my admission is twisting into something new: discovery, and the thrill that comes with it. But the next question is tender for both of us. "Your voice, the way you're talking to me—does it have anything to do with what happened at Hell's Court?"

Another long silence. "Yes."

Slowly, I stand, almost without meaning to. "Why didn't you tell me before now?"

"I only just learned myself," he says, his voice touched with bitterness. "I'm not the expert, am I?"

Frustration makes a knot in my chest. "Unfortunately, neither am I."

"Just tell me," he says. "Can you ready the flying machine at midnight tomorrow?"

I wet my lips, unsure. How will I get past the guards? "Maybe. It would be easier if I had the whole book."

"Leo was worried the general would search the room," he says. "But I'll see what I can do."

My heart beats faster. If Leo brings the book, it will be proof my brother's voice was real. "And then?"

"Then we get out of the city and go to the rebel camp."

"We?" I bite my lip—the last flying machine only had room for three. Was the new one any bigger? I can't remember. "You, me, and Papa? What about Leo?"

"Papa isn't well enough to travel. Leo's made arrangements for someone to care for him in the capital."

"So Leo's coming with us?"

"Learn your part," he snaps at me. "And let everyone else play theirs."

The admonition is so familiar that I almost laugh. How many times had he told me so, as we elbowed each other backstage? But I smother the giggle—this is serious. "The flying machine. Midnight tomorrow."

"See you then."

"I hope so," I say, but there is no response. In the quiet

of my room, it's easy to doubt he'd spoken at all. Taking a deep breath, I smooth the crumpled flyer and fold it neatly around the little book of armée matches—I'll use them to free the soul when I need to. Then I tuck the bundle into my pocket, in case the soldiers decide to search the room after all.

When I appear in the doorway, the guards draw back a little, gripping their bayonets tighter. They weren't half so afraid of a nécromancien as they are of a mad girl. I lift my chin, striding down the hall toward the sanctuary, the flask of elixir banging against my hip.

My footsteps slow. The bottle contains roughly two weeks' worth. Is stealing more elixir part of the plan? I whisper my brother's name, hoping to ask him, but no answer comes. The silence feeds my doubts, but whether or not my brother's voice was only in my head, I can't leave Hell's Court without more elixir. Not when my malheur could put the rebellion at risk. But where will I find it in the sprawling workshop of Hell's Court?

The answer comes with striking clarity—the locked room in the dining hall. Theodora had told me herself: the chemicals are stored inside. Might my elixir be there among the oil and kerosene? I have till midnight tomorrow to find out. But if the keys were back on Theodora's desk among the shifting piles of paper, it wouldn't be too difficult to spirit them away.

Confidence blooms as I continue down the hall, then dies on the vine when I enter the sanctuary. The room is overrun with Aquitan soldiers. My veins thrum like plucked strings at the sight of so many armée men, but they are too busy stacking crates on hand carts to look my way. There are two men supervising. One, an officer who holds a clipboard and a pen as though furious with both. The other is the Chakran boy—Camreon, Theodora had called him. The one designing machines to plant rice. To judge by his face, he'd rather be laboring in the fields than standing here.

They are arguing over the crates—or, rather, the officer is arguing. Camreon is only nodding, his head bowed, his eyes on his paperwork. The scene is uncomfortably familiar—why do the Aquitans always think that raised voices will change facts? But I do not want to make it worse by staring. Instead, I look at the boxes. There are so many of them. What do they contain? Bullets? Rifles? Bombs? My jaw tightens, but when Theodora looks up from the letter she is penning, I'm surprised to see frustration on her face as well.

"Jetta!" She beckons me over with one ink-stained hand. "I've been waiting for you all morning. I want to talk to you more about . . ." She glances over at the officer, hesitating. "About what we discussed yesterday. The quartier-maître is nearly done."

Reluctantly I approach, but when the officer hears her voice, he turns away from Camreon mid-sentence. "I'll be done as soon as you clear the discrepancy between the quantity of munitions listed and the quantity received," he says through his teeth. "Cha doesn't seem to understand the problem."

At the slur, I look to the Chakran boy—I can't help it. Apparently, neither can he. Our eyes meet for an instant before he glances away. Still, there is comfort in the glance—the shared connection of two strangers who, for a moment, have everything in common. La Fleur doesn't even look up from her letter, though her own reply is sharp. "If you'd let me know you were coming, we could have sorted it out ahead of time. As it is, most of my staff is making room so we can accept my uncle's delivery. Besides, it's your list that has the discrepancy. Camreon cannot clear a problem he did not create."

The Chakran boy keeps his expression carefully neutral,

but the officer's chest swells. To my surprise, he turns to me—does he recognize me as the nécromancien? Or only as another Chakran in the room? "What is more likely? That I've made a mistake? Or that things would go missing with cha underfoot?"

I know better than to answer. Theodora replies instead, with a smile that doesn't reach her eyes. "Rumor has it you're more comfortable with riflery than recordkeeping."

"Take it up with your brother," the soldier snaps at her. "He's the one who put me behind a desk."

"I don't think he was wrong, Lieutenant Pique." Theodora's smile does not falter, but the name sends a chill through me—this is the man who razed the peaceful village of Dar Som. La Fleur sets aside her letter to take the clipboard from his hand. Then she crosses out the number there and writes her own, along with her initials. "Mistakes are easier to correct in ink than in blood."

Pique takes the clipboard back, but his eyes stay on me. "Spilling ink won't solve the problem."

"Take it up with my brother," Theodora says coolly, sitting back at her desk. "Your general. Now if you'll excuse me. I'm writing to my uncle with an update on our progress here. I'll send him your regards."

The lieutenant clenches his jaw at the invocation of the Aquitan king; at last he stalks away, shouting at the men with their handcarts. The Chakran boy too disappears back into the temple. La Fleur does not watch as they clear out. I do, though. I want to know the lieutenant has left before I turn my back. It's only once he follows his men out of the temple that my heart starts to slow. "Was it really him?"

"Pique? Unfortunately yes."

"I thought he would have been . . ." My voice trails off. What had I thought? Imprisoned for the atrocities? Sent back to Aquitan in disgrace? "Punished."

"For men like him, a desk is a demotion." Theodora must see the expression on my face, because a faint blush comes to her pale cheeks. "He's been an officer longer than I've been alive. Xavier can't dismiss him without extreme measures."

The rage flares in me, too hot to tamp out. "Dar Som was an extreme measure."

"And nothing like it will happen with him behind a desk," she says. I grit my teeth.

"He should be in a dungeon somewhere."

"To Pique, a desk is worse."

"Is it really?" My question hangs in the air, long enough

for me to reconsider asking. Have I grown too bold? I am only Chakran, after all—more prisoner than peer. But Theodora pauses as she signs the letter.

"I prefer engineering to politics, Jetta, but it's all gears and levers. And instead of steel, they're made of loyalty and pride and distrust and resentment." She tosses the pen down with a grimace; it rolls off the edge of a folded square of canvas—the carcan, picked up off the floor and subsumed in the pile. But is that the set of keys I see peeking out underneath? "If you want the truth, appointing him quartier-maître was already a stretch. Pique is the most experienced officer we have, and the men look up to him. Which is one reason he can be so bold. We may need him back in the field, and he knows it."

The thought makes me cold all over. "You would do that?"

"Me?" Theodora scoffs. "No. Besides, it's Xavier's choice. But we're doing things my way for now. To wit . . . where is my notebook?"

She searches through her papers, but her words ring in my ears. "Is that a threat?" I say. "The general will let Pique massacre a few more villages if I don't cooperate with you?"

La Fleur's hands still. She sighs. "Though you may not

believe it, Xavier is a good man. But even good people can do terrible things when they have no other choice."

Her look is pointed, and how can I argue? Besides, my real fight will be outside these walls, and I can only hope that Pique will be my first target. Theodora frowns at the disarray of her desk, still searching, but my eyes are on the keys, gleaming gold in the electric glow. How can I slip them into my pocket without her noticing?

The sound of soft footsteps interrupts my planning. Is it Leo? No . . . only Camreon, pushing a handcart with a box on it. "Miss Theodora." He gives her an apologetic look, gesturing to his haul. "I'm so sorry. The lieutenant was right. I found this under one of the tables."

I tense, expecting her to be angry, but La Fleur only gives him a rueful smile. "He'll be insufferable next time. Do you want me to come with you?"

"No, no," he says, to my disappointment. "You work too hard as it is. I'll catch up with him and come right back. After all," he adds then, his look turning hopeful. "I'm eager to see what your uncle sent."

"Aren't we all?" she says, and he makes another low bow before he goes. Does she watch him a little longer than she needs to? I press my lips together. The boy is handsome, to be sure, short and compact, with dark brown eyes and fine features and a soft voice that's practically a purr. I can't exactly blame her for staring. But his behavior offends me: his open admiration as he acts as her delivery boy. To Lieutenant Pique, no less!

Theodora turns then—have I made a sound? Color touches her cheeks, but she lifts her chin. "Do you have something to say?"

I take a breath. Have I embarrassed her? "I'm surprised to see a Chakran working here."

"Camreon used to work at the palace," she says. "We've known each other for years. He's quite a brilliant thinker."

Is that why he's running her errands? I cannot ask. "I meant in Hell's Court."

"Ah. Well." The pink in her cheeks deepens. "He's brave too."

I bite my lip. The boy strikes me as more shy than anything else, though of course I haven't known him as long as La Fleur. Maybe it's not what she knows, but what she feels. Am I the same way about Leo? Perhaps love is its own madness.

The thought spins through my mind before I can stop it. Horrified, I push it away. Not love. Not Leo. Still, I feel the flush creeping up my own neck. I take a breath—where was I? Before I can remember, more voices drift across the sanctuary. There is a disturbance among the guards at the door.

Almost gratefully, I turn to watch; the men shout and gesture at something at the base of the stairs. I stand, leaning out, and see a crate large enough to hold a horse sitting on a dolly. The argument unfolds in Aquitan, but I can make out most of it—the men delivering the box demanding help to haul it up the steps, the guards at their posts declining to stoop to such labor.

When Theodora goes to see what the trouble is, I see my chance. The noise of the argument covers the rustle of pages and the jingle of keys as I snatch the ring from the altar. "What's this?" La Fleur says, and I jump, but she's speaking to the soldiers.

The men all reply at once. She holds up a hand to stop them, then points at one of the guards. "We brought these up from the dock," the soldier says. "But the crates are too heavy to get up the stairs without help."

"Crates?" Theodora glances out through the wide doorway and gasps. When I follow her eyes, I do too. There must be two dozen of the boxes in the plaza, with more coming up the central path on wheeled carts, each pushed by four men. My stomach clenches—the supply ship has come in. How many weapons does this represent? La Fleur shakes her head, but her expression is resigned. "We'll open them out here, then. I'll have my staff help bring the supplies in piecemeal."

"That won't work," one of the men calls up from the plaza, wiping sweat from his brow. "Not unless you want to take these things apart."

Theodora frowns. "What do you mean?"

"See for yourself," the man says as he climbs atop one of the wheels to push the heavy wooden lid aside. Theodora walks down the steps just far enough to see into the crate. Then her mouth falls open. There is a long silence, then she swears.

Curious, I stand, hoping to catch a glimpse, but Theodora turns, coming back up the stairs. I try to look small—disinterested and uninteresting—but she nods toward the hall as she takes up her pen. "I'm sorry, Jetta," she says grimly, searching for a fresh sheet of paper. "You should go back to your room after all. I may be a little while."

I hesitate—will she notice the keys are missing? She doesn't seem to, and I make my way back down the hall as her pen scratches furiously across the page.

Dear Uncle Antoine,

Your delivery arrived today, and I am, for want of a better word, overwhelmed.

What you may have intended as a show of strong faith has arrived a display of fervent hope. To put it mildly, your engineers took great liberties with my design. I know my schemata were unfinished when my father sent them to you. That should have been a sign to proceed with caution, not to send half a hundred models based on an unproven prototype. Moreover, the ship was so stuffed with these strange avions that there was no room for the medical supplies or raw materials I requested.

Please read this gently, Uncle, as I know you are still grieving. But you and I have ever been blunt—it was your honest reports that allowed me to discover the lytheum cure in the spring at Les Chanceux. So let me be honest now: I fear it is the destabilizing effects of grief that may be clouding your mind to the realities of the situation. Are you listening to your seneschal and maintaining the treatment?

I know you want a decisive blow in Chakrana, but if physics has taught me anything, it's that any force will result in an equal and opposing reaction. As such, I will be disassembling the avions for their parts, and will follow this letter with an updated list of the need that remains. Please address it in your next shipment.

Yours,

Theodora

ACT 1,

SCENE 10

Late afternoon. The general's office at the barracks in the stone fort at the mouth of the bay. XAVIER is at his desk, poring over a map of Chakrana with the aid of LIEUTENANT FONTAINE. A knock at the door.

XAVIER: Entre! Ah. Quartier-Maître. Come in.

Grizzled and war-weary, LIEUTENANT ARMAND PIQUE is conspicuously older than the man he must call his superior. One might be able to discount the lethargy of his salute as old age, but for the fire in his eyes as he looks at the general.

PIQUE: If you are otherwise occupied, I can return in an hour.

There is a pause so slight that to point it out would be its own humiliation.

Sir.

GENERAL LEGARDE clenches his jaw.

XAVIER: No need for that. Lieutenant Fontaine was just leaving to prepare for his journey. He's assuming your old post.
FONTAINE: I've heard of your exploits in Le Verdu, Lieutenant. Do you have any advice for me?

PIQUE looks his replacement up and down, from his pale face, untouched by the jungle heat, to his shiny boots, still polished from life in the capital. Then he turns toward LEGARDE as he answers.

PIQUE: The enemy can be hiding anywhere in Chakrana. Watch your back.

FONTAINE's eyes flick from one man to the other.

FONTAINE: As you say. Sir!

He nods at both men, then exits. The silence is thick and unpleasant as the humidity.

XAVIER: Reportez, Quartier-Maître.

Gritting his teeth at the title, PIQUE hands over the papers he holds.

PIQUE: The paperwork from your sister's workshop, and the bill of lading for the latest transport from Aquitan. I can't help but notice there are no reinforcements aboard.
XAVIER: My uncle's last letter mentioned we were expecting supplies instead.

He glances at the bill of lading, then frowns.

This can't be right.
PIQUE: I counted them myself.
XAVIER: Fifty of the things?
PIQUE: Steel and brass, shaped like eagles. Fearsome, if you could ever get them off the ground.

XAVIER blinks at the page, reading it again. His other hand creeps up toward his medallion.

XAVIER: Theodora's working on it. Though the bottleneck is still the nécromancien. If we want to use nécromancy, that is.

PIQUE: There's nothing you can do with machinery that you can't do with enough men in the field. Though I can see why recruitment has flagged. They're going to be slaughtered led by children like Fontaine. Especially without intelligence from the questioneurs.

XAVIER looks up from the page, taking a deep breath.

XAVIER: Fontaine is two years my senior, Pique.
PIQUE: As you say.
XAVIER: Nevertheless, Quartier-Maître.

He tosses the paper on his desk and drops his hand.

Slaughter in the field is no longer your concern.
PIQUE: The field is where the fight is.
XAVIER: I'm not so sure, Pique. The fight seems to follow you.
PIQUE: It must look that way to one so comfortable behind a desk.

Slowly, XAVIER stands, stepping into the open with the barest limp in his wounded leg.

XAVIER: I didn't stop the abomination in Luda with paperwork. Nor was it comfort that made me cut short my convalescence to haul you and your battalion out of Le Verdu. I don't bother chasing glory either, Quartier-Maître. I go where God sends me. And right now, he needs me to oversee progress in the workshop.

PIQUE smiles thinly.

PIQUE: Yes, someday you'll be quite well known for your oversights. The discrepancies continue in your sister's little domain.

The general stiffens.

XAVIER: Theodora's talents do not lie in recordkeeping.
PIQUE: Her cha keeps those records, General. Your sister is too busy scribbling love notes in her diary to do figures.
XAVIER: She's designed half the weaponry we're using these days.
PIQUE: She's also done half a dozen sketches of her secretary's profile.

The lieutenant reaches into his jacket pocket, taking out THEODORA's notebook and tossing it on the general's desk. XAVIER looks down at the book in shock.

XAVIER: You stole this from my sister? Put it back on her desk now, or your next post will be digging latrines.
PIQUE: I still won't be half as deep in it as you, if you let cha turn your sister to their side.

He flips open the notebook to the most recent page—there, indeed, is a likeness of CAMREON beside a labeled sketch of the crank of a rotary cannon. XAVIER clenches his jaw, his mouth tight as he considers the sketch. Then he flips the book shut.

XAVIER: These are clearly drawings of her fiancé, Pique. The Boy King. Who she must miss very much. I've heard you say yourself that Chakrans all look the same.

He holds up a hand to forestall the lieutenant's arguments.

Nevertheless. When I go to return her property, I'll speak to my sister about focusing on her work.

PIQUE: You'll speak? (*He laughs.*) In your father's day, generals led. Of course, back then, rank was earned.

XAVIER: You're dismissed, Quartier-Maître.

The general goes to the door, opening it to show the old lieutenant out. Then he returns to his desk, considering the notebook. After a long moment, Xavier picks it up, sitting down to read.

CHAPTER
ELEVEN

It is late evening when Theodora comes to the door of my cell, and I am sure from her face that she has discovered the keys missing. La Fleur is paler than usual, and her chin is dimpled from clenching her jaw. But she does not mention my theft as she beckons me out past the guards. "I'm glad you're still up," she says, running a hand through her mussed curls. "The day got away from me, but I have some more questions."

"Why am I not surprised?" I give her a casual laugh as I follow her toward the sanctuary, trying to keep the keys from jingling in my pocket. "What about?"

"Your brother," she says, and my steps falter. "He wasn't the first man you resurrected, was he?"

The accusation surprises me, though perhaps it shouldn't. "He was."

Theodora glances sidelong at me. "Then what happened to the questioneur in Luda?"

"Oh." I blink at her—at those ghost blue eyes. In my memory, I see another pair. Eduard, the soldier who had tried to bring me in after my first brush with the rebellion. I had been so desperate to escape. Anger rises in me, flooding past the guilt; after all, the man was a questioneur. "He wasn't dead. At least, not when I marked him. I put another soul in his skin. A n'akela. The spirit of one of the boys he tortured."

"While the questioneur was still living?" Now it is Theodora's turn to look surprised. She takes a breath, about to say more, but instead she stops in her tracks and swears. Then she turns and leads me back toward my room. "Wrong way."

"Why?" I peer over my shoulder toward the sanctuary at the end of the hall—there is activity there, despite the lateness of the hour. The hum and murmur of many people. "Pique?"

"Almost as bad," she says, making a face. "It's the delivery from my uncle. It's completely thrown off my routines."

A pang of real sympathy hits me: routine used to be my only barrier against my malheur. "How so?"

In response, she flings out an arm as we enter the workshop—I am surprised to see it empty. Anticipation twists a knot in my gut. I let my eyes pass casually by the locked room in the corner as Theodora nods at a table piled high with her papers. "To start with, my filing system has been thrown into disarray. Secondly, my notebook is missing, though perhaps that's only part and parcel of my first problem. But lastly, my entire staff is arguing the merits of building a ramp over the front steps of the temple versus widening the path through the gardens. Most of my staff," she adds, more quietly now.

I follow her gaze and see Camreon. He sits on the floor beside the table, holding the aides à la mobilité, tinkering with a wheel on the chair. "What are you doing here, Cam?"

Pushing his hair out of his eyes, he blinks up at La Fleur; there is a spot of grease on his cheek. "Sorry, Miss Theodora. The sanctuary was rather crowded. I know the saying is that too many cooks spoil the soup, but I'm fairly sure that too many engineers can spoil something too."

"Possibly the appetite," she says, peering at a tray shoved into a bare spot on the far end of the table. On it, a heap of wide noodles tossed with fresh vegetables and roasted pork, a plate of crab and herbs rolled up in rice paper, and a black rice pudding sticky with coconut milk.

"To be fair, that might have been Pique." Camreon gives her a winsome smile. "I couldn't help but notice in all the back-and-forth earlier, you forgot to have lunch."

She smiles faintly. "Is that why I'm so irritable?"

"If I had to guess?" Camreon lowers his voice like a conspirator. "I'd say that's probably Pique's fault as well. Then again, it could be that you never sleep. Your schedule will be the death of you."

Now she laughs, though her look is rueful. "You worry too much."

"I like my job," he says. Then he leans into my line of sight—that's when I realize I've been staring at the pudding. My mouth is watering. It looks so much better than the dry Aquitan bread. "I made more than enough to share, lailee."

Though the boy is not my brother, the honorific is

touching. Still. "I thought you were an engineer, not a cook," I say. "Do the Aquitan workers do double duty?"

"Of course not," Camreon says with a straight face. "Haven't you heard what everyone says about Aquitan laziness?"

My eyebrows shoot up, but to my surprise, La Fleur's lips twitch. "To say nothing of our avarice," she says, echoing Xavier's insult to me earlier. She takes a plate from the tray, handing me one, and Camreon another. "You best take some before I seize all of it."

Their rapport is so comfortable that it leaves me feeling at loose ends. To cover, I pick up a crab roll. "You're very young to be so accomplished," I say pointedly, but Camreon only tilts his chin, running a finger along his jaw.

"I'm older than I look," he says with another gentle smile. "No beard."

My hand goes still, hovering over the food. But hadn't Theodora said he was brave? He must be, to call her attention to what the Aquitans would call his crime, with their obsession about bodies over souls. But La Fleur only returns his smile. "Not to mention the extra time he has, since he hasn't got to shave."

They lapse into companionable silence as they eat. How

mundane it is for the two of them, that he trusts her with his life! Is he only naive, or has she earned it? There is more to Theodora Legarde than I had expected. As I take little bites of the delicious black rice, I am absurdly grateful that I didn't kill her last night.

Then her brother's voice rings out across the hall.

"Theodora?" The sight of the general makes my stomach clench. Camreon scrambles to his feet. Theodora's reaction is more subtle—a graceful movement as she shifts her weight, putting space between herself and the Chakran boy. But Xavier is only looking at me. "Why is she out of the carcan?"

"Good to see you too," Theodora says smoothly as she puts down her plate. "We were just having dinner."

"And I was just having a conversation with Lieutenant Pique." The words come clipped through his teeth. The general looks from her, to me, to Camreon, who doesn't meet his gaze. But to my surprise, the boy speaks up, though it looks like he's talking to his shoes.

"It was my fault, General, sir. The missing supplies were stacked where we usually keep the raw materials. Once I located them, I brought them to the lieutenant right away."

Xavier only clenches his jaw. "If I need an answer from you, I'll ask."

"Camreon, perhaps you should go help with the ramp." At Theodora's suggestion, the boy practically flees down the hall. When he's gone, La Fleur sighs. "What is it you need, Xavier?"

"To talk." He flicks his eyes at me. "In private."

Theodora grits her teeth, her good mood soured. But she tosses back her hair and jerks her chin toward the hall. Turning crisply on his heel, Xavier follows. She leads him to the first cell, pulling the door open; as they step inside, I can hardly believe my luck. The workshop is empty but for me.

Is it a trick? Some ploy to catch me red-handed? But I can hear their heated voices almost immediately. The roofs of the cells are only canvas, though the stone is still thick enough to muffle their words. Tossing aside my own plate, I shove my hand into my pocket for the keys, but my fingers meet the flyer first.

No—it's too early to ensoul the flying machine. Akra had said to wait till midnight tomorrow. Instead, I pull out the ring of keys. There are quite a few of them, and the door of the locked room gives no indication of the right one, so I start with the heaviest. The key doesn't fit, so I try the next, and the next, but the longer it takes, the more my hands shake. Should I use the flyer instead? Put a soul into the lock?

I swear it is the last key on the ring that makes the heavy iron tumblers fall. Eagerly, I grasp the handle. As the door swings wide, I curse—there is another just behind it. Iron bars, closely spaced, and locked as well. But behind them . . . behind them . . .

It is not the storage room I expected—no cramped closet reeking of oil and chemistry. Instead, an electric bulb hangs from the ceiling, illuminating a narrow teak bed, pale clean sheets . . . and a Chakran man with his head on the pillow.

His hair is short and clean, going gray at the temples; he is thin but not painfully so. His face is unlined, and his skin is a bit pale—but that isn't surprising, considering he hasn't seen the sun in years. There is a heavy set of manacles around his ankles, and a short chain connecting them to a ring in the floor. Aside from that, he looks like just another man. Someone's uncle, napping. Someone's father.

Mine.

I don't know if I've made a sound, but all of a sudden, the man opens his eyes and I startle. I had half expected the bright blue irises of vengeful ghosts, though I am not so lucky. It is something worse. His eyes are a warm brown, wide and intelligent and too familiar. I've seen them every time I've looked in a mirror.

Le Trépas sits up and smiles at me.

I vomit on the floor.

ACT 1,

SCENE 12

THEODORA and XAVIER in the ruined cell. Three scarred stone walls; the fourth is reduced to rubble where the rambunctious garden is already starting to intrude. The general shuts the door behind them, then looks carefully at his sister over his steepled fingers as though wondering where to start. At last he lowers his hands.

XAVIER: Setting aside Pique's accusation that you're going native, I'd like a report on the progress you're making with the nécromancien.

THEODORA: "Going native?"

XAVIER: Setting it aside—

THEODORA: You just set it directly between us!

XAVIER: Would you prefer to address it, then?

THEODORA: It's as ridiculous as he is.

XAVIER gives her a long look, but she lifts her chin, defiant, though her cheeks are pink. Is it anger or shame?

THEODORA: Look, Xavi, just because I've spent some time getting to know the people I work with—

XAVIER: There are three dozen Aquitan engineers working on your ramp, and I find you eating curry with the two Chakrans?

THEODORA: You prefer bacon that's been marinating in bilge water for a week?

XAVIER: I prefer the company of my kind.

The general sighs.

I don't blame you for it, Theodora. You were even younger than I was when our mother went back to Aquitan. Of course the various women our father brought on as caretakers had an influence on you. Not to mention his constant visits to that cathouse.

THEODORA: To Le Perl, you mean. The theater.

XAVIER (*ignoring her correction*): So it's natural, in a way. Your . . . fascination with the locals. And I know that you and Leo have always been close. But you must make a distinction between comfort and collaboration. We're not all on the same side.

THEODORA: But you and I are trying to be. Aren't we?

XAVIER: The nécromancien could help get us there. Especially now that we have the flying machines.

THEODORA clenches her jaw.

THEODORA: Pique told you about those too?

XAVIER: I saw the bill of lading. How soon can you get the avions commissioned?

THEODORA: I thought you called the fantouches abominations?

XAVIER: Theodora—

THEODORA: It won't work. You heard her as well as I did. Her blood gives her control of the machinery.

XAVIER: What if I use it to draw the symbol instead?

THEODORA's mouth drops open at his suggestion—so similar to the one she'd written in her notebook.

Well?

THEODORA: What makes you ask that?

XAVIER: Have you tried it?

THEODORA: Why are you reading my notebook?

XAVIER: Why are you keeping secrets?

THEODORA: They're not secrets, they're theories! Untested, I might add.

XAVIER: Then test them! Our foothold here is tenuous at best, Theodora! If we lose control of the country, God knows who or what will take our place. I want an update this evening.

THEODORA: It would help if I had my notebook back.

XAVIER pulls it from his jacket, tossing it to her.

XAVIER: Keep better care of it. Pique found it while he was here this morning.

THEODORA: Where? On my desk?

XAVIER: He didn't mention. But he also saw the drawings of your fiancé.

The general gives her a significant look. THEODORA opens her mouth, but before she can say anything, a scream splits the air. JETTA's voice. Brother and sister look at each other for a moment; then XAVIER rips open the door and dashes into the hall, followed closely by THEODORA.

CHAPTER

THIRTEEN

Pounding feet—people running—someone is screaming—
is it me? With a strike like a punch to my shoulders, the
general shoves me away from the iron grate. As I stumble
backward, he kicks the outer door shut with a clang. "Putain,
Theodora, you should have known better than to trust her!"

La Fleur is just behind him. She draws a handkerchief
out of her pocket, using it to pluck the ring of keys from
the noxious puddle on the floor and lock the heavy door.
But what is the look in her eyes? Not disgust. Regret? Guilt?
Fear? "You sound like Pique," she says to her brother.

"He was right, wasn't he?" Xavier grabs me by the wrist,

wrenching me around to see my audience: when had they appeared? The guards from outside my room . . . Camreon too, and a few of the other engineers. They must have come running when they'd heard my screams. The general yanks me around again, his face pale with rage. "What were you doing in there?"

"I thought I would find my elixir," I pant. I can hardly breathe, much less speak. My fingers tingle; there is a roaring in my ears. "You told me he escaped!"

"We only printed it on your recherche," Theodora corrects me, but she has the good grace to look ashamed. Still, Xavier turns to her, incredulous.

"You don't need to justify yourself to her, Theodora!"

My laugh is a wild thing, bouncing off the stone walls. "And you claim you can't trust *me*?"

"I think it's clear I've been too lenient with everyone," the general growls. "How did she get the keys?"

Theodora's response is pointed. "Probably the same way Pique got my notebook."

"You should never have let her out of the carcan," he shoots back. Then he narrows his eyes, turning back to me. "But since you are, we might as well see what you can do. Where is the note you wrote to the Tiger? Summon it."

I open my mouth to protest, but all that comes out is a hiss as he twists my arm. The bones of my wrist creak in his grasp. "Come," I whisper, and soon enough, I catch sight of the dirty recherche, fluttering toward us in the hall.

What does he want with it? The general snatches the scrap out of the air as he drags me, stumbling, toward the flying machine. Theodora frowns, following him. "Xavier—"

But the general ignores her, calling to one of his men. "Alec! Your lighter!"

One of the guards steps forward, but I cannot stop staring at the sleek wings of Theodora's invention. Is Xavier foolish enough to let me ensoul the thing? I do not protest as he nicks my finger with the knife at his belt: here is my freedom before me. I can already imagine the flame pouring from the twin barrels on the front. I will raze the place to the ground—Le Trépas too. The general is mad himself, to think I won't. But to my surprise, he curls his lip and dips his own finger in the blood on mine. Then he pushes me into the waiting arms of the guard. "Hold her."

The soldat obeys, digging his hands into the flesh of my arm. But I stare at Xavier, half mesmerized as he lifts his hand. Still, he hesitates. On his face is a look of distaste— not at my blood, but for the magic it holds.

Behind me, Theodora shifts on her feet. Her face is troubled as she stares at the avion—the metal wings, the hooked beak. "If it doesn't work—"

The general lifts his clean hand sharply, cutting her short. But he takes hold of the medallion at his neck, whispering a prayer to his own god before he paints the symbol on the leather wing. Then he wipes the blood from his hand as though it carries a curse.

As he holds my note to the Tiger over the flame, I tense, ready to leap to the flying machine. As the soul spirals up and flashes into her new skin, I whisper to her: "Fly."

The avion only shudders, shaking her wings. Xavier gives me a look. "Fly," he repeats grimly, and the bird spreads her wings.

They beat—once, twice—the wind moving through my hair. I feel dizzy as the machine begins to lift from the stone. Surely it is a mistake. The soul only hesitated—she was late to obey the command *I* gave. But Xavier puts his hand out to stop her, and the machine drops down and folds her wings.

Then he turns to me, and the look on his face is less triumphant than resigned. "Theodora, have your men unbox the rest of the shipment on the plaza. Jean, send for the armée docteur," he adds, turning to the second guard.

Then he points to Camreon. "You. Go to the dovecotes and bring me all the messenger pigeons. And for god's sake, someone put her back in her cell."

The threat jolts me into action. With a burst of strength born of panic, I pull free of the guard and run toward the far hall. A gunshot stops me—a crack like a snapped bone. "Consider," Xavier says as I skid to a halt. "I don't need you alive to take your blood."

I sway on my feet; when a guard prods me with his gun, I nearly tip over. As he marches me back to my room, my eyes dart left, then right, searching the corridor fruitlessly for a way to escape. But the general follows just behind me, as does Theodora, like a kite on a string.

"Xavi, please." Her tone is an attempt at calm. "You can't rush these things."

"It's been more than a month since Father was killed," he says. "Long past time for action."

"But you've barely tested the first avion! You don't know if you can command two at once, much less fifty."

"I'll order each bird to obey a handler," Xavier replies.

"But what if something happens to you?" she says, her voice rising with desperation. "If the whole flock is under your control, you're a target for kidnapping, or worse."

"I'm already a target, Theodora." He slows as we approach the door to my cell. "Any other excuses?"

Anger flashes in La Fleur's eyes. "They aren't excuses, they're concerns."

The guards push me through the open door, shutting it behind me; the jingle of keys in the lock makes my heart pound. Still, I can hear her through the heavy wood.

"I'm trying to save you from making a mistake!"

"I don't need you to save me, Theodora. . . ." Xavier's voice fades down the hall. I try the door, just in case, but it is definitely locked. Dare I open it with the hawk's soul in the flyer Leo had sent me? No—the guards will be right outside and I have no way to fight past them. Better to get a message to him—or to my brother. Unless . . . "Akra?" I whisper the name at first, but there is no answer. "Akra!"

My voice echoes in the stone cell, and despair rises in my heart. Maybe it really was a hallucination.

Still, I have a way to get him a message. Pulling the flyer from my pocket, I cast about for something to use as a writing utensil, but there is nothing in the room. I check the lamp for ash, but I've never lit the wick. Then my heart skips a beat—what about the book of matches?

Striking one at a time and waiting for them to cool, I

use the ash like a crude pencil. I cannot write much—x ENSOULED MACHINE, NEW PLAN? But between my message and the flyer itself, Akra will surely be able to guess that something has gone wrong. But before I can finish the letter, the keys jingle in the lock once again.

Hurriedly, I shove the paper into my pocket moments before the door opens. A stranger stands there, sweating in a foreign suit. "The docteur," Xavier announces as he follows the man into the room. Then the general wrinkles his nose at the sulfur smell of the matches, glancing at the scattered sticks on the stone floor. I bite back a curse as he picks up what's left of the matchbook and puts it in his own pocket. He only gives me a look. "Sit."

I have little choice. The docteur sets his leather case beside me on the pillow. My heart pounds as he unbuckles the clasps and rummages inside. Then he draws a long needle from his case.

At first I think he means to take my blood with it. Instead, he pushes half a dram of cold liquid into the crook of my arm. My stomach drops as my head starts to float. My eyes are fluttering as the doctor draws a thin lancet out of his case; it's so sharp I don't even feel the cut. Blood runs down my forearm: a red river into a glass jar.

The smell sickens me . . . iron and soil. When the jar is full, the docteur hands it to Xavier and bandages the wound. The general carries the jar away—toward the sanctuary, toward the waiting avions. As my eyes slide shut, I can't tell if I am dreaming when I hear the sound of wings beating.

Wings

music and lyrics by
Mei Rath

With mon-ey, we could build a

pal-ace, and live our lives like kings. With

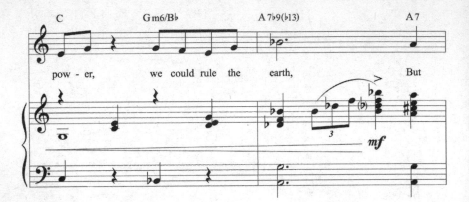

pow - er, we could rule the earth, But

what could we do___ with wings?___ With

jew - els, we could wear our rich - es in neck - la - ces___ and rings.

With ar-mies, we could con-quer worlds, But

what could we do with wings?

Some peo-ple say love's not e-nough, a

girl should ask for more. _____ But love is all I want,

_____ and you're the one that makes my heart soar.

And is - n't it a love

geth - er,   your   love   will

give   me   wings._____

ACT 1,
SCENE 14

Night at Hell's Court. In the plaza outside, the electric bulbs are blazing, and extra torches have been lit for the workers still disassembling the crates. THEODORA is watching over her engineers, her face grim, her arms folded. But the sanctuary is practically deserted. Only XAVIER is there, leaning against the altar on which the glass jar rests, wrapped in a clean white handkerchief and brimming with clotting blood.

The sounds of work drift in from the plaza, but XAVIER is very still. For a while, he contemplates the stone floor where his father died. Then he looks up, searching, as though he can see the stars through the armée green canvas of the roof.

XAVIER: Holy Father in heaven, sacred and glorious, your will be done on earth and in heaven.

His voice falters. He takes a breath as he searches for the right words.

XAVIER: Guide my footsteps, oh my God, on this shadowed path, and reveal to me why you have brought the nécromancien under my control.

He closes his eyes, bowing his head again.

Am I meant to use her blood to do your will, or am I putting my soul in peril by participating in dark magic? Give me a sign, my Lord. Show me the way.

THEODORA (*off-stage*): Xavi?

The general opens his eyes, blinking, as THEODORA comes to the entrance of the temple. If anything, her expression is even more sour than before.

XAVIER: Yes?
THEODORA: Pique is here.
XAVIER (*frowning*): Why?
THEODORA: God only knows.

The general's hand travels to his medallion as he follows his sister outside. Indeed, LIEUTENANT PIQUE has arrived, pushing a handcart stacked with bamboo cages. Each one holds a dark gray pigeon. Wings rustle as golden eyes peer from the depths. The general looks from the birds to PIQUE and back.

XAVIER: I asked one of the engineers to fetch the birds.

PIQUE takes a breath, choosing his response carefully. When he speaks, his tone is crisp—respectful. So different than before.

PIQUE: As quartier-maître, I'm in charge of supplies. It was my duty to make sure you got the pigeons. And as you know, the . . . engineer in question has already misplaced several boxes.
THEODORA: And found them again.

PIQUE raises an eyebrow.

PIQUE: That's news to me.

La Fleur frowns, but PIQUE presses on.

Speaking of news, sir, rumor is you plan to create a special force to fight by air. As the most experienced officer in Chakrana, I'd like to be considered to lead it.

The general blinks at the man.

XAVIER: You?

PIQUE draws himself up.

PIQUE: I've spent nearly two decades traversing this country. I know it north to south. When you're a hundred feet above the jungle, you can't spend time peering at a map. And not only am I the most experienced officer in the country, but with Fontaine gone, I'm also the only man above sergeant in Nokhor Khat. Aside from you, sir. And we can't risk you.

The general looks at THEODORA.

XAVIER: My sister said much the same thing.

La Fleur's eyes narrow; she speaks under her breath.

THEODORA: I didn't say to share command with Pique.

The general turns to her sharply.

XAVIER: I don't follow your orders.
THEODORA: But you'll follow his?

She glares at PIQUE, speaking through her teeth. XAVIER's reply is stiff.

XAVIER: I'll follow God's.
THEODORA: And what are God's orders now?
XAVIER: I'm still trying to figure that out.

The general takes a deep breath, and turns back to PIQUE.

One question, Quartier-Maître. What makes you volunteer? Is it service to the armée? Or glory for yourself?

PIQUE hesitates, considering his answer.

PIQUE: It's salvation, sir.
XAVIER: You've never seemed like a godly man to me.
PIQUE: I don't know much about God, sir. But I know

about Chakrana. This country needs saving, and I'm willing to do whatever it takes. Are you?

A pause.

XAVIER: Yes. Yes, I am. Lieutenant?

PIQUE straightens up at the title, saluting sharply.

PIQUE: General, sir?
XAVIER: Unload the cages. Put one by each avion. I'll bring the blood.

CHAPTER FIFTEEEN

When I wake, it is from a dream: it is the dry season, and I am eight years old. Akra is teaching me how to work the puppet of a butterfly as we roll down the road on our way to a show. The roulotte is rocking under us, and the sweet smell of rumdal floats in on the breeze.

Akra holds the wire; on the end is a little scrap of mulberry paper, trembling with the tiny motions of his hand. He is so good with the fantouches—gentle and steady. But when I take it from him, the wire bends in my hands. The fantouche falls, and I try to catch it. Instead, I crush it in my fist.

When I open my eyes, it is dark. How long have I slept? I blink, still nauseated. Is it the blood loss or the lingering effect of the drugs? Is it the theft of my blood itself? My hand goes to the bandage tied around my elbow—the memory makes my skin crawl. The dark red liquid in the clean glass jar, the stink of iron threaded with the stench of sulfur . . .

I take a deep breath, trying to clear it, and hear the crinkling of paper. Frowning, I slip my free hand beneath the pillow and find a whole stack of it.

My heart pounds along with my head as I pull out the book of souls—the rest of the flyers, sewn together with red ribbon. Laying the book on my lap, I flip through the pages: here, the soul of a friendly dog that used to belong to our neighbor, and here, the soul of an armée horse that I'd found running through a rice field. The playful soul of a lemur from the jungle up the hill behind our village, a multitude of birds.

The pages rustle; I hug them tight to my chest. Old friends in this deathly place—and more than that. I had not imagined my brother's voice, and nothing can stand between us now. The locks are no obstacle—nor are the walls, if it comes to that. I could destroy the whole workshop by slipping spirits into the columns along the halls—or the bricks of Le Trépas's cell. And this time, I would make sure the old monk was killed in the collapse.

In fact, I could kill him now—burst through the door with one soul, bend the bars with another—if I was brave enough to touch him. To wrap my hands around his neck.

What am I thinking? I shudder, appalled at the violence I feel. With Legarde, I had rationalized my actions as my malheur—as a choice made on the spur of a terrible moment. Could I go so far as to plan out a murder? To open Le Trépas's door again, to walk into the cell where the old monk sits, to . . . to . . .

My mind balks. I don't want to see him again, much less wrench his soul from his body. Perhaps it is best to focus on my own escape. What time is it? I squint through the window, but though it is dark, I cannot see the moon. I don't have time to dawdle.

I have to get out—but how? The flying machine is no longer an option. Did my brother and Leo have another plan? Slowly, I stand, making sure I am steady on my feet. Then I try the door. To my surprise, it is unlocked, and though the guards hold their bayonets a little tighter when they see me, they don't bother to hide the bottle they've been passing. "What's the time?" I ask carefully, but Jean only shrugs.

"Nearly midnight," he says, and my stomach drops.

"I slept a whole day?"

Alec only gives me a knowing look, lifting the bottle in a mock toast. "What you got from the docteur was much better than wine."

Inside, I curse; outwardly, I smile. I need to get them away from the door. "Less filling, though," I say, but he only offers me the bottle. I raise my eyebrow. "On an empty stomach?"

"Come now. It's a celebration!" He shakes the bottle again, the dark liquid sloshing against the green glass. This time, I take it, pretending to drink, trying not to stare at the stains on his teeth.

"What are we celebrating?"

"The end of the war," Jean says, and I nearly drop the wine. "The rebellion is as good as over now that we have the avions."

Despair is a dark threat; my hand comes up to cover the bandage over the crook of my arm. But things can only get worse as long as I'm here at Hell's Court. "Can I go check the kitchens?" I say—a long shot, but I have to get out. "There might be some food left over."

"I don't think the general would like it if we let you out for a little stroll." Alec laughs again, and I grit my teeth. But then he takes the bottle back from Jean and frowns when he finds it empty. "C'est tout? Ah, well. If I have to go back to the kitchens anyway, I'll bring something for you as well."

"Alec," the other guard says, a warning. "I don't think it's wise to part ways."

Alec only winks at him, setting the bottle down by the door. "Don't worry, my friend. I'll bring something for you too!"

He starts down the hall as Jean chews his cheek, adjusting his grip on his weapon. Is the soldier afraid of me? I suppose he should be. But with only one guard to deal with, I might not even have to kill him.

Stepping back into the dubious privacy of my room, I swing the door nearly closed, till all I can see is a thin slip of Jean's back. Then I pull out my book of souls, flipping through till I find what I'm looking for: the soul of a boa, sleepy but strong.

Quietly, I yank the gauzy mosquito netting from over

my bed and roll it lengthwise, knotting it every few feet, to keep it together. Then I tear out the page, but where will I find a fire? As though in answer to my unspoken prayer, I hear the sound of Jean's lighter; in another moment, the familiar smell of smoke wafts in. Chewing my lip, I fold the flyer and roll it tightly. Tucking it between my fingers and holding it just so, it looks a bit like a cigarette.

Leaning out into the hall, I wave the rolled paper at Jean. "Do you have a light?"

Now he laughs. "Where did you get that?"

I shrug, affecting nonchalance. "The docteur said it would calm my nerves."

"That it will." He reaches into his pocket and pulls out the lighter. Three clicks to a flame, and the end of my rolled flyer goes up in smoke.

"Thank you, merci." I duck back behind the door before he can ask why I'm not smoking the thing. Cupping the paper in my hand, I coax the flame to life. Soon enough, the flyer blackens to ash, but I have already moved on to the netting. It doesn't take a lot of prodding at the tender wound on my arm to draw blood. Wincing, I dab the gauze with the mark of life. When the snake soul tumbles free of the flyer, it slithers immediately into the fabric.

The length of netting twists, rolling in my hands. "Wrap him up," I whisper, setting the fabric down at my feet. "Hold him tight."

The soul of the snake slips out through the crack in the doorway. A moment later, I hear a cry. The bayonet clatters to the floor as Jean struggles, and though he wraps his hands around the sheet, he can't choke something that does not breathe. The silk winds tighter and tighter around his ribs, and soon he is the one choking. When I open the door, he looks up at me with bloodshot eyes. "Aidez-moi," he wheezes. "Help me."

Instead I pick up the man's bayonet. But glancing down the hall, I hesitate. The gun might not be as helpful as his lighter. Turning back, I whisper to the snake's soul, "Not so tight." Jean drags a shallow breath as I dig through his pockets. Just as my fingers close around the metal, I hear a shout. "Jean!"

Alec is running back down the hall, leveling his weapon. I bring up my own, but I fumble with the trigger and paw at the safety. I have no idea how to fire this gun.

"Stop where you are!" Alec's command echoes down the hall as he drops to one knee to take aim.

I cast about wildly, but there is nowhere to hide in the

starkly lit hall. A wild hope: can the shadows protect me? Grabbing my weapon by the stock, I swing the tip through the glowing glass of the nearest electric lamp. The bulb shatters in a shower of sparks; all along the hall, the other lights flicker and die.

The soldier roars a curse in the dark. I blink, but the only thing I can see is the afterglow of the explosion. All the lights in the building have gone out. I can't see my hand in front of my face, much less find my own way to the workshop. Turning the lighter over in my hand, I flick it to life: a lone flame in the dark.

But before I can get my bearings, the click of metal on metal echoes down the hall—too familiar. Dropping to the floor, I smother the light a moment before the crack of the gun. The echoes fade into shouting and cursing—the workers in the cells are waking in a panic. "Stay in your rooms!" Alec calls, but I can hear the sounds of doors opening in the hall.

"Who's shooting?"

Jumping, I stifle a scream—but it is only my brother's voice. "Akra," I whisper. "Where are you?"

"In the back of the temple. The workshop. Are you hurt? What happened to the lights?"

"I'm fine," I say through clenched teeth. It's not a lie . . . yet. "I have bad news about the flying machine."

"I know," Akra says grimly. "The Tiger told me."

"The Tiger?" My exclamation was too loud; I bite my tongue. In the silence, I hear Alec reloading.

"We're all here," my brother says. "Where are you?"

I take a breath, chastened. I need to get to my brother's side, but the hall is so dark. Damn Le Trépas for chasing all the souls away. I could use one from my book, but it would only flee if I didn't trap it first. Frowning, I feel my way across the floor. Where is that wine bottle?

My searching hands brush the stone, the broken shards of the electric bulb, Jean's leg, now still. Then—yes. The empty bottle. It rocks as my fingers graze the glass, but I snatch it up before it tips over.

Scrambling to my feet and pulling out the cork, I tear a random page from my book and stuff it into the mouth of the bottle. All along the hall, doors are creaking open, people peeking out. Would Alec be reckless enough to fire toward a crowd? I decide to risk it, setting the flyer aflame. For a moment, I see the frightened faces of the engineers, pale in the light, all turning my way. But I am only another shadow among them. "Get back in your rooms!" Alec shouts. "The nécromancien has escaped!"

A shocked murmur goes up around me, but soon enough, the flame snuffs out. I jam the cork back into the bottle, trapping the soul in the glass. By the dim light of the spirit, I flee as fast as I can.

How soon until the light is restored? Can we slip out the back door in the dark? But when I reach the great hall, all the questions fly out of my head as I skid to a halt, unmoored. Gone are the plows and the gunnery and the open work spaces scattered with gears. Theodora's other projects have been cleared aside to make room for the avions.

The machines stand in eerie rows, and in the green glow of my makeshift lamp, they are unmistakably alive. They do not hop or sway—but in the shadows, there is a rustle of metal wings, the creak of joints that need oiling.

They chill me, these enormous creatures—and so many of them. Tentatively, I approach the machine closest to me, reaching out a gentle hand. "Come," I whisper. At the sound of my voice, there is another ripple of movement through the flock. One even ruffles its wings, like a dove does when her sleep is interrupted. But they are only responding to the noise—the creatures do not obey my command. Though my blood is on their skin, they do not belong to me.

I can't help it; I shudder. I understand it now—the general's fear of what I can do. What had he called it? An abomination. Is that what they are? What I am? I don't know—but in the armée's hands, it is sure to mean destruction. "Akra?" I whisper. "Where are you?"

Even though I'm expecting the answer, I still jump at the response. "Down here. At the west end of the hall."

I change course, dodging through the machines as fast as I can, panting under my breath. "We have to do something with them, Akra. We can't just let him have—"

"I know, Jetta! It's being taken care of. Just hurry! I hear guards!"

"Taken care of?" The only answer is a shouted order in Aquitan and the sound of booted feet echoing down the hall. Gritting my teeth, I pick up the pace, my mind working furiously. It would take coal or gas to make a fire hot enough to destroy the avions. Or kerosene—but where is Theodora hiding the chemicals, if not in the locked room? Then I see another light moving slowly—a narrow beam from a thief's lamp. When I see the man holding it, my heart skips a beat: Leo, his violin case slung on his back, the shape of it silhouetted against the dim glow. He has the lamp's shutters cocked to shine on a thick spool of copper wire, and the two careful hands paying it out along the floor. "Camreon?"

"Jetta." Without glancing up, the Chakran boy inclines his chin as he walks slowly backward. The wire is thin—almost invisible in the dark—as it coils toward the nearest flying machine. But when I raise my own lamp, I can follow the gleam of the metal in the soul glow, linking each avion to the next. A chill goes through me. The most notorious saboteur in Chakrana is the leader of the rebellion. The Tiger. I look at Cam with new eyes. He smiles back at me—or at least, he shows his teeth. "For all your talk about joining the rebellion, you're terrible at following orders."

"I should think a rebel leader would appreciate dissent," I hiss, but now is not the time to pick a fight. "Where is my brother?" I ask instead, and the Tiger jerks his chin toward the stone archway leading to the garden.

"Waiting by the back door," he says. "Lucky I'd already cut copies of the keys you stole."

I clench my jaw, biting back a retort as I leave him to his work. And there is Akra—the sight of him is a weight off my shoulders. He is standing behind a wheeled chair—is that Papa sitting in it? It must be the device that Cam was working on earlier. A grateful smile tugs at the corners of my mouth. But the green light of my lantern reveals a different man sitting there. His head is covered by a black linen bag, and his arms swathed in a carcan, but I recognize the manacles on the feet.

Le Trépas. Outside his cell.

My spirit lamp shatters on the floor as I reel; the soul inside spirals free, fleeing down the hall. Someone grips my shoulders; I wrench away, but it is only Leo. His hands are up, placating, as he speaks. "We can't let them use your blood. And we certainly can't let them use his."

I gape at Leo—I can't think of my own solution, but I don't like his. "So you'll set him free?"

"He's hardly free," Leo says. "And Akra will be guarding him to make sure he doesn't escape—"

"So *when* he gets out, he'll kill my brother first?"

"No," Leo says delicately. "He can't take a soul that you've already put back."

I stare at him, wild-eyed. "How on earth can you know that?"

"The myths written in the walls," Camreon interjects.

"Theodora may have told you she had a translator working on them."

I blink at him, incredulous. "You?"

"Me," he says, passing by with the wire. "I'll tell you all about it when we're not so pressed for time."

I want to scream at him, at all of them. How dare they keep this from me? How dare they risk all our lives? And how dare my brother go along with it? But before I can say anything, a new voice makes us all turn.

"I'd like to hear it now, actually." Theodora appears at the edge of the circle of lamplight, and though her voice is firm, there is real sorrow in her eyes.

"Miss Theodora." Camreon's voice is oddly tender as he straightens up to meet her gaze. "What have I told you about getting more sleep?"

"Did you think I was a fool?" Her voice shakes—from sorrow, or anger? But as she raises her hand, the light shines dully on the barrel of a pistol. "I spoke to Pique today, Cam. He never got the box you claim you brought to him. So I checked the supply room. We were missing a box of lytheum. You're the only other person who ever seemed interested in the formula. And I started to wonder why the rebels were so good at explosives."

Torchlight bounces down the hall as the soldiers draw near. There is pain on Theodora's face, but her aim is steady. Slowly Camreon sets down the spool. He walks toward her on steady feet, till his chest is pressed against the barrel of her weapon. Was this the bravery La Fleur so admired? Camreon gives her that winsome smile. Then, quick as a viper, he grabs her wrist. She pulls the trigger, but the weapon only jams.

"I'm also the only other person who knows you keep your gun under your pillow." He twists the pistol out of her grip and ducks under her wrist, pushing her arm up behind her back until she cries out.

"Don't hurt her!" Leo steps forward, a warning in his voice, but the Tiger gives him a look as he pulls his own gun from a canvas satchel slung over his shoulder. The weapon is a strange-looking thing, with a barrel half as long as a rifle's.

"I could never," he says, but he brings the weapon up beside La Fleur's head. "She's too valuable."

"You can't take me with you," La Fleur says without flinching. The gun stirs the gold curls of her hair. "I'll betray you the first chance I get."

"You're too smart for that," Camreon replies.

"Smart enough to know that if you won't shoot me now, you won't shoot me at all."

"You're right," he says as she renews her struggles. "Come, Jetta, and bring your pin."

I stiffen, and even Theodora goes still at the tone of his voice. Gone is the shy Chakran boy, his eyes so full of stars. There is fire there now, and when he waves me over with the gun, I obey. La Fleur wets her lips then. "Cam—"

"You have been so invested in practical experience, Miss Theodora. Can you imagine what might happen if Jetta marked your skin?"

"There are no souls here," she says, but her protest sounds feeble even to me. Camreon only shrugs.

"I brought Jetta a whole book of them. What would it be like to share your mind with a worm? Though a moth might suit you better. Still striving toward the light, though you might no longer know why." His tone is so casual, as though contemplating the color that best complements her skin. "Legarde may have made you brave enough to face death, Miss Theodora. But I don't think he taught you much about not being in control."

The Tiger pushes her toward me; I catch her by the wrist. La Fleur trembles, shrinking from my touch; I too am horrified at the thought—at being used as a threat. But she doesn't know that. "I'll cooperate," she whispers, and I nod. But as the Tiger goes back for the spool of wire, a shout echoes through the room.

"Allez, vite! Search the hall!" Lieutenant Pique's voice makes me shudder. How did he get here so fast? "The cha girl has to live. Shoot the others, but if you kill her, you're next!"

My hand goes to the bandage in the crook of my arm. I never thought I'd prefer Pique wanting me dead to wanting me alive. But can we leave without destroying the birds? I look at Camreon, the question in my eyes. He shakes his head. "Go."

The Tiger grabs La Fleur and pulls her through the open gate. Leo follows, and I pelt after him. Behind us, the soldiers are shouting; one fires a shot. Hot chips of stone explode from the pavers at my feet. I bite off a scream as I duck through the doorway; behind me, a cry and a sound like a slap. Then Pique's voice. "Not the girl!"

We flee across the plaza. Akra and Le Trépas were first through the door, and the chair bounces and judders over the cracked stone. But they fall behind as Akra eases the contraption off the plaza's edge. The wheels sink into the loamy garden path, pitching the chair sideways. Swearing, Akra leaves off his pushing, lifting Le Trépas and throwing him over his shoulder. Chains clanking, my brother carries the man through the brush, but I won't leave the chair behind. Not when Papa needs it.

I grab the handles and drag the chair behind me. It's lighter without anyone sitting in it, but the wheels tangle quickly in the undergrowth, catching against thick roots. Leo notices when I fall behind. "Leave it!" he whispers, rushing back to my side.

"Papa needs one!"

"He needs you more!" Leo tugs at my arm. I shake him off, but now the soldiers are spilling from the building.

Leo draws his gun, firing back over his shoulder. He doesn't bother aiming in the dark, but the guards don't know that. Cautious, they take cover, and Leo shoves his gun back into his pocket to pick up the front of the chair. Together, we wrestle it through the greenery.

We've fallen far enough behind Le Trépas that the little souls once more light our path. At first I think Camreon has chosen the way at random, but at a break in the overgrowth, I catch a glimpse of the Ruby Palace and find my bearings. We are headed toward the entry gate—the quickest way back to the slums. Back to Papa. And by the sound of it, the soldiers are falling behind. Then Camreon stops, holding up a hand, and we all stumble to a halt behind him. "What is it?" I whisper, and he shoots me a look of caution. Then he nods down the path.

"More guards at the main gate. I was hoping the explosion would lure them up to Hell's Court, but of course the explosion never happened."

"Can we go over the wall?" I ask without thinking—but of course not, not with Le Trépas in the carcan. Dare we let him loose? He'd need his hands to climb, and this is a man who rumor says can kill with a touch. What can I do instead? I cast about the garden, looking for roots or vines— something to bind the guards, like I did with Jean. Or could I distract them? A rustle in the greenery? A figure in the shadows? I reach into my pocket for the book of spirits, but Camreon is already taking aim. "Cam—"

My protest is cut short by a shot . . . and another . . . and another. Sharp, swift, and oddly soft. What magic has he worked with the barrel of his gun?

And like magic, the guards at the gate have fallen, leaving the bright columns of akela standing as though in shock. I stare at the Tiger wide-eyed as he tucks the gun back into his belt. When he catches my eye, he only gives me that winsome look. "That's three less I'll have to kill later."

He starts off down the road, and I follow, but only because I cannot go back.

ACT 2

ACT 2,
SCENE 16

In the garden by the gate. The bodies of the guards lie in silence, their souls already drifting toward the temple. Distant shouting echoes along the path as PIQUE and the soldiers approach. Closer, something rustles in the greenery.

In the moonless shadows, a figure lurks. It might be mistaken for a living man, if not for the smell. One hand is raw and black, with old blood where the bony fingers have grappled for hours with the locked grate of the old well.

As the revenant approaches the bodies, he reaches out with his good hand, scraping a symbol into the blood leaking from a bullet hole: life. But it is not JETTA's blood, nor LE TRÉPAS's, so the souls in the garden ignore the offering. Then the revenant reaches up to draw a new symbol on his own forehead. Death.

The rotting body falls, leaving the soul standing, blue as gaslight. The n'akela pours itself into the fresh corpse. For though the blood is not LE TRÉPAS's, the soul might as well be: the last life it lived was as one of LE TRÉPAS's nameless children. The one JETTA met in the well. The old soul shudders in his new body as the soldiers burst through the greenery, led by PIQUE. The men stumble to a halt, staring at the carnage.

SOLDAT: Putain.
PIQUE: Allez! We'll make them pay for each bullet twice over.

The soldat peers more closely at the nearest body.

SOLDAT: Junot is still alive!
PIQUE: We can't wait. We have to stay with the nécromanciens!

The soldiers start forward again, more hesitantly now, but from the dark path, the general's voice comes.

XAVIER: Arrêt! Who's there? Pique?

The quartier-maître bites off a curse as the general appears, breathless, down the path from the palace. XAVIER's hair is

mussed from sleep, and his uniform jacket is unbuttoned—he
has come directly from his bed.

PIQUE: Sir! We're in pursuit!
XAVIER: Of who? I heard the alarm. What's happening?
PIQUE: Each minute we delay, your sister gets farther away.
XAVIER: They have Theodora?

The general stares at PIQUE. For a moment, XAVIER looks
no older than his nineteen years.

Allez! Go!

Led by PIQUE, the soldiers race through the gate; the sound of
boots fades down the road. For a moment, XAVIER watches
after them, his hands in his hair, as if wondering whether
to follow. Then he whirls, heading toward the temple. As he
disappears down the path, there is stillness . . . silence. The
revenant sits up, smoothing the wrinkles out of his armée
uniform and opening his ice-blue eyes.

CHAPTER

SEVENTEEN

Careening through the deserted streets, we make our way back toward the slum. I am grateful now for the armée's false claim that Le Trépas was on the loose, for there is no one out so late to give them our position. Only the dead know what's coming. As we run, the flickering embers of vana race away along the gutters—the spirits of vermin. The arvana of cats scramble up the trunks of trees, the souls of birds cant upward till they seem to float among the scattered stars.

Reaching the river, we duck into the crook of the muddy path, skidding between the shacks. I never expected the slum to feel like home, but as we pass the burned-out hull of *La Rêve*, my heart clenches with the familiarity of it all. Has it only been three days since the fouilleur led me to Leo? When I see the pale boards of our shack, a smile tugs at the corners of my mouth. "Papa?"

But as I pull aside the tattered cloth that covers the doorway, panic flickers in my chest. There is a stranger sitting there beside Papa . . . a boy in nondescript clothing, though there is something terribly familiar about him. No—about her.

"Tia!" She clambers out of the lean-to, grinning. Her lips are bare now, as is the rest of her face. Without the makeup, without the wig and the padding, any Aquitan would think she was a young man. She'd even let the stubble grow on her jaw, deepening her disguise. Is it because she feared being recognized as one of Leo's showgirls? Or because the risk was even greater if the Aquitans in the capital recognized her as someone breaking one of their many laws? Either way, I am more than glad to see her. "May I?" I say, opening my arms, and she wraps her own arms around me.

"Of course." She pulls me close. "Are you all right?"

I nod. "All things considered. You?"

She steps back, making a face and gesturing down at her disguise. "All things considered."

"How are the others? Cheeky and . . ." My voice breaks; I clear my throat. "And Maman?"

"They're alive and well. But you'll see them soon enough," she adds, her gentle smile turning wry. "As long as the rest of the plan goes better than the first part."

"None of the plan involves talking," Camreon interjects, looking up from reloading his weapon. "We'll head east toward the warehouses and cut toward the docks. The streets back there are a warren. They can't follow all of us if we scatter. Our meeting place is Le Livre, the inn. Tia, you have the box in there? Hurry. The soldiers will be on our heels."

My head is swimming with Cam's instructions, but Tia ducks back inside and hauls out a crate—the same one I'd seen Camreon claim he was bringing to Pique. The Tiger kneels in the mud, tossing the lid aside. I peer over his shoulder, unsure what to expect. Guns? Munitions? But he only pulls out a thick glass jar filled with some kind of oily liquid. "What's that?"

"Your lytheum," he says as he tucks the jar inside his satchel. My eyes go wide as understanding dawns.

"You mean the elixir?" Before I can thank him, the Tiger swears.

"Let's move. Tia, you too." Leaving the empty box behind, he starts down the street, pushing Theodora before him. Akra follows, still carrying Le Trépas, but Leo hesitates, glancing back at Tia and me. We haven't budged from the doorway of the lean-to. "Hurry," Cam calls, a warning in his voice. "The general's coming."

Whirling, I peer down the street, half expecting a cadre of soldiers, boots churning the mud, bayonets gleaming in the low light. But the street is still empty. "I don't see him."

"Up there." Camreon points. Not at the street, but toward the stars. I follow his gesture to see the flying machine circling above the temple, gaining height. For a moment, I watch in awe. Is this one of the new avions? No—as the bird turns, I see the pale color of the canvas wings. This is the contraption I was meant to steal, the one Theodora had built. It is far more graceful than her prototype was. This one toys with the air like a real bird. My own fantouches were never so nimble—or so fast. "We have to move," Cam says again.

"I'm not leaving Papa behind," I spit back. "He's already lived through questioning once."

"I can shoot him instead." Camreon gestures so casually

with his gun. My hand darts out to wrap around his wrist.

"If you do, he'll be wearing your skin before dawn," I snarl.

"Bien," Cam says, more quietly now, turning back to the sky. "But if we let the armée catch up, a quick death might be the best we can hope for."

Letting go of his wrist, I dive through the doorway of our lean-to. Papa is sitting up, and the sight startles me. Was he so thin when I left? So sallow? Or is the picture in my mind's eye only an image of the man he used to be? But I haven't seen him this alert in weeks. He must have heard what Cam said—had he heard my threat as well? But he only smiles when he sees me. Then he lifts his hand to hide his mouth. "Go," he says, but I shake my head.

"I won't leave you a second time." Kneeling in the mud, I snake one of my arms under his. The other, I slide beneath his knees, but despite his frailty, he is heavy—or perhaps I am only weak. Tia goes to Papa's other side, and together we help him to his feet.

He grimaces as he supports his weight on the crooked bone of his left leg. When we reach the chair I've stolen, he sinks into it with a sigh. Then he opens his eyes, and the relief on his face turns to fear.

The flying machine has reached the east side of the slum. How close are the soldiers? Hope wars with dread in my stomach—can we slip from hut to hut, hiding from Xavier as we make our way to the dock? But as the avion skims the tops of the buildings, flame bursts from the barrels at the front.

My breath catches in my throat; beside me, Leo swears. The fire pours like syrup into the street. Quickly, it licks up the sides of the shacks—delicate at first, rising quickly to a wall of crackling heat. Screams rise along with it. The whoosh of flame fills my ears. Then the smell hits me. Burning hair and acrid smoke. Or is that only the memory of the fire I'd battled in the theater? My hand goes to the scar on my shoulder. Will the general set the whole slum alight?

No—when he reaches the waterline, he pulls up to circle back around. "What is he doing?" Leo shouts, anguish in his voice.

Camreon's reply is grim. "Cutting off our exits."

"Can you shoot him?" I say, my voice hoarse, but Leo turns, wild-eyed.

"No!"

I stare at him, but why am I surprised? Leo hadn't been able to shoot his father, even when the general's gun was turned on him. But Cam shakes his head. "A few bullets can't bring down an avion. Better to save them for the soldiers on the main street. It looks like we'll be fighting our way to the inn," he adds, louder now. "Don't let them have the nécromanciens. And Jetta—if we fall, don't stop to bring us back."

My eyes widen as his words sink in, but before I can respond, Leo jerks a thumb toward the sky. "Xavier's coming back."

Hands shaking, I push Papa's chair, but mud sucks at the wheels. "Tia—"

"I've got it," she says, taking one of the handles. Papa grasps the wheels with his gnarled fingers, and the three of us struggle through the alley, the heat of the fire at our backs. All around us, people stumble through the choking haze. Others drop to the mud to smother the clinging flame as Xavier circles above us, searching. At least the smoke gives us some cover. He is faster on the wing than we are on the ground, and already I can hear the distant soldiers closing in.

How many are there? And how many bullets do Cam and Leo have? The odds aren't good. Tia could likely escape, maybe even Papa. Neither of them has a recherche. But the rest of us are wanted—not all of us alive.

Our only other path is the river, but we can't swim it. Then, in a burst of inspiration, I realize we don't have to. "Follow me!" I shout over my shoulder as I wrestle Papa's chair through the mud. "We're going back to *La Rêve*."

"Where is that?" Cam says, but my answer is cut short by the crack of gunshots. Not Camreon's muffled weapon—Leo has taken aim as the avion passes by. Sparks fly from the hammered metal protecting the hull. The bullets barely make a mark. "Save your ammunition!" Cam says again.

With a curse, Leo jams his gun back into his belt. His eyes are rimmed in red. Smoke, or tears? "Come on, Leo," I say, beckoning him over. "You and Tia help Papa. I'll go get the ship ready."

At his nod, I start down the muddy path, dodging residents of the slum as I veer toward the cove. But in the smoke and the confusion, the path seems to twist in my memory. Am I lost? Surely the ship wasn't so far the last time. As I push through the haze, the screams crescendo behind me. Turning, I see Xavier's avion circling back through the smoke. Will the flame come again? No— something is dripping thickly from the scarred belly of the machine: the accelerant.

My relief is short-lived as the shouts of the approaching soldiers drift through the cacophony. They've cut off the exit to the street.

Stumbling through the shifting shadows and the billowing smoke, I reach the cove at last. Most of the residents of the slum have continued toward the main road, unaware or uncaring about the waiting soldiers, but there are a few who have stopped at the water. Their bodies are scattered along the bank, or drifting in the current. Smoke still rises from charred hair, singed clothes, burned flesh: a sour haze. A few of the prone forms are groaning, but most lie far too still, and the eerie blue light of their vengeful souls gleams on the lacquered scales of *La Rêve*.

They turn as I pass—do they hope I can help them? What would happen if I brought them back into their bodies? If I sent them to stop Xavier as we fled? I push the thought out of my mind. That is something Le Trépas might do. Not me.

Instead, I splash down the bank, but bile rises in my throat as hair brushes my leg. A memory bursts behind my eyes—the muddy pit outside Dar Som, where the villagers lay piled like cut cane. Shaking the scene out of my head, I pull myself through one of the holes in the hull.

It is high tide, and brackish bilge makes a puddle that reaches my knees. My hands are trembling as I flip though the book of souls. Have I got one that swims? I'm almost sure I have a turtle somewhere, but I'm going through the book a second time when I see the long, glowing spirit moving through the reeds.

Had it leaped from the bank when Le Trépas passed by? Now the crocodile's soul is drifting closer, drawn by the scent of blood—I've acquired half a dozen scratches as I fled Hell's Court. It is the matter of a moment to draw the symbol on the hull of the ship. A flash of light illuminates the smoky haze as the soul slips inside.

"Won't this tub sink in deeper water?" Tia calls from the bank, but Leo only splashes into the shallows to help Theodora aboard. The Tiger comes after, lifting the satchel high above the surface of the river.

"Don't let it get wet," he says as he hands it over. I nod, looping the strap over a splintered piece of wood high above the waterline.

Over the crackle of flame and the cries of the injured, the shouted orders of the armée ring out through the slums. Will they search street by street? Tia scrambles in next, swearing, but Papa is still on the bank, along with Akra and

Le Trépas. My stomach clenches; the n'akela have turned to the old monk. Frantically, I wave my companions closer, grateful for the carcan and the blindfold the man is wearing.

Camreon has the good sense to help Leo lift Papa up into my waiting arms. Tia takes over then, ushering Papa away from the bilge as Akra wades into the water. Le Trépas is still slung over his shoulders, and my brother tries to hand the man up to me. But even though the old monk is bound, I cannot bring myself to touch him. Gritting his teeth, Akra heaves Le Trépas up through the hole in the hull. The man grunts as he falls through in a jumble, facedown in the black water.

When I see him struggling, I panic. Pulling him back by the shoulders, I prop him up against one of the ship's curved ribs. But the wet linen of his mask clings to his face, and he sputters, still struggling to breathe. My skin crawling, I reach out with two fingers and pull it from his head. Then I scoot backward, putting some distance between us as he takes deep breaths through his nose.

I cannot look into his eyes, so I focus on the white strip of cloth tied between his teeth. I'm grateful for the gag. I do not want to hear his voice. His threats. His thanks. Standing, I wipe my hands on my coveralls as Akra and Leo lift the wheeled chair through the hole. "Hurry," I urge as the n'akela drift closer. I reach out to Leo, who helps Akra up after him. Then I whisper to the crocodile's soul. "To the open water," I say, and she's only too glad to obey.

As we scull into the dark mirror of the bay, I can see the small body turning in our wake. A stray fear: is it the fouilleur? Why hadn't I tried harder to learn his name? But is his death worse than any other child's?

A voice echoes across the water: "Arrêt! Stop!" Are the soldiers talking to us? No—as we move out toward the bay, the wind shifts, pulling back the smoke like a curtain. They have set up a cordon at the mouth of the slum to detain people as they flee. They are relying on the blaze to keep the crowd from escaping. And of course no one dares to swim the river—not in the dark. So the soldiers are not looking at the water, and they do not notice the listing wreck in the moonless night as we float into the bay.

As we pick up speed, water flows like a stream through the hull of the ship, passing in one hole, rippling over the ballast and out through another. It washes over my feet as I watch the scene at the slum. Silhouetted by the blaze, it reminds me of a shadow play. Shouted orders are a staccato song echoing across the water. This far from the crush of the crowd, the movement could almost be a dance.

But this is no passing fancy—no one here is acting. There are more souls now, a few akela like columns of fire. The lucky ones. The rest blaze cold and blue: the ones who died in pain. Turning from the shore, I catch the old monk staring at me. Is that a smirk behind the gag?

Stepping over his prone form, I nod over my shoulder toward the far-off n'akela. "Some of yours back there."

His response is muffled by the cloth. Do I want to know what he said? The monk's dark eyes gleam in the reflected glow of the fire, waiting, but I do not want to touch him. After a moment, my brother reaches over, pulling the strip of silk out of the old monk's mouth. Le Trépas gives him a little nod, a strange gesture from him: gratitude. Then he looks back to me—is that sorrow in his eyes? "I said, not as many as there will be, before this war is over."

I had expected a hiss—a sibilant whisper, the hush of the dead, but his voice is low, almost rich. "Is that a threat, old man?" Akra glares at Le Trépas, but the monk only looks back at the shore. At a loss, I follow his gaze to the n'akela, still standing where they died, and I am not naive enough to disagree with his claim.

Help Me, Brother

REV. FREDERICK KARL   H.R. BENEDICT

1. Help me, broth-er, in the dark - ness, Of all
2. Lead me, broth-er, past temp - ta - tion, On the
3. Save me, broth-er, from my tor - ment, Walk with

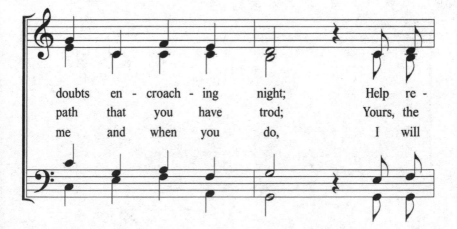

doubts en - croach - ing   night;   Help re -
path   that   you   have   trod;   Yours, the
me   and   when   you   do,   I   will

mind me   of   God's   love _____   That
shoul - der   I   will   lean on;   And
pray to   find   a   mo - ment   When

warms us   with   a   ho -   ly light.
bring me   clos - er   thus _____   to God.
God will   let   me   save _____ you too.

CHAPTER

EIGHTEEN

It is too uncomfortable to stay in the bilge, so we make our way upstairs to what used to be the dining room. The fine crystal, the velvet chairs, the polished wood tables—the gilding that had decorated *La Rêve* has been stripped and scavenged. What is left is a cavernous room with water-stained carpets, moldering drapes, and barely enough broken furniture for kindling.

The berths are just as empty, though Tia finds one that still has a mattress in it. We shake out the family of mice living inside and drag it into the dining hall for Papa. He is already exhausted by the move from the shore to the ship, and as soon as we lay him out on the mattress, he closes his eyes. I squeeze his hand before I go to help the others get situated, but when I try to let go, he won't release me. "Papa?"

He opens his eyes again, and I step back; there is a look in them like I've never seen. He clenches his jaw and takes a breath, but when he speaks, the words come all at once and in a rush. It is the most he's said in weeks, though I can't understand him through the shush and slur of his mangled tongue. But as I follow his gaze, the words become clear: "Stay away from the other side of the ship."

There, on the far end of the dining hall, Akra is guarding Le Trépas. They have staked out a spot well away from the rest of us. Is it for everyone's safety, or Papa's comfort? Either way, I'm grateful. But hearing the venom in Papa's voice, questions bubble up, unbidden. The whole country feared Le Trépas, but this is anger. It must have to do with me . . . and Maman . . . and what happened sixteen years ago, when we fled Hell's Court.

I know the rough outlines of the story—that rather than bury me with the other temple children Le Trépas killed for their souls, Maman had spirited me out of the city. In the confusion of La Victoire, she had fallen in with Papa and Akra, never to return.

But now is not the time to ask for more detail. "Yes, Papa," is all I say, and only then does he release my hand.

Still, I wait until he's asleep before I join the others in searching the rest of the ship. We haven't got more than what we fled with—little ammunition, fewer weapons, no clothing or bedding. Most of what remains aboard is broken glass and debris too damaged to steal. Cam does find a rusted machete, and we scrape together enough ruined carpet and curtain to make up some crude beds. The one thing we do not lack is food: the pantry holds cans and cans of tinned victuals that the scavengers from the slum had no idea how to open. As Leo reads off the labels, my stomach growls, but I have no idea how to open the tins either. Theodora is the one who finds the can opener. She even knows how to use it.

Leo builds a little cookfire atop a platform of ballast stones, and La Fleur open stacks of the tins without making a dent in the supply: fish and fruit and the pureed livers of duck. Enough to last weeks. The bounty had been meant to supply a royal journey from Chakrana to Aquitan— the voyage *La Rêve* was built for. What does Theodora think, hauled aboard the ruined ship that was built for her wedding, a prisoner rather than a princess? But she is quiet as she helps supply our makeshift dinner, and her face gives nothing away. Unsurprising—she was born to politics. And either way, there are more pressing issues than a cancelled wedding. "Where am I taking us?" I ask instead.

"Up the coast to the Coffret." Camreon frowns into a can of pineapple as he fishes for a slice. "Raik has set up headquarters above the abandoned sapphire mines."

I cock my head. "So far away?"

"Remember, we thought you'd be going by air," he says with a wry look.

"Me, Akra, and Le Trépas." It's difficult for me to imagine being crammed in a flying machine, trying to flee the city with the old monk breathing down my neck. I glance once more toward the other side of the dining hall. Leo is distributing tins across the ship, but of course Le Trépas's hands are bound. As I watch, Leo hands the food to my brother, who lifts a tin to the old monk's lips.

"Getting him out of armée control was vital," Camreon says, and I frown.

"Leo mentioned they might find a use for his blood."

"They were already considering it," Cam says grimly. "An armée of the dead."

"Xavier would never." Theodora's interjection is

unexpected; she doesn't even look up from her work.

"You might have," the Tiger replies. "Especially knowing Jetta brings them back to life."

"You've done worse to try to end the fighting." With a pop, she presses the metal opener through the lid. "I would have done the rebels more good as a queen than as a hostage."

"Who's to say there won't be a wedding?" The Tiger raises an eyebrow. "Raik is waiting in the Coffret. But any marriage treaty will be on our terms, not Aquitan's. Especially now that we have the nécromanciens."

I can't help but stare at Camreon. He is so casual as he brokers the marriage of the girl I'd been so sure he loved. But La Fleur turns away, as though she can't bear to look at him. "And you," she growls at Leo as he approaches. "After tonight, even our father couldn't deny that you're his son."

Leo slows, clenching his jaw. The struggling flame throws eerie shadows on the water-stained walls. In the dim light, his eyes look hollow. "Xavier might be the one to disagree this time."

"How could you lie to him?" she says. "How could you lie to *me*?"

Leo looks at her, incredulous. "You're angry at me

for lying when our brother just set fire to a camp full of refugees?"

"Our brother isn't here," she says. "Besides, what did you expect him to do? You kidnapped me!"

"An eye for an eye will make the world blind," Leo says darkly. "Didn't he used to believe that?"

"That was before she killed our father." Theodora glares darkly at me. The accusation sparks anger in my chest—I want to fling my hand out toward Papa, toward Akra, to remind her what the old general did. But isn't that the same argument Theodora is making?

Instead, I take a breath, trying to control my anger. "I'm going upstairs to take a look at the coastline," I say at last. "Make sure *La Rêve* is headed in the right direction."

"Good thinking," Cam says mildly. The Tiger drains the last of the juice from the can and tosses it into the corner. "Akra, sava bien with Le Trépas? Good. I'll watch Theodora. The rest of you, get some sleep."

La Fleur isn't ready to let go. "All of this for your precious Boy King," she mutters bitterly. "When he was willing to sign the country over to Aquitan for a lifetime supply of champagne."

Cam's voice lowers dangerously. "But he didn't."

Theodora scoffs. "Only because he learned that my father was going to kill him before he had to order a new crate of the stuff."

"Yet here you are," Camreon says, incredulous. "Surrounded by the enemy, and still arguing for your side!"

La Fleur opens her mouth, taken aback. "I never thought of you as the enemy, Camreon."

"No," he says pointedly. "It was just all those *other* Chakrans."

He might as well have slapped her, the hurt is so plain in her eyes. In the silence that follows, Leo sighs, rubbing his forehead. "Why don't you let me watch her instead?" he suggests. "After all, we have things to discuss."

"Better you than me," Cam replies.

Leaving the others to make some beds, I pick my way up the wide stairwell. The steps are soft with water, and portions have burned to char in the fire that took part of the ship. I hold tight to the curve of the carved banister as the night breeze catches my hair—refreshing, after the muggy warmth and tension below.

Taking another deep breath, I survey the proud ruin of *La Rêve*: the tattered remains of the red silken sails, the dragon head at the prow. The shape reminds me of my dragon fantouche—the great leather creature, gold and scarlet, ensouled with the spirit of a kitten. I had fashioned it in the hopes it would make the Boy King take notice, and he had, if not exactly how I expected.

Though the fantouche was with him now, I had never spoken to Raik myself. What is he like, the Boy King? Or the Playboy King, as the joke went. I had assumed his libertine ways were encouraged by the Aquitans to keep him from meddling with their policies, but after his escape, I had wondered if they were only a cover to hide his involvement with the rebellion. Was Theodora right? Had Raik only sided with the Tiger as a last resort?

As the deck moves beneath my feet, I can't help but feel as though I've stepped into uncertain territory. Perhaps the murky waters of politics runs deeper than I'd thought. Still, I can't exactly go back. Across the water, the fire still glows as red as coals along the ruins of the slum. Forcing myself to turn away, I face the far horizon instead.

Nokhor Khat is cupped by the remains of an ancient crater that rises sharply past the fort. I point the soul in our ship toward the dark silhouette that the jagged hilltop cuts from the starry sky. The wreck moves as quietly through the water as any crocodile would. For a while, in the blissful silence, I simply breathe. Then, soft as a kiss, the first few notes of a song drift up from below: Leo and his violin.

My muscles tense—sound carries across water. Will the soldiers hear it at the fort? But Leo plays quietly, and we are far away. I do not recognize the song; it sounds foreign. Aquitan. With the stately, measured pacing of one of their hymns. Still, there is a longing to it. Incongruous after the fire, the escape, the fighting. As I listen, a smile touches my lips. I hadn't realized how much I'd missed music. Had Theodora requested a song, or did Leo know what we needed to soothe the strain of the day?

He goes through the verses, spiraling out through variations—low to high, thirds, fifths, a falling waterfall of notes that sounds much more effortless than it is. Was it only a few months ago I first saw him play at Le Perl? His silhouette swaying, a shadow on the scrim . . . when the song ends, I feel adrift in more ways than one.

Will he continue? Hopeful, I lean on the rail, and though I am listening, I do not hear Camreon approach until he speaks. "You should eat."

I turn, startled. The boy is standing so close he could touch me; in his hand is an open tin. Trying to hide my discomfort, I force a laugh. "I had assumed it was your ruthlessness that earned your nickname, but perhaps it's your quiet feet."

"Alas, it's neither," he says easily, though I note he does not tell me what it really is. He holds out the tin again. "You need to keep your strength."

"Fair enough," I say, not wanting to argue. I take the tin from his hands, hoping he'll go back below. Instead, he leans on the rail beside me, watching the dark water pass beneath us.

"Is this as fast as the ship will go?"

"This is cruising speed for crocodiles," I tell him primly. "I can push the soul faster, but not for long."

"Do the dead get tired?"

"They think they do," I say. "I've seen plenty of cat souls playing at sleep."

"Let's save our speed, then," he says, watching the distant shore. "We may need it later."

Awkwardly, I hold the tin, waiting for him to go so I can pitch it over the side; after a day like today, the smell of it ties my stomach in knots. But the Tiger lingers. The only sound between us is the gentle lap of water. His silent presence is maddening.

"How *did* you get your nickname?" I say at last. "Or did you choose it yourself?"

"Camreon is my only chosen name." He cocks his head, curious. "Why does it matter so much to you?"

"Just trying to make conversation," I say. "But you're good at sabotaging that, too."

"Touché." He gives me a wry smile. "I suppose I've gotten too used to keeping secrets."

"I can only imagine," I say. "Theodora said she'd known you for years. How did you hide what you've been doing?"

"She was just as busy as I was," he says. "Dances. Functions. Her father. Her work. And I invented family too, for an excuse to leave the palace grounds. They always needed help in the paddies during the growing season."

"And thus the automated planter," I say, and there is the winsome smile I'd seen before. Even though I know it's an act, it's hard not to let it draw me in. "If you hadn't chosen a life of actual crime, you could have made a killing on the stage," I say, and he laughs. "How did you keep all the stories straight?"

"It's easiest when the people who can prove the lie are dead or imaginary," he says with a shrug. "I should have known she'd go to Pique. She's too clever for me."

I give him a sidelong look. Is that admiration in his voice, or am I only imagining things? "If I hadn't found Le

Trépas while Xavier was at Hell's Court, things might have gone differently," I say at last. "I wish I'd known you had the elixir sorted out."

The Tiger smiles thinly. "I almost didn't. Faced with the avions, I considered using it to blow them apart. It reacts with water to produce a flammable gas," he adds at my quizzical expression. "But your medication was part of the deal."

"Deal?" I ask, but of course. "With Leo."

"And I don't dare go back on it." Camreon makes a face, but my own heart is sinking.

"Because it's a prerequisite?"

The Tiger shakes his head. "Because he's already angry enough about his sister."

"Well." I fold my arms. "Can you blame him? Your threats broke her heart. I was so sure you were in love."

His look is whimsical. "You're not the only actor in the world."

I don't know why his nonchalance offends me, but it does. "Out of everything I've seen you do, leading her on might be the cruelest."

"We've only just properly met. Give me time." Camreon's smile shows too many teeth, but it dies quickly. He looks back across the water. "But I never said that being in love was the part I am pretending."

"I find that hard to believe."

"Good." The ghost of the smile returns. "Matters of country outweigh matters of the heart. Theodora knows it too. After all, she was willing to marry my brother without being in love with him."

The claim takes a moment to digest. Above, the wind whispers in the shredded sails. "Your . . . your brother?" I turn to him, blinking. "Raik is your brother?"

"My younger brother, in fact," Camreon says. "Though only by a few minutes."

"Twins?" I stare at Camreon, uncomprehending, but when I'm looking for it, the similarities are so clear. The same eyes, the same nose. Once he'd cast off the persona he'd worn in the workshop—the humble servant, the chaste boy in love—he had given orders like someone born to lead.

And he had been.

"Younger brother," I repeat softly. "The throne is yours?"

"Ah." The Tiger raises an eyebrow. "That's where it gets complicated. For sixteen years, Raik has been the Boy King. As for me? Very few people know I survived La Victoire."

The story floods back—everyone knows it. Assassins

with knives, sent by Le Trépas. The Ruby Palace was red with blood that day. The horror of it all was the final straw—the Chakrans petitioned the armée to end Le Trépas's reign. The Aquitans replaced it with their own. After all, the Boy King was only three at the time; he needed advisers, and everyone else with royal blood was dead. Or so the story went. "But how?" I whisper at last. "How did you escape?"

"I begged," Cam says simply. "What can I say? I was a child. I begged, and he let me live."

My eyes widen—I cannot imagine Le Trépas showing mercy. But half the stories I'd heard about him must have come from the armée. Were they only more propaganda? "Did he tell you why?"

Camreon stares at the fort, his voice soft. "I always imagined it was because I was about the same age as Miss Theodora. Besides, Legarde saw me as a girl. And the Aquitans don't think a woman can rule a country. I wasn't a threat like the rest of my brothers."

"Wait—the Aquitans?" I frown. "Why would Le Trépas listen to the armée?"

"Le Trépas? Oh, no." Camreon laughs, the sound dry and hollow. "You don't believe that old story, do you? Le

Trépas had nothing to do with the assassins. Why on earth would the nécromancien bother with knives?"

"It was *Legarde* at the palace?" I blink at him, reeling. But it is so obvious—why had I never questioned the story myself? And it would hardly have been the only lie the Aquitans had told. How convenient, this one, to rid the country of all its rulers in one night.

"Do you really want to know how I got my nickname?" Camreon doesn't wait for an answer. He tugs at the buttons on the front of his coveralls, peeling the sleeves away from his shoulders and turning to show me his back. Peeking out from beneath the pale silk of his binder, long scars shine silver in the starlight. "It's the stripes."

My jaw drops—I try to imagine him then. Barely three years old, bleeding from a dozen wounds. I see now why he had shot the guards at the gates without hesitating—how he so quickly did the calculus of casualties of war. I can almost forgive him for telling me to leave Papa. Almost.

As he pulls his shirt back on, I find my voice. "Do the others know who you are?"

"Everyone but Miss Theodora," he says. "Though Leo said he'd tell her."

"And the Boy King?"

Cam's expression does not change, but his tone does. There is tension in it. "He knows."

I chew my lip; in my mind's eye, I can see him. Young, proud, handsome—the picture of a ruler. "And . . . how does he feel about it?"

"He's the one who found me a position in the palace three years ago."

I narrow my eyes. "That's not exactly an answer."

The Tiger sighs, buttoning his coveralls. "Raik was raised to take the throne. Trouble is, he was raised by the Aquitans. But he's still one of us, and we'll never rid ourselves of foreign control if we spend our energy fighting each other."

My eyebrows go up. "You don't want the throne?"

"I want peace more," he says simply.

For a moment, there is silence again. Still, the question tugs at me. "So what should we call you, then?"

"Camreon, of course." He grins. "The Tiger, if you must."

"Not 'my king'?"

His smile deepens. "Not if Raik's around."

I smile back, tentative. I can't help it—I like him. But before I can say so, a column of flame erupts from the water just behind the ship. Red as blood, tall as the soul of a giant.

Except it isn't a soul—I know because Camreon sees it too. "What is that?"

The soul in our boat surges away from the flame, fearing fire as it did in life. Is the ship alight? We rush to the rear to check, but no—it is the sea. I have never seen water burn. The heat of the flame prickles my skin, and the ocean boils at the base of the column. For a moment, I fear we are about to be consumed by a tower of flame. But as quickly as it rose, the fire dies, as do the bubbles, and the rush and crackle of flame is replaced by shouting downstairs: Theodora and Leo, arguing.

"How could you?" he demands, and I've never heard him so angry.

Theodora matches him in volume. "If we go back to Nokhor Khat, we can easily get more!"

"We're not going back! You think Xavi will be reasonable? After what he did to the slums?"

"That's exactly why we have to end this war!" Her voice echoes up from below. "If Cam is really the rightful king, he could finish this today!"

"What happened?" I call to them, my heart still pounding, but I don't think they hear. Beside me, Camreon grinds his teeth.

"I'll go check," he says. Then he looks up at the distant shore, gauging the distance to the fort. "But it might be wise to push a little faster, now."

"Right." Heart still pounding, I return to the prow, murmuring to the soul as I go. The boat picks up speed, but we haven't gone far when a boom like thunder rolls across the water. I frown, looking back, but the water is dark. Until a moment later, when something big and heavy splashes down from the sky.

I have time enough to curse before it explodes.

Properties of Lytheum

—The metal has similar characteristics to the more common alkalis.

—(Highly reactive to water, even to the small amounts found in the air.

—(Is the relatively high humidity in Chakrana a factor in this?)

—Are the volatile properties of the material a factor in its ability to treat "volatile" personalities, or is this only coincidence?

Store the material in oil.

CHAPTER NINETEEN

White spray swamps the deck. The boat rocks in the water. From below, I hear the others shouting. What was it? I cast about wildly, but Camreon takes my arm and points to the fort. "Artillerie!" As he speaks, I see the flash, hear the boom. "We need to move!"

I am already ahead of him. With my hand on the rail, I urge the soul faster, faster. Smoothly, the boat accelerates, slicing through the churning water as we turn away from the fort. When the next shell hits, we've gone far enough to outrun the ripples of the wave.

With the shell after that, we are not so lucky.

It hits the rear of *La Rêve* and bursts apart in light and heat. Below, the shouts have turned to screams. I want to rush down to check on the others, but there will be another shell any moment, and I can't take my eyes off the fort.

The wind shifts; I smell smoke. "Get down there!" I shout to Camreon over the ringing in my ears. "Make sure the ship isn't burning!"

"I'll take care of it," he says, looking sharply toward the shore at the next crack of the cannon. "To the left!"

I send the soul sideways; as the ship jerks in the water, the shell falls where we would have been. The explosion rocks the boat, but we keep our course, safe from the blast.

"Keep dodging," Cam says as he hurries to the stairs. "When they fire, they're aiming for where they think we'll be. Most ships don't sail like crocodiles swim."

I nod, stroking the rail absently, watching the fort. When the next flash comes, we dart right; for the one after that, I hold my breath while we stop dead. The shells go wide, and there is a fierce victory in every miss. Is the artillerie cursing me as he peers through his binoculars, wondering what tides we are riding? And when the last bomb falls far behind our wake, a wild pride swells in my chest. We have passed out of range of the cannon—nearly out of the harbor, to the freedom of the sea.

My smug satisfaction lasts until I look at the sky above the fort. Dawn is approaching, and against the lightening sky, three avions make ominous silhouettes. And this time, it is the metal flying machines we will face. Setting the crocodile's soul on a course toward the open water, I hurry downstairs. A hazy smoke still hangs in the air below. "Camreon! Where are you?"

"Back here!"

I find the others at the rear of the ship, where the shell hit. There is a new hole rimmed with jagged boards, charred and splintered, and I can see down through the carpet into the bilge. Smoke still drifts up from below, but at least the fire is out—without the soul buoying the boat, we'd sink in an instant. "Is anyone hurt?"

"No," the Tiger calls up. "Are we out of range?"

"Not for long," I say. "There are avions coming."

Akra clenches his teeth. "How many?"

"Three, for now," I call back. "How many bullets do you have left, Leo?"

"Not enough," he says grimly. "What about you, Jetta? Any ideas?"

I blink at him, then pull the book out of my pocket, flipping through. A pangolin, a horse, a dog, some birds . . . I chew my lip, thinking, and into the silence, an unfamiliar voice falls.

"You could kill their creator." Le Trépas's suggestion. He even sounds regretful as he makes it.

"You mean me." The thought shakes me painfully familiar. An echo of the lies my own malheur whispered from time to time, before the elixir silenced their siren song. But is Le Trépas telling the truth?

"I meant the general," he says—is that reproach in his eyes? "Isn't he the one who ensouled the creatures? But now that you mention it, yes. Your death would drop the birds from the sky like stones. It's your blood on their wings, after all."

"That's not an option," Leo says through his teeth, but Le Trépas only shrugs.

"She could try to pluck the souls out by hand," he replies. "But there's no guarantee she'll live through that either."

"Your sense of strategy leaves much to be desired," Cam says, but I am only half listening. Something is tugging at the corners of my thoughts . . . dropping the birds like stones . . .

"The ballast," I blurt out, tearing one of the pages from

the book—a hawk's soul. Hadn't I meant to do the same thing with the supply ship? "We'll use them as our own artillerie."

Cam gives me a nod, approving. We leave Akra guarding the prisoners. Leo, Cam, and Tia rush down to the bilge while I go above. By the time they bring me the first round of blocks, the avions are far too close for comfort. "Cam! Your knife!"

He hands it over quickly; he's kept it very sharp. With the guard's lighter, the page, and a drop of blood, I transfer the soul of a hawk into the first stone. As the flying machine comes tearing through the sky toward us, I send the rock up. Improbably—impossibly—it lifts into the air, circling just the way a hawk would. "Higher," I whisper, and the soul inside obeys.

The ballast block spirals up as though caught in a whirlwind, until it is above the flying machine. Then, at my command, the stone tips and stoops as though remembering it is of the earth and not the sky.

Down, down, down—the granite strikes the avion like a fist. In a heavy crunch of metal, the wings splay sideways, the machine tumbling through the air. Liquid spills from the split hull like milk from a cracked coconut, pooling like oil on the surface of the sea. The soul inside the metal body tries to right itself, but I send the rock circling around. The next hit smashes the machine down into the water.

The metal fantouche struggles to rise again, churning the waves into whitecaps with her twisted wings. Without fire, the soul will be trapped in the metal body even when she sinks below the sea. It seems a cruel fate. "Have any of you got a kerchief?"

Tia passes me a folded square that still smells faintly of perfume; quickly, I knot the silk and light the end. Cocking my arm, I aim for the spreading oil around the wreck, but just as I release the flaming kerchief, a man clambers out from the bucket of the cockpit.

Was Xavier foolish enough to come himself? No—it is just a soldat. A stranger to me. Is it only fear that makes him look young? "Allez!" he shouts desperately, urging the bird upward. "Go, go!"

The creature struggles fruitlessly to obey his command. I blink at the soldier. Is he the one who ensouled the avion? Then the accelerant goes up in flames around them, and the soldier dives into the foaming sea. He comes up gasping, covered in the oily stuff, and the flames cover him too, like a mantle. My stomach twists as he shrieks; the scar on my shoulder seems to burn under my sleeve. Fire isn't quick.

Will the man rise again as a n'akela, and follow me till his soul fades? But the soldier's scream is cut short as Camreon raises his gun; the soldier's head jerks back, and his body tips to float in the burning water. It takes me a while to find his soul among the flames—gold as dawn. A small mercy.

Beside the body in the water, the avion's struggle continues—at least, for a little while. The accelerant burns so hot. But the Tiger jerks his chin toward the sky.

"Look out," he says. "Here comes another."

I grit my teeth, marking the next block. "So let's give them a show."

With the smell of blood and smoke in my nostrils, I send up two more stones. One goes straight through the joint of a metal wing, and the avion twists and bucks in the air before the second stone takes it down. But then the last pilot has learned—the avion dodges and dances; the stone follows, but not fast enough. The flying machine swoops down toward us, gaining speed as it skims low over the surface of the water. Flame drips from the barrels, and in the wake of its passing, fire rises from the surface of the sea.

"Leo!" I scream. "Shoot him!"

As I smear blood on the next stone, a shot rings out—

and another—and another—loud enough to make me jump. But these avions are much stronger than the one Theodora built. Bullets ping off the sculpted metal that shields the pilot in the cockpit. The avion does not turn, even as Leo's pistol clicks on the empty cartridge.

"Where's the Tiger?" I do not dare take my eyes off the avion as I urge the stone after it. "He has a gun!"

"I do," Cam calls back, his voice almost calm. "But I'd rather not use it just now."

Beside me, Leo curses. The Tiger is advancing across the deck with Theodora before him, his gun once more to her temple. Fury rises in me—how can he have spoken so sweetly of love, while daring to treat her this way? But together they face the flame: a challenge.

The avion stands down first, banking hard as my stone shoots past. The ballast block makes a pale blue streak in the sea as it plunges into the water. Frantically, I coax it up again as the avion circles around. But to my surprise, the flying machine slows as it nears the ship. The ocean's surface ripples out in waves at the great backbeats of the metal wings.

I recognize the man in the cockpit: Lieutenant Pique.

"Hand over La Fleur at once," he calls over the rush of

wind, the pounding of my heart. "The nécromanciens too. Return to Nokhor Khat and face trial for your crimes. I can promise you justice, and swiftly."

"I prefer *La Rêve* to the prison ship," Cam calls. "And if you sink her, I'll sink La Fleur. As much as you'd enjoy that, I don't think the general would."

Cam's suggestion makes me shudder—I am half sure Pique will call his bluff. But he only shouts back, "I give you one last warning. Return to the port or face the consequences."

"I'd prefer to face the open sea, Lieutenant!"

"Ah well," Pique calls, and though it may just be the way the sound carries, he does not sound disappointed. The thought chills me. What are the consequences he is threatening? The rock is rising out of the water—will I be able to knock the lieutenant from his perch? But the soul inside the ballast block is weary, and Pique turns the avion quickly, leaving ripples over the water as he goes. I call the stone back to rest on the deck, but Camreon doesn't drop the gun till the lieutenant is out of sight.

When he does, Theodora pushes him away. Her blue eyes flash—fire on water. But before she can speak, Leo steps between her and Camreon. "I told you not to hurt her—"

"And I told you to guard her." The Tiger shrugs. "Who broke the deal first?"

"Here's a new deal, then," Leo growls. "If you threaten her again, I'll kill you."

"Wanting me dead is practically tradition in your family," Cam says. "But if it makes you feel any better, my threat was empty too."

"What are you talking about?"

"Show him, Miss Theodora," Cam says. Theodora's face is a mask, but she opens her fist. The bullets from the Tiger's gun gleam there on her palm.

Leo looks from Theodora's hand to the Tiger's face, his anger banked, still hot. "You agreed to this?"

Cam makes a face. "It's the least she could do, after flagging them down in the first place."

"I thought Xavier would have the good sense to send a ship after us," Theodora says through her teeth. "Not avions."

"This wouldn't be the first time Pique took the initiative," Leo says, but I am still staring at Theodora.

"The column of fire," I say, putting two and two together. "Just before the artillerie. It was a signal? How did you make it?"

Theodora hesitates, so the Tiger answers. "Do you remember what I said about keeping the satchel out of the water?"

"What do you mean?" My heart sinks at the guilt on Leo's face. He sighs.

"She threw the lytheum in the water while my back was turned."

"Only half!" Theodora protests, but I stare at her.

"Why?"

"Because the fastest way to end the fighting is for the rightful king to make a truce," she says, glaring at the Tiger. "One thing I know you've never lied about is loving your country. We used to imagine such bright futures for Chakrana, Cam." Her voice breaks like a heart on his name. "I can't believe those were only fiction."

"Unfortunately, none of those futures includes Xavier." Camreon slots the bullets back in his gun. "And I don't think he'll go back to Aquitan."

"Why does he have to?" she asks, but he laughs.

"Has your own propaganda fooled you, Theodora? You know Xavier holds your father's legacy as sacred as he holds his god. And both of us know what your father did to win this country," he says darkly. "I don't trust the new general any more than I trusted the old one."

"Don't talk to me about trust," she scoffs. "You've pretended to care for years while plotting behind my back."

"You've done much the same with my country," he says, but he can't meet her eyes.

"A person and a country are two different things."

"Don't be ridiculous." The Tiger slams the chamber shut and shoves the gun into its holster. "You can't pretend you designed weapons to shoot at the landscape."

Theodora takes a trembling breath through her nose. Then she whirls, fleeing down the stairs. Leo hesitates before he follows, leaving me alone with Cam on the deck. The Tiger shakes his head. "He shouldn't go after her."

"No." I give him a look. "You should."

Cam raises his eyebrow, and as if on cue, shouting echoes up from below. Theodora's voice. "She needs space."

"So do I!" I snap, and he blinks. I try to relax my shoulders, my jaw, my neck. "Besides, you were right. Leo isn't the best guard when it comes to family."

Cam sighs as he stands, but he does not protest. "Wake me if anything else happens. You should try to rest, yourself."

"After all this?" My laugh is bitter as he makes his way down. The worst part is, I know he's right, but there's no chance of sleep. Not now. My blood thrums in my veins, and the fiery scenes replay whenever I close my eyes: the slums, the explosions, the young pilot floating in a pool of flame. The scar on my shoulder itches, as though in sympathy. But more than that—there is something under my skin. A tingling tension, a buzzing feeling. Adrenaline that will fade, or my malheur creeping back?

My hand falls to the flask at my hip—have I taken today's dose? Certainly I must have skipped yesterday's. I take a sip, then heft the bottle, trying to gauge how much is inside. Especially now that Theodora has tossed the lytheum overboard.

It shakes me—the realization that so much of my supply has gone up in a flash of smoke. But the quantity was finite the moment we left Theodora's workshop. Suddenly, I want what's left of it. I need to hold it in my hands. To keep it safe. I run down the stairs, casting about for the satchel. I catch sight of Leo instead, sitting cross-legged, running a polishing cloth over his violin. "Where's the lytheum?"

He looks up from his instrument, his expression resigned. But he nods toward a broken table in the corner, the missing leg replaced by a stack of tin cans. Atop it: the jar. Gingerly, I pick it up. In the dim light of the dying fire,

I see a lump of something floating inside. Metal—the size of a bullet, and dull as lead. Except for one side, gleaming silver. "What is that?"

"That's the lytheum. The kerosene in the jar keeps it safe from humidity," Leo says. "Unless someone chops off a piece, drops it in a can of river water, and lights the resulting gas on fire. I should have been watching more closely," he adds apologetically.

"It's not your fault," I say, holding the jar close—protective. The weight of it is a comfort to me. "If it weren't for you, I wouldn't have any of it."

"I promised I would help you." Leo brings his hand up to cover mine, and his voice is protective too. My heartbeat is so loud in my ears, and there is something warm in my belly—a familiar feeling . . . magnetic . . . and as strong as if we hadn't spent any time apart. As though he'd never left in the first place. But he had. And standing there with the jar in my hand, I can't help but wonder why he only came back once he knew I would have the elixir—and what would he do when I ran out.

"Thank you," I say, but the words are stilted. His own face falls, and after an excruciating moment, I draw my hand back and return to the deck to be alone.

ACT 2,

SCENE 20

A ruined berth, the walls peeling and spotted with mildew. The door has been pulled from the frame, along with all the other trimmings and trappings, leaving only a small window to decorate the room. THEODORA stares out through it, watching the shore sliding by.

In the hall outside, CAMREON approaches, tapping softly with a knuckle against the doorframe. THEODORA doesn't turn from the window.

THEODORA: Why do you knock at an open door?
CAMREON: I miss when we pretended to be civil.
THEODORA: I was never pretending.

La Fleur sighs, rubbing the bridge of her nose, as though fending off a headache.

The worst part is, I know you're right. I knew what the armée did with my inventions, but I kept going anyway.

CAMREON: Why did you?

THEODORA: Maybe it was inertia. An object in motion staying in motion. When I was younger, I thought I was helping Chakrana. After all, I was going to marry the king.

CAMREON: You did help. Where else could I have learned so much about explosives?

THEODORA snorts.

THEODORA: Yes. You've always been my most unbalancing force.

A smile whisks across CAMREON's face, then vanishes.

CAMREON: I'll take that as a compliment. But I don't believe your behavior was mere mechanics. You care about your brother. You don't want him to fail.

THEODORA: Does he have to lose for you to win?

The Tiger sighs, shaking his head.

CAMREON: That's the problem with you Aquitans. You think peace requires victory.

THEODORA: I don't.

CAMREON: He does. And as long as he's trying to win, the fight will continue.

THEODORA throws her hands in the air, frustrated.

THEODORA: What's your endgame, then? Rounding all of us up and marching us into the Hundred Days Sea?

CAMREON: We could use the prison ship.

That faint smile returns.

But you misunderstand me, Theodora. Peace doesn't require the Aquitans to leave. It only requires you to surrender.

THEODORA: Surrender . . . what? Land? Money?

CAMREON: Control. Power.

THEODORA: To who? Raik?

She laughs, short and bitter.

He'll be just as bad a king as your father was.

The Tiger goes still.

CAMREON: Careful what you say.

THEODORA: I'm not the only one precious about my brother.

CAMREON: I have respect for the king.

THEODORA: And what if his leadership paves the way for Le Trépas to return to power?

CAMREON: That's a daring accusation, knowing you've considered harnessing his power for yourself

THEODORA raises an eyebrow.

THEODORA: It's your own religion.

CAMREON: Le Trépas twisted it through a foreign lens. There was balance before the Aquitans came. Now your people and mine see death as vengeance. It's only when you put up your white flag that we can put down our weapons.

THEODORA: And that's when you kill us, I suppose.

CAMREON: Why would we kill our queen?

La Fleur stares at him.

THEODORA: You actually expect me to marry Raik.

CAMREON: You'd be safe from being marched into the sea.

THEODORA: What about Xavier? Can he stay too?

CAMREON: That's up to the general.

THEODORA wets her lips, unsure.

THEODORA: We should go back to Nokhor Khat. I can talk to him, Cam.

CAMREON: Or he could have me questioned and shot.

THEODORA: I won't let him do that.

CAMREON: You've been so sanguine about your father's plan to kill Raik. What makes me different?

THEODORA hesitates—the admission is difficult.

THEODORA: I never loved Raik.

CAMREON closes his eyes, taking a deep breath and hanging his head before he sighs.

CAMREON: I know. But I do. He's the only family I have left.

When he looks up again, his smile is sad.

Though if negotiations go well for a marriage treaty, I look forward to gaining a sister.

LEPHARE JOURNAUX

Mercredi le 21 Octobre 1874   *Prix cinq étoiles*

FLYING MACHINES TAKE TO THE AIR IN AQUITAN

Late last night, one of the machines designed by our beloved roi returned to Lephare from its journey to far-off Chakrana. There, armée engineers fitted the avion with the capability to fly, and sent a pilot soaring triumphantly across the sea to bring the news!

Remy Mathiue, nineteen, is the first known man to fly from one country to another. He is also the first to make the journey across an ocean. The young soldier is currently a guest of Le Roi Fou, and has been granted an Order of Merit for his bravery.

This is only the latest triumph from the armée under the guidance of young General Xavier Legarde and his sister, the prodigy Theodora, known as the Flower of Chakrana. Possibilities are boundless, not only for Aquitan interests across the Hundred Days Sea, but for those closer to home. Young men are clamoring to make their names in the new air corps forming across the sea, led by decorated Lieutenant Pique, and recruitment offices have reopened across Lephare. The next ship leaves within the week, and excitement is high in the . . .

continued

CHAPTER TWENTY-ONE

The shore slides by as we move up the coast, a patchwork of gold sand and green jungle during the day, and a black-and-blue backdrop at night. Though the sea is calm, the rain continues in typical seasonal fashion. Despite the grim conditions of the erstwhile dining hall and the closeness of the quarters, the space is oddly cozy in a downpour. Above, drops pound the deck like a drummer; the wind hisses on the water like it used to in the mango tree outside my old window. On days like this we would gather inside, working on fantouches or costumes—me, Akra, Papa, and Maman. She would play the bird flute, and Papa used to sing.

But Maman is not here, and these days, Papa is silent. Still, music follows him; I find him with Tia, and she is humming a little tune from Le Perl. Papa sits in the wheeled chair I liberated for him, and to my surprise, he is working on one of the armrests with a knife.

Under the steel blade, a carving of a flower is taking shape. It is cruder than the work he used to do: the rich carvings on our wooden fantouches, or the fine scrollwork on the roulotte he built—the roulotte we burned on our long trek to Nokhor Khat. Is the plainness of the work due to his simple tools, or his missing fingers? Still, there is grace to the petals as they emerge from the polished wood. "Will you decorate the whole thing?"

Papa only shrugs, but Tia tilts her head. "Not all at once, certainly." She runs a gentle hand over her close-cropped hair. "He's promised me a comb when I get back to my wigs."

I smile at the girl—grateful for her grace, and guilty too. I should have been the one coaxing my father to return to his art. "When will that be?"

"As soon as we get to the Coffret," Tia says. "When Cheeky and I parted ways outside of Nokhor Khat, she was *generous* enough to cart away all my pretty things. For my safety, she said, but if she doesn't give them back, she'll be the one in danger."

"And Maman?" I press. "She's there too?"

"Cheeky promised to look after her," Tia says. "Meliss seemed eager to get away from Nokhor Khat."

"Ah." Deliberately, I keep my eyes on Papa—on his work. I do not turn to look toward the back of the ship, where Le Trépas lurks. Though I know why Maman wanted to run, and it has nothing to do with Nokhor Khat. What will she do when we arrive at the camp with the old monk in tow? I don't dare ask Papa.

He too prefers to ignore the man sitting in chains on the other side of the boat, but I don't know if he's pretending or only lost in his art. His hand moves in small, precise gestures; little curls of wood drop to the musty carpet. But as I watch, I can imagine the chair when it is done—a lacy, graceful thing, even more beautiful than the roulotte was.

Suddenly my own hands are itching with the need to create. "There must be tools there at the rebel base," I say softly. "Maybe when we get there, you and I could work together."

"Do you expect to have spare time?" Camreon's voice floats across the hall. He has taken up a position near La

Fleur, and I can't quite tell if he's guarding her or keeping her company. "Art must wait for war."

"I know," I say, still watching Papa work. What would I be creating instead? How will my fantouches change when they are made for defense instead of display? In my mind, I conjure up a fantastical armée: something even larger than the mechanical birds, ensouled with an eagle's spirit, to hunt them out of the sky. Or something smaller—like a mosquito—though instead of drawing out blood, it could draw out the accelerant. But leather and bamboo are no match for fire and steel. And out in the jungle, metalworks are in short supply. I chew my lip. "Do the rebels have the resources to make weaponry?"

"Raik is the one overseeing the supplies," Cam says, making a face. "I'm sure he has ideas, but they'll be much improved by your own. He's never been one for working with his hands."

I can't help but glance at Theodora. "Will she help too?"

"She can't hurt," Theodora interjects drily.

"Speaking of Raik . . ." Cam lifts his hand. In it is a piece of red cloth. He must have torn it from the sail. "Can you send him a letter?"

I come to his side, reaching for the fabric. "What does it say?"

He gives me a look. "It says, 'I wrote this in old Chakran so no one but my brother could read it.'"

"Old Chakran?" My eyebrows go up—I unfold the letter, peering at the writing.

"It's an update," Cam says, taking pity. "Remember, Raik was expecting you and Le Trépas on the wing. Instead, he's getting all of us weeks later by boat. Including La Fleur," the Tiger adds, his smile falling again, though I am only half paying attention. "So he has some options to weigh."

Despite his explanation, I can't help but stare at the letter. Would Papa be able to read it? He'd studied the language in his youth, as had most people in his generation. But for those of us who grew up after La Victoire, the old ways were forbidden. "Where did you learn, Camreon?"

"When I was quite young, my caretakers hid me in the old temples," he says. "Along with the rebels and the remaining monks. A lot of my bedtime stories were myths read from the carvings on the temple walls."

"So were mine," I say, remembering. "Myths, I mean. Of course, they were from shadow plays instead of temples."

"That's how the old stories survived after La Victoire," Cam says. "Some of them, anyway. Most of the temple art is lost forever. And who knows what disappeared with the scrolls the Aquitans burned?"

The question is rhetorical, but an answer comes to mind: Le Trépas might. In my mind's eye, I see the beautiful mysteries carved into the ceiling in Hell's Court. Is that how the old monk had cultivated his powers? Interpreting old legends . . . daring to push the limits of what he knew, what he could do. I glance toward the back of the ship only to find that Le Trépas is looking right at me. My stomach drops. Had he heard my thoughts? Or just the conversation?

Quickly, I turn back to the letter in my hands, knotting the scrap of cloth in the center, so the two ends flare like wings. Then I reach into the satchel at my side, pulling out the book of souls, tattered and torn. Flipping through the pages, my brow furrows. "I'm out of birds . . . no, wait." In my pocket is the folded flyer—the one I'd found tucked under my pillow. The one they'd meant me to use for the flying machine. "One left."

"Good," Camreon says, but my hands tighten on the paper.

"What if we need it for something more important?"

Cam cocks his head. "Can't you get more?"

"Not with Le Trépas so close."

"What about the ballast stones?" Theodora says. "You can take the souls from them."

"We might need them for the avions. Besides, I don't think we can make a fire hot enough." I trail off, looking back at Le Trépas again. What was it he'd said about the avion yesterday? That I could pluck the souls out one by one . . . Le Trépas is rumored to kill at a touch. Is this a skill I really covet?

"Theodora," I say at last. "Did Le Trépas ever say how he pulled souls out of bodies?"

"No," she replies, curling her lip. "But he liked to offer to show us."

I shudder, Papa's warning still ringing in my ears: stay away. "What about the translations, Cam? Did they say anything about . . . about killing at a touch?"

"Symbols and blood," he says. "The stories are just that. Stories. Not instruction manuals. Send the letter," he adds then. "It's important."

My eyes narrow. "I thought it was just an update."

The Tiger gives me a look. "I may be the leader of the rebellion, but Raik is still the king. He'll be expecting word."

With a sigh, I turn to the little cookfire, readying my pin. But as I transfer the hawk's soul to Camreon's note, my eyes drift back to Akra and Le Trépas. The flame rises, the ash curls, the spirit flashes into her new skin. It would be more than useful to be able to do these things without fire.

Whispering instructions to the spirit, I release the note, watching it spiral upward into the pale sunlight streaming through a hole in the deck. Then I turn my attention to Papa. He is still lost in his work. Curls of wood fall around him like petals. Would he notice if I ignored his warning?

The thought itself feels like a betrayal—of him, of Maman. Of myself. But I had risked so much to learn about my powers from Theodora. Isn't it worthwhile to try to learn from one of her sources? Giving Papa one last glance, I stand, the muscles in my legs twinging, and make my way across the room.

At the back of the ship is an open hole that used to be a glassed-in balcony. The glass is long gone, but the balcony remains, overlooking the shimmering wake of our passing. Le Trépas sits cross-legged on the carpet, facing the sea; his arms are in the carcan, wrapped around his belly, and his fetters are locked to a beam. No chance of him escaping. Especially with no souls about. Akra too is gazing out at the water. And though the mildewed carpet muffles my footsteps, I can tell by the shift in my brother's shoulders that he knows I am behind him.

Is it his time in the armée that made him so perceptive? Or is it what I did at Hell's Court? Perhaps I should ask Le Trépas that too. But it is the old monk who speaks first. "Come where we can see you, girl. You have such a pretty face."

"Teh-twa," Akra says softly to the monk. Le Trépas's demand only makes my lip curl; I do not move from where I stand. My brother folds his arms. "What do you want, Jetta?"

"To talk to Le Trépas."

Now Akra turns, looking at me askance. "Why?"

"He mentioned a way to pull the souls out of the avions," I say, trying to keep the defensive tone out of my voice. "I'd like to know what it is."

Akra's eyebrows go up, but Le Trépas replies. "Without dying, you mean?" I can hear the smile in the old monk's voice. "You'd need to get closer than the avions will allow."

"Close enough to make a mark." I flex my hands as he nods; my knuckles twinge, scarred and scabbed. Life and death—everything begins and ends with blood. "But what symbol?"

"You can't guess?" Le Trépas sighs. "I had hoped you would be more clever."

"It's death, isn't it?" The answer comes in a flash. The approval in his eyes aggravates me. I press my lips together, disappointed that I rose to the bait.

"Do you know what it looks like?"

"I do." Maman had taught me the symbol of life, but the sign for death was something I'd only seen drawn in ash on the foreheads of the dead. These days, not everyone can afford enough dry wood to burn a corpse. The superstitious say that it's to keep a restless spirit from sneaking back into a body. Could it be so simple? The knowledge the Aquitans worked so hard to forbid, turned into a funeral rite? "And . . . will my blood work?"

"Try it and see," Le Trépas says.

"Don't," Akra blurts out, his voice a touch too loud. Then he takes a breath, softening. "Don't trust him, Jetta. He's pulling your strings."

"I'm trying to teach her," Le Trépas protests. "She has a lot to do and little time to learn. Besides," he adds with a pointed look at my brother. "You know better than most what happens when she acts in ignorance, on impulse."

Akra stiffens, but I clench my teeth. Had the old monk

somehow seen what had happened the night I killed Legarde? No . . . Theodora must have told him. "What sacred knowledge did you trade to the Aquitans for that little tidbit?"

Le Trépas only shrugs. "Nothing as sacred as a pint of your blood."

My hand goes to the crook of my arm—the bruise there is fading, but the memory still haunts me. "Our blood," I say softly. "The blood you would have killed me for sharing."

"Better you than all those people in the slums," he says.

"Teh-twa," Akra says, louder now, but I grit my teeth.

"This, from a child killer?" I growl.

"Their deaths served a purpose," the monk says. "That's all any of us can ever hope for when the time comes. There will be plenty of blood on your own hands before it's done, Jetta. Pray that it's more of theirs than ours."

There is a sour taste on the back of my tongue. It makes me want to spit. "I serve the rebellion. Not your bitter god."

"My god? Oh, Jetta." Le Trépas's laugh is full and rich, and loud enough to be infuriating. "You don't serve the King of Death."

I clench my jaw—I don't want to ask. Everything

in me tells me to turn, to walk away, to not give him the satisfaction of the question. No . . . not everything. "What do you mean?"

"Death begets life," he says. "You serve the Maiden. Though not very well."

My eyes go wide. The Maiden—life? I take a breath to ask, but the silence is broken by a shout from up above. "Avions!"

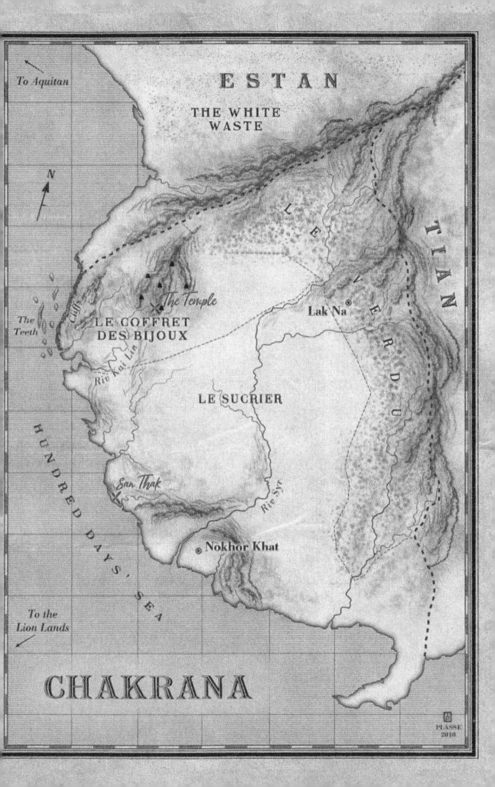

CHAPTER TWENTY-TWO

They skim over the green tangle of the jungle, fast and sleek: a flock of avions. Far too many to fight off—five . . . no, six—soaring north from Nokhor Khat. Has Pique changed his mind about attacking *La Rêve* with Theodora aboard?

Racing to the deck, I am already urging the ship's soul to flee. But it's pointless—the avions move far faster than *La Rêve* can sail. What else can we do? Jump into the waves and scatter? Swim for the distant shore? The specter of the pilot bobs up in my memory: the body in the water, wreathed in unquenchable flame. But after a moment at the rail, gripping the cracked wood, I frown. The avions are keeping their course over land, moving parallel to our ship.

A glimmer of relief—but what are they after, if not us? Half a dozen is too many to use for spying. As I watch, they bank in unison, just as living birds would, wheeling above a spot in the jungle. Unease grips me as avions gambol over the fluffy green clouds of the tree line. They are so graceful— even beautiful, until the fire comes.

Like a sudden storm, flame rains down. It spirals and tumbles through the air like silk ribbons; it uncoils like my mother's hair as she lets it down her back. Black plumes of greasy smoke billow up to meet it. Fire licks the treetops as embers rise to the darkening sky.

"What are they doing?" I frown, puzzled, as the avions circle back, passing through the smoke with another gout of flame.

The Tiger reaches into one of his pockets, pulling out a folded scrap of the oily armée paper: a map. He peers at it for a moment, his expression darker than the drifting ash. "Putting on a show," he says at last.

I cock my head, trying to understand. "We already know what the avions can do."

"Yes," he agrees softly, passing me the paper. "This is about what the armée is capable of."

I search the map, trying to place us along the jagged line of the coast between the mountains of the Coffret and Nokhor Khat to the south. Camreon must see the confusion on my face, for he reaches over to point at a dot inland. "San Thak," he says. "A village too unimportant for the armée to name."

"A village?" My stomach drops as I look back at the conflagration. We are far enough out to sea not to hear the whoosh of hot air or the crackle of flame or the distant screaming of the people as they burn. The jungle hides the huts and fields and the lights of the souls, gold or blue. But though the wind is blowing in from the water, I swear I can smell the sooty reek of smoking hair.

Whirling, I reach for one of the ballast stones, but Camreon puts his hand on my arm to stop me. "There are three stones and twice as many avions," he says.

"Then I'll take them down three at a time!"

"It will be over before the first stone reaches them," he says. "Besides, the souls inside may be too tired to come back, and what if we need them later?"

I stare at him, uncomprehending. "You want me to do nothing?"

Cam's eyes are flat. "Sometimes that's all you can do."

I feel dizzy, sick; the scar on my shoulder seems to burn. I wrap my arms around my stomach, as though I can hold myself together if I squeeze. "This is my fault."

"No." The answer makes me turn—not Cam's voice, but Theodora's. She stands there at the top of the stairs, watching the flying machines. "It's mine."

"Your brother is the one giving the orders," Cam says.

"Or Pique," she shoots back, her voice too loud.

"It's all of us," I snap, before they can continue bickering. "But without the Aquitans, none of this would have happened."

"It's true," Leo says. I hadn't seen him come above. He sighs. "At least now we know what the consequences are."

I swallow, still tasting smoke. "Will they come again?"

Cam sighs. "Unless the general gets what he wants."

Longingly, I look back at the ballast stones, but already the avions are wheeling away from the conflagration. They leave a plume of black smoke behind as they turn toward Nokhor Khat. Cam was right—they were too far away for me to stop them. "Show's over," he says, following Theodora below. Leo goes too, but I stay on deck, watching the smoke until it disappears over the horizon.

The guilt chases me long after. I stare at the water,

the setting sun igniting the waves. I should have done something, though I don't know what. A laugh bubbles out of me—how could Le Trépas claim I served the Maiden when Death seems to follow me? I'd be a fool to trust a word he says. But as my laughter fades, I look back at the ballast stones. What if he was telling the truth?

If there is a way for me to pull souls from their skins, I could have freed all of the arvana from the avions before we'd left Hell's Court. I could have taken all the souls from my fantouches without having to burn them. I could have killed Pique too, just by reaching out to touch him. The thought is darkly comforting.

Is it worth it to try my blood on the stone? To learn what I can do?

Do I dare not try it?

The pin is in my hand; I kneel beside the stones. With a wince and a hiss, I prick the pad of my smallest finger. Blood wells up, and I mark the stone with a symbol I have only seen but never drawn. A circle with a short tail, like a staring eye, or a bullet wound. Death.

Pulling back, I steel myself, but it is less shocking than I fear. The soul simply uncoils from the stone, stretching golden wings. It hovers for just a moment before turning toward the open sea; with a start, I race to the tattered sails. Tearing off a piece, I write life on the silk and wave it like a signal flag. The soul circles back reluctantly—afraid of Le Trépas, or of me? But I am patient, and at last it dives into the fabric. I watch it flutter, marveling. Could the spell really be so painless?

"I'll never get used to that." Leo's voice makes me whirl. He stands behind me on the deck, his expression a mystery.

"The best acts are ones that amaze over and over again." I clear my throat, my voice still hoarse from cursing. The silk trembles in my hand; gently, I fold the fabric, hushing the soul inside before I tuck it into my pocket.

"Would you mind an encore?" Leo approaches. He gestures with a piece of canvas covered in his neat handwriting.

I wet my lips as his last note comes back to me: au revoir. "You have a letter for me to send?"

"To my brother." He passes it over and leans on the rail, looking out at the silent shore. Night's curtain is falling, soft as velvet, with no stars and no souls in sight. I toy with the cloth, curious, but unwilling to pry. My silence speaks for itself, and after a while, he fills it. "It's true what you said. None of this would have happened without the Aquitans.

Then again, I wouldn't be around to see what might have been instead."

Hearing my words repeated back to me, shame echoes where anger had been. "You're not one of them, Leo. They'd be the first to tell you that."

"I'm not exactly one of 'us' either." He shrugs one shoulder, giving me a half smile. "But if I have to pick sides, I'll stand with you."

His voice is soft and earnest, but something in me pulls away. I turn back to the ballast stones to cover my confusion. Marking the note with life and the second stone with death, the soul leaps from the ballast to the canvas, and soon it is winging across the water, back the way we came.

"Is it difficult?" Leo says then as we watch the letter go. "Being surrounded by the dead, I mean?"

"You are too," I tease gently. Leo's lips quirk. "At least, when Le Trépas isn't near. It's actually stranger without them. Somehow the world is less alive without the spirits around."

Leo nods slowly, but does he understand? "I suppose if they need you, it's only fair you need them."

"It is best when it goes both ways."

"It is." He pauses then, hesitant, and at his look, I brace

myself. "I am always happiest being needed," he adds.

"I know," I say softly, and what I wouldn't have given for this moment weeks ago. The pounding of my heart, the earnest look in his eyes, the soft breeze and the sickle moon, and all of it before he'd run from me. Au revoir—until we meet again. What next? "That's why you came back when you knew I needed the elixir."

He blinks at me—is he surprised that I have guessed? "I came back because I needed you too," he says, and the words strike a chord in me. But there is a note that doesn't ring true.

"I don't need you," I say, but that too feels wrong, and not just because of the hurt in his eyes. "I can't. You left when I needed you most."

"I know." He drops his eyes, ashamed. The silence grows between us—I half wish he would make excuses, or find some explanation. But I know them all, don't I? His maman, and how he lost her to her own madness. His father, who he lost, in part, to mine. "I'm sorry," he says, and I shake my head.

"I can't blame you." I squeeze his hand, running my thumb over the callus on his third finger—the one he's earned from bowing his violin. "But I can't let myself need you anymore either."

"Then . . ." His voice trails off; he looks out at the water as though he can't bear to face the thought head-on. "What now? Should I stay away? Keep apologizing? What do you want?"

I hesitate, suddenly unsure. Can I have him near without learning to rely on him? Then again, is it fair for me to demand what I can't offer? I don't know exactly how long the elixir will last, or what will happen when I run out. But neither does Leo, and he came back.

Would he stay?

"I want you never to leave again," I say at last.

He looks up, hope in his eyes. "I won't," he says, too quickly, but I am cautious—I have to be.

"Don't tell me," I say. "Just . . . show me."

"I will," he says fervently, wrapping his arms around me. He holds me so tightly I feel for a moment he will never let me go. It is exactly what I want—exactly what I need. "One day at a time."

I am the one to pull back, looking into his eyes as he does into mine. I have kissed him before—once on a whim, twice on a dare. But now? The kiss we share is a promise, and he tastes like seawater and gunpowder and the distant perfume that drifted backstage at Le Perl.

We only part when Tia clears her throat. "There's dinner downstairs," she says, half delighted, half disgusted as she stands at the top of the stairs. "If you're still hungry after *that*."

I flush, but Leo laughs; together, we make our way belowdecks.

To my surprise, the dining hall has been converted into a miniature workshop. There, a pile of nails pulled from some of the old crates downstairs. Here, a stack of tin cans, drained and cleaned through narrow holes punched in the tops. "What is all this?" I say, watching Papa. He has left off his carving to drop nails into the cans.

"Grenades," La Fleur says primly. "Or they will be, when they're finished."

"Grenades?" I turn to Camreon, unable to keep the admiration off my face. "I should have known the Tiger would have a plan."

"They aren't my design," he says, looking up from his work shredding carpet into fiber. "They're Theodora's."

I blink, surprised, but La Fleur only makes a face. "Well," she says, in a tone that sounds like she's about to apologize. "I had hoped these would be a collaboration."

"With me?" The surprise is short-lived. "You'll need to animate them."

She nods. "To get them to the avions, yes. But . . ." She hesitates, her eyes traveling to the satchel at my side. "We also need a bit of explosive."

"What?" I clutch the strap as I understand her meaning. "No."

"I know it doesn't look like a lot in the jar," she says quickly. "But just a small piece of lytheum produces quite a bit of the elixir."

I narrow my eyes. "And how much do you need?"

"I don't have to use all of it," she says, which is not an answer. "What if we only made . . . say, ten? That would put a dent in Pique's next volley."

"You keep blaming it on Pique," Cam mutters, but Theodora ignores him.

"It would still leave you . . . oh, another month's worth. And I know where the source is. After this is over, we can go get more. Please, Jetta." There is desperation in her voice. My reluctance feels selfish. Hadn't I wanted to do something?

Still, I hate that she's asking. Better that she take the elixir away than make me give it up. "What happened to the elixir being a prerequisite?" I mutter, but I pull the bag from my shoulder and set it down roughly beside her. Then I turn to the little makeshift fireplace where the food is warming.

Picking out a can of turtle soup, I wrap my hands around it, but it doesn't comfort me as much as I want it to.

"One last thing?" Theodora's voice is tentative, reluctant. I turn back, smothering a sigh with difficulty.

"What?"

"We'll need more souls. You only have three birds left in the ballast stones, isn't that right?"

"Two now," I say tiredly, taking a small sip of the soup. "But I can keep looking for more as we sail. Or you could put me down ashore. With Le Trépas on the ship, it wouldn't take me more than a few minutes to gather more."

"That's a last resort," Cam says. "We don't know when the avions will be back. I don't want them catching you there while we're out here."

"Well," Theodora says again. The tone of her voice makes my heart sink—as does her glance down the hall at Le Trépas. "It's possible there's another way to summon souls."

"Blood and symbols?"

"*His* blood," she says, softer now. "And a piece of something dead."

My lip curls. "Like what?"

"Hair. Teeth. Bones." She shrugs, uncomfortable. "I never dared to test it."

"And you want me to?"

"Only if you're willing." She gives me a look; when I sigh, she nods, satisfied. I take another sip of the soup and start toward the back of the ship. But when I pass Papa, he sets down the tin he's working on and covers his mouth with his hand.

"Jetta," he says softly, the name soft as butter in his mangled mouth. But his tone is so reproachful he needn't say more. Excuses bubble up in me, followed by apologies. But I can't give up now.

"We have to stop them, Papa." I take a breath—how to explain? Had he seen the avions circling San Thak? Smelled the smoke of the burning village? But he didn't have to, did he? "You know exactly how cruel the armée can be."

"I do." His fists clench in his lap, the scars of the missing fingers whitening over the stumps of the knuckles. "But . . . *he* is too."

"I won't forget," I say, and he does not protest further. Instead, he turns back to his work, pushing nails into the tin.

Despite my bravado, I am not eager to visit Le Trépas. Akra too—what will he say to see me back so soon? *Don't listen to him—don't let him pull your strings.* But this is for the villages. For the rebels. For the rebellion.

"I saw the smoke," the monk calls when I approach. "It seems like the young general is eager to fill his father's shoes."

"I'm not here to talk about the armée," I say tersely. I have no love for Xavier Legarde, but I know it's harder for Leo and his sister. "Theodora says there's a way to summon souls with your blood."

Akra narrows his eyes, but Le Trépas only lifts his arms to press against the carcan. "Let me out and I'll show you."

"Not a chance."

"You expect me to simply share my secrets?" He sighs, almost theatrically. "If you weren't my daughter, I'd send you packing."

I bite down on the words—"I'm not your daughter"—lest he follow through on his threat. "But you won't," I say, and he shakes his head.

"No."

I wet my lips, afraid to ask the obvious question. Afraid to learn the answer. "Why not?"

Le Trépas raises an eyebrow. "Haven't you ever wondered why you lived when so many others didn't? Why the gods intervened on your behalf?"

"Maman intervened," I shoot back. "Not the gods. And that isn't an answer to my question."

The monk smiles. "I don't have all the answers, Jetta. But I believe you have a higher purpose."

Gritting my teeth, I take a deep breath through my nose. I can't tell if the monk is playing at mysticism or madness, but either way, I can tell he's not in earnest. It's not worth it to argue with him, as long as he tells me the truth about the spell. "So how do you do it, then?" I say. "How do you summon souls?"

"My blood and the symbol of life," he says, as though the answer is obvious.

"And something else," I say pointedly. "Something dead."

"Yes," he says. "But you do the same, don't you? Aren't most shadow puppets fashioned out of leather?"

I frown. "Theodora said you can't make fantouches."

"I can't," he says. "This isn't creating life. This is calling the dead. The material you choose will summon a similar soul. Is there flesh in the soup you're drinking?"

I grimace at the tin, my appetite gone. "We need birds, not turtles."

"Then fetch me a feather," the monk says.

"Where do you expect me to find a feather on the ship?" I mutter, but Akra shakes his head.

"This is a bad idea, Jetta."

"I know," I say—I can feel it. A mounting sense of dread. But hadn't I felt the same way at the thought of using the symbol of death? "But so is ignorance."

So I set off toward the corner of the dining hall where Papa's mattress lies. Digging my hand into the hole in the covering, I pull out a handful of damp feathers. When I bring them back to Le Trépas, he raises an eyebrow. "So many?"

"You didn't say how many we needed."

"As many as you need spirits," he says. "Count them out."

I pick the ten largest feathers and lay them on the damp carpet. They tremble in the breeze off the sea, and I can't deny it—the feeling of excitement sparking in my stomach. How long had I waited for this kind of knowledge? "Now what?"

The chains clink gently as Le Trépas shifts his weight, stretching his leg out before me. I gasp. It's lined with scars—the methodical wounds of a man with a knife and need for his own blood. They are so much more orderly than mine, but I have seen scars like this before, on the tender thigh of the first girl who turned my head. She had her own malheur. The memory brings a stab of compassion, though I don't know if the monk deserves it. "Do you have a knife?" he asks.

With reluctance, Akra pulls the blade from his belt and holds it out. Still . . . I hesitate. Why? How many times had I drawn my own blood? But though Akra's weapon is clean and well kept, when I take it, the handle feels slick and sticky on my palm. I drop it to the carpet, scrubbing my palm on my coveralls. "I can't do it," I say, feeling queasy.

Without a word, my brother picks up the knife and makes the cut for me. Le Trépas hisses, but he jerks his chin toward the blood that's running down his ankle. "Now the symbol," he says through his teeth. "Life on each feather."

Steeling myself, I dip my finger into the warm blood, trying not to cringe. How different it is, when it is not my own. The feathers stick to my hand as I try to paint them; the symbol is little more than a smear. When I am done, I wipe my fingers clean on the carpet and sit back. Nothing happens. "Where are the souls?"

"Just wait," Le Trépas says, drawing his leg back. The cut was shallow, the blood already slowing. "They're coming."

There is something in his tone—or his smile. It makes my gut twist. I glance over the black water, but there are no souls in the sky. I pick at my hem; I comb my fingers through my tangled hair. How long will it take? Trying to distract myself, I turn back to the wound on Le Trépas's leg. Is there something I can use to bind it?

I cast about, but aside from the mildewing carpet, there is nothing to use. Is there a clean patch on the tattered silken sails? I stand, but Le Trépas looks up sharply. "Don't go now," he says. "They're coming."

In spite of everything, a thrill goes through me. But when I see the first soul, my mouth goes dry. Fluttering over the water, it approaches: amorphous, flickering, and the color of sapphires.

My stomach drops as the spirit sweeps through the open balcony toward the bloody feathers. But instead of diving inside, it draws the bit of down up in its wake. The soul circles, as though waiting for my instruction. I draw back. Not even in the butcher's market have I seen the vengeful soul of an animal.

Another approaches then, and another; they swirl

toward the feathers, all of them waiting, all of them full of rage. "Why do they want revenge?" I say as the fourth soul appears over the water.

Le Trépas looks at me, surprised. "Because of what you did."

"What?" My stomach twists; I look at Akra, but he looks just as uncertain as I am. "What did I do?"

"You've called them out of the lives they were living," Le Trépas says. "These feathers are more than three days old. Where did you think their souls would be?"

"I . . . I killed them?" I stare at the old monk, horror quickly turning to rage. "Tell me they were only birds!"

"I don't know what they might have been," he says. "But you can tell yourself so."

Dear Brother,

You have tried to be my keeper. I owe it to you to be yours.

    If you do not stop, I will come and stop you.

    I am trying to be better than my blood. Will you?

—Leo

CHAPTER TWENTY-THREE

The first thing I do is feed the bloody feathers into the fire. The flames engulf the souls and the quills alike, and when the spirits spring free, they are the bright color of arvana. I am grateful for this reprieve, but I will not forget my crime so easily. I tuck each spirit into a tin grenade, and soon enough we have almost a dozen waiting for the avions.

The next thing I do is take my dose of elixir. The act itself calms me, but only a little. And I take a bit less than I know I need, not quite half, but not quite three-quarters, either. Better to ration than to run out—I know this from the Hungry Year.

When La Fleur returns the jar, the little lump of lytheum

floating inside is no bigger than a fingernail. "You should have at least six weeks left in total," she says.

"And less if we need more grenades."

"There isn't enough in the jar to bother with more," she replies with a twist of her lips. "Let's just hope I was wrong about the birds coming back."

"Let's hope," I say, staring into the fire, but neither of us is so foolish as to actually do such a thing.

The pile of grenades is shockingly small. Theodora transports them to a berth on the far side of the ship—away from the water, out of the weather, and far enough from the rest of us that if something goes wrong, the explosion would be as contained as possible. Still, I can see them in my mind's eye. Ten tin cans, packed with fire and iron and the soul of something I killed.

Ten dead, just like that. Who or what, and where? I'll never know. It might have been ten birds. Or ten beetles. Ten eyeless crawling worms, their wet bodies already returning to the soil. But it could have been ten soldiers. Ten mothers. Ten children.

Is saving a village worth the price? Of course it is. Of course. I tell myself that, again and again, as I watch the fire dance.

"Jetta?"

I look up, but there is no one beside me—it is only my brother's voice. I almost don't want to answer; I know what he will say. "Don't tell me," I say under my breath. "I should have known not to trust him."

"You know now," he says, and the sadness in his voice is thick as burned sugar. "You shouldn't dwell on it."

I stifle a laugh. "I'm supposed to just forget?"

"Only the dead forget," he says. "Or monsters passing as men. You're not a monster, Jetta. Stop thinking that you are."

"How do you know what I'm thinking?" I say, heat rising on the back of my neck. Can he spy on my thoughts?

"Because I've killed too." His tone brings me up short—I knew that already, but I'd never heard him say it quite so softly. Not a boast or a threat, but a confession. "Le Trépas was right about one thing, Jetta. In war, everyone has blood on their hands."

"Some of us more than others," I mutter, looking down at the scabs on my fingers, the cuts on my palms. But the sound my brother makes is cut short, bitten off, and I can't tell if it was a laugh or a sob. I look for him over my shoulder, trying to get a glimpse of his face across the hall, but Akra is facing the water.

"Trust me, Jetta," he says at last. "You haven't done half so much wrong as I have."

I take a breath—the memory surfaces. The rebel woman in the camp outside of Nokhor Khat, her teeth bared as she spit Akra's rank back in his face: capitaine. The story she'd told, her village razed, her parents killed. But looking at my brother's back—his bowed head, the slope of his shoulders—all I want to do is comfort him. He is the still the boy who'd taught me to hold a paper butterfly so it trembled like a living thing. The boy who sang in the fields. The boy who joined the armée to save my life.

Looking down at my own battered hands, I think of Akra's scars. The terrible things he had done left marks on his body—none worse than the scar that marked what I'd done to him. Only the dead forget, he'd said. Sometimes, not even then.

"You're not a monster either," I say softly, and I hear his sigh, see his shoulders rise and fall.

"I'll try to remember that," he says.

"Why don't you sing anymore?" I ask. "You used to do it all the time, do you remember? While you worked. While you carved. When you were trying to flirt with Mina Amadee and her brother shook a cleaver at you because he said you sounded like a dying rooster."

"Thanks for reminding me," he says, and now I can hear the hint of a smile.

"I still heard your voice after you left," I say, softer now. "Singing in the fields. I never told you. But your voice was the first one I heard when I . . . started hearing things."

"And I thought war was hell," he says mildly, and the joke is so unexpected that I have to stifle a laugh.

"I wasn't ready for you to go," I say, the words rushing out. "I wasn't ready, that night at Hell's Court. But it wasn't my choice to make."

"I'm glad you did it," he says, and I blink.

"You wouldn't have preferred to . . . to forget?"

"What I have instead is a chance to make up for some of it," he says. "Maybe that's better."

"Maybe," I say. How much will I have to atone for by the time this war is over? But I know now why Theodora is so eager to blame Pique . . . why Leo couldn't shoot his father . . . why Cam glances at La Fleur out of the corner of his eyes. Perhaps none of us are righteous when it comes to the ones we love.

Akra's voice interrupts my musing. "Didn't I start this entire conversation by telling you not to dwell?"

I fling up my hands, exasperated. "What do you want me to do instead?"

Heads swivel—Theodora, and Camreon, and Tia too. Leo murmurs something to them, an explanation—and for a moment, the feeling is too familiar: whispers and silence and significant looks. Strange that magic can look so much like madness. A blush starts across my cheeks, but then my brother's answer rings out across the room so everyone could hear it. "How about a little music?"

Tia perks up at the question. "Now that is a good idea."

There are still no souls about, but somehow Akra's suggestion has brought life aboard. Almost immediately, Leo snaps the clasps on his violin case, and Tia hums scales while he tunes. Even Papa sits up on his mattress, an eager smile on his face. Though it is late, I can feel my exhaustion easing with each note that shimmers in the air.

The warm-up always thrills me. All excitement, no pressure. I want to join in. My hand itches for a fantouche, but all I have are the grenades, the ballast stones, the tattered book of souls . . . and the scrap of red silk in my pocket.

I am a better puppeteer than a dancer, but even before the music starts, my body aches to move. I pull the silk from my pocket, running it through my hands; the fabric flutters, more graceful than I am. When Leo finishes tuning, he lifts his violin. The first few notes are a salve, and when I hear Tia's smoky voice, I am transported back to Le Perl.

The flicker of the candles, the smell of perfume and backstage dust, the way the glitter stuck to my skin long after we'd left it behind. But Le Perl exists only in memory now: Tia and Leo conjure it with their music. As the harmony wraps around us, the run-down dining hall is transformed. The musty room feels intimate, and the dim light of the smoky cookfire casts the splintered walls into a dramatic light. And in the makeshift spotlight, I dance.

Tossing the red silk up, the soul of the hawk takes to the air; at my whisper, she banks, the scarlet fabric streaming like a ribbon as I whirl. When I make circles with my hand, she swirls like a conjuring; I throw up my hands, and she snaps her silken wings wide.

All around me, the spirit soars, my feet turn and flicker across the soft floor as my blood thrums to the melody. It has been too long since I felt so alive. But as I turn, I catch sight of Akra. He has cocked his ear to listen to the music, and even across the room, I can see the dreamy smile on his face.

Will he sing? I hope so. But each song moves into the next as the moon rises and falls in the sky, and I do not hear Akra's voice. Not even in my head.

Days later, the avions return.

We are nearing our destination—only another few days, according to Cam's map. The rain has cleared for a while, and Papa and I are taking a halting stroll across the deck when he sights the flock. He clenches his hand around my elbow and hisses through his teeth; that's when I look up and see them too.

They approach at speed—another cadre of six—and this time their target is clear: a pretty fishing village tucked into a cove. I call to the others as I hurry Papa down the stairs; my heart is pounding, but I force myself to go as slow as he needs. Once he is safe below, I make a beeline for the stock of grenades. Theodora is already there.

"You have to fill the can with water and light the wick," she says as I pick one up, pointing at a long piece of twine dangling from the tin.

"I thought lytheum explodes in water." I look at her askance, but she shakes her head, frustrated.

"It's a chemical reaction that creates a flammable gas.

The water left behind is actually the elixir—"

"We can go over chemistry later," Cam interjects, gathering an armful of the grenades and starting toward the deck.

Gingerly, I pick up two cans and follow. "Once we light the wick, how long do we have?"

"I'm not exactly sure," Theodora admits. "Just try to keep the fire away from the gas."

"You're not sure?" My head reels—ten grenades suddenly seems far too few. But the avions are already too close to the village; when we reach the deck, Cam starts lining up the grenades, and Leo meets us with a lighter and a bucket full of water. "Hurry," I say, and he dunks one of the tins into the bucket.

Immediately, air starts hissing through the hole in the top, where the wick protrudes. "Should I light it?" Leo asks, nervous, but I coax the soul upward till the twine is dangling beneath—away from the gas. Gritting his teeth, Leo flicks his lighter to life; we hold our breath as he lights the wick and I send the grenade spinning toward the first avion.

"Another," I say, and Cam dunks the next tin into the bucket. But the metal birds fly far faster than my little grenades. I only have three in the air by the time the avions start to circle above the village. I send up a fourth as the massacre starts.

Cozy grass huts burst into flame: two hundred souls scatter as the avions chase them down the beach. Soon the shore is a conflagration, from the coconut palms to the long bamboo pier. Families flee to the brightly painted coracles, pushing them out on the water only to have the sea catch fire beneath them. The sight of it all snaps something in me; enraged, I send the last ballast stone after the birds as Camreon prepares another grenade.

By now, the first explosive has reached an avion. I send the spirit down into the cockpit to wait—and wait. Has something gone wrong? I am only half watching as I send the other bombs to chase the rest of the avions—my eyes are riveted to the first as my target pours another gout of flame down on the village. I have started to despair when the bird judders in the sky.

Above the screams and the fire, I hadn't even heard the far-off explosion. But I can see the smoke drifting from the avion as it banks—is that blood gleaming on the metal wings? The remains of the pilot slump in the cockpit; the avion wheels away from the fire, no longer so keen to attack the village without orders. But she doesn't fall, either. Xavier must have ensouled all the avions himself.

I don't have time for frustration. Instead, I urge the rest of the grenades nearer to their targets. One of the bombs bursts too early—I see the flash of fire, then the soul rising like a phoenix from the explosion. Another grenade misses the mark as an avion swoops: I send the bomb around again, but the wick has burned too close. The explosion is hard to see through the thickening smoke. The next shot is luckier—my fourth grenade shatters the glass of the cockpit and the skull of the pilot. Red bursts across the steel as the avion beats her wings in panic. Then, to my dismay, the rest of the warbirds wheel south, speeding back toward the capitol.

The ones without pilots follow, as do the grenades. The next explosion sends its target reeling as the rest of the flock pulls ahead; this time, the flame reaches the accelerant in a blast that seems to shake the ship itself. I shout in triumph as pieces of metal spin away to splash into the water—one avion down.

But the rest of the grenades are lagging, and one by one, they burst ineffectively against the sky. The ballast stone is my last chance for a final strike, and I sent it plunging through one avion's metal wing. The creature goes spinning through the air, but with a few frantic wingbeats, it rights itself and trails after the others. I watch the sky, but I've lost sight of the stone. In the end, all that is left to send after the birds is my curses.

My heart sinks; my eyes burn. I stare at the remains of the village, the charred bodies bobbing in the shallows. Some of them are so small. "Maybe Le Trépas was right," I say softly. "Maybe it would be best if our blood had never fallen into the wrong hands."

"Jetta . . ." Leo reaches for me, but I step back.

"I don't want comfort," I say, but what I mean is I don't deserve it.

"I can improve the design," Theodora says, staring resolutely at the remaining grenade. There is only one left. And are those tears in her own eyes? "As long as we get more lytheum."

"Take it all," I say, slinging the satchel off my shoulder, but she shakes her head.

"I told you," she says. "There's hardly enough left to make a difference—"

"I don't care!" My shout brings her up short. I bite my lip, ashamed. I'm not mad at her. I lower my voice, holding out the satchel again. "Even one more avion down is worth it."

"No, it isn't," Cam says firmly. "We need you, Jetta, like

it or not. Between you and Le Trépas, we'll bring them all down. But we won't win every time. You need to get used to that."

I stare at him, bitter. "Why should I?"

"Because there will be another fight," he says. "And another and another. And we can lose most of them and still win the war. But if we lose hope, we've lost everything."

I grit my teeth, turning back toward the rail, the satchel still gripped tightly in my fist. Half of me wants to sling it, along with the elixir, into the foaming sea. Near the shore, waves toss the burning coracles. For a moment, I imagine the rest of the avions plunging down among them—the entire flock, blasted from the sky. At first, it tastes like justice, but by the time the smoking village passes over the horizon, I know by the bitterness in my mouth it is only vengeance.

ACT 2,

SCENE 24

XAVIER's office at the barracks. The general toys with a pen. On his desk is his brother's letter, fluttering weakly, pinned to the scarred wood with a letter opener. There is a piece of paper beside it—a letter in response, along with what's left of the jar of blood—but XAVIER hasn't gotten past the first words: "Dear Leonin . . ."

A knock at the door, and the general stirs, wincing at the twinge in his knee. He has been sitting here for quite some time.

XAVIER: Yes?

The adjutant peeks in.

ADJUTANT: Lieutenant Pique, sir.

The general pulls the letter opener out of the wood and stuffs the note in his pocket. Then he flips over the sheet of paper and nods. At the gesture, the adjutant ushers PIQUE into the room, shutting the door behind him.

XAVIER: Reportez.

PIQUE: The second sortie has just returned. This time, the rebels had explosives. We lost three pilots, and one of the avions.

The general's jaw tightens as he curses.

XAVIER: Putain.

PIQUE: Evidence carried back in the empty avions shows the devices were somewhat sophisticated, considering the supplies they had to work with. Your sister's work, most likely.

The general looks up sharply.

XAVIER: Are you implying my sister is a traitor?

PIQUE: No, sir. After all, the last I saw, the Tiger was holding her at gunpoint. But this does illuminate how far the rebels are willing to go. Sir . . .

As the lieutenant trails off, XAVIER narrows his eyes.

XAVIER: Spit it out.

PIQUE: I know there will be . . . serious casualties, but if we burn the ship, we could take out the Tiger and the nécromanciens at the same time. It would also prevent La Fleur from being further used by the rebels.

The general clenches his jaw.

XAVIER: My sister is not a "casualty."

PIQUE: As you say, sir.

The answer frustrates the general. He slaps his hand on the map and stands, an accusation in his eyes.

XAVIER: You said if we made it too costly to keep her, they'd bring her back.

PIQUE: The price is higher than I imagined, General. But I'm happy to increase the sorties. We'll have to, once the rebels go to ground.

XAVIER: We can't burn the whole country, Pique.

PIQUE: I don't like it any more than you do. But if the rebels won't hand her over, we risk losing them all in the jungle.

The general glances back down at the map, chewing his lip.

XAVIER: We should have someone following them by air.

PIQUE: Not with the way the nécromancien can attack.

XAVIER: I would risk it. I should be the one going after her.

PIQUE: Your father trusted you to lead the armée, General.
Not to chase down your sister.

XAVIER: It was easier when he was in charge.

*The general glances out the window to the courtyard below. It
used to echo with the sound of drills: men preparing to deploy,
sergeants shouting at their platoons. Now it is empty—the
soldiers have been sent to hold the sugar fields in La Sucrier,
where they are spread much too thin.*
PIQUE takes a breath in the silence—cautious. Hopeful.

PIQUE: With permission, sir?

A silence.

XAVIER: What is it?

PIQUE: I can't presume to know what your father would
advise if he were here now. But I did serve with him for many

years, and saw him make good use of the questioneurs.

XAVIER narrows his eyes, but PIQUE presses on.

I know that you indulged your sister's request to have them reassigned, but your father had a firmer hand. And if we can get an idea of where the Tiger is headed, we can concentrate our forces.

Another silence.

XAVIER: Take care of it.
PIQUE: Yes, sir.

The lieutenant smiles, pleased. Then a knock comes at the door. Frustrated, Xavier answers.

XAVIER: What?

The adjutant enters, a folder in his hand.

ADJUTANT: A letter for you, sir.
XAVIER: A letter?

The general glances at the note on his desk—the response he is still trying to pen. Frowning, the general takes the folder, flipping it open.

XAVIER: From Aquitan? I wasn't expecting a ship.
ADJUTANT: It came by avion, sir. The one Lieutenant Pique sent to Lephare. It's returned.
XAVIER: Ah. Thank you.

With a salute, the adjutant exits. Xavier opens the wax seal on the letter and reads. The lieutenant watches the general's face as his frown eases into a look of relief.

PIQUE: Sir?
XAVIER: From my uncle. Recruitment is up. We can expect reinforcements within two weeks.
PIQUE: That's good news, sir.
XAVIER: It's a gift.

XAVIER's hand goes to the medallion on his necklace.

Or a sign.
PIQUE: Sir.

The general looks sharply at PIQUE, but the lieutenant returns his gaze frankly. XAVIER drops his hand to his desk. Plucking up the unfinished note, he crushes it in his fist and tosses it into the wastebasket in the corner.

XAVIER: I want daily reports on the intelligence.
PIQUE. Yes, sir.

PIQUE salutes and exits to find the questioneurs.

CHAPTER TWENTY-FIVE

We continue north, watching the sky with dread, but we reach the mouth of the Kai Lin—the Gods' Tears—without seeing another flock. It is late afternoon when *La Rêve* tucks herself into the calm waters of the quiet inlet. Though the bay is protected from the sea, there are no villages along the golden shore. Not anymore.

The river got its name from the sapphires that used to litter the bed—stones the size of snails, and just as common. The Aquitans quickly snapped them from the water, then cored into the mountains looking for more. The runoff from their mines silted the bay, killing the coral that sheltered the fish. The villages soon went the same way. The landscape has long since been ceded to the jungle, though signs of habitation remain: an abundance of fruit trees, tangled and wild, the old walls of a mill nearly covered with bromeliads, the drooping lines of an abandoned telegraph.

Initially, I had hoped we might ride the boat at least partway up the Kai Lin, but the silty riverbed is much too shallow. Besides, *La Rêve* would be quite visible from the air. Rather than leading the armée right to the rebel camp, we disembark on the shore of the bay. Keeping an eye on the sky, we unload as many tins as we can fit onto a tabletop I ensoul to carry them for us. When we have all our supplies ashore, I give the cracked hull one last pat and send the boat cruising slowly toward the Teeth. Then we sweep our footsteps from the beach as we retreat to the cover of the trees.

The sand is difficult for Papa's wheels—he opts to walk, leaning on me as Tia and Leo drag the chair up the shore. He is stronger now after our time at sea, where he'd been able to stroll slowly around the deck and work with his hands, far from the damp miasma of the slums. But he still sinks gratefully into the chair once he reaches it—the pain in his twisted leg is not something that fresh air and exercise can fix.

As I open a can of soup for his dinner, Theodora's suggestion returns to me—the one she'd made about the other aides à la mobilité. To fill them with a soul bound by the person using the aide. Would Papa want to ensoul his chair? He has never forbidden me from using my magic— not like Maman did. But it is blood magic, after all, and from the blood I share with a man he does not like or trust . . . with good reason.

I could do it for him and tell it to obey his orders. The avions Xavier had ensouled seemed to listen to their handlers. But the thought makes me uneasy: better for Papa to have complete control. I page through the book of souls as I heat his soup. By the time the food is warm, I have found the perfect arvana. So I go to Papa, the tin in one hand and the flyer in the other.

At first, I think he's dozing, but when I approach, he sits up straight, opening his eyes. "I brought some dinner," I say, handing him the can. "And something else."

He only raises an eyebrow, looking first at me, then at the page.

"It's for your chair," I say, so he doesn't have to ask aloud. "The arvana will make it easier to lift and push. And if you use my blood to write the symbol, the soul will answer to your commands. It's the one from our roulotte," I add then, glancing down at the carved flower on the armrest of his chair. "A dog's spirit. Loyal and friendly."

Papa takes a sip from the can, as though to cover his hesitation, but I can see the uncertainty in his eyes. Is he squeamish about the blood? About the nécromancy itself? He does not say, but after some consideration, he nods. Almost eagerly, I pull the pin from my hem. Papa balks, but only for a moment. When he is done, I feed the flyer to the flame. Brightly, the dog's soul bounds free, leaping into the wooden chair.

Papa can't see the spirit, but can he tell the difference? I want to ask, but I know he doesn't want to talk. Instead, I watch as he takes a breath, putting his left hand on the wheel. As he pushes, the faintest sound creeps through his lips—not loud enough for me to make out, but I am not the one he's talking too. The chair turns to the right, and even I can tell it's moving much more smoothly. Papa's smile is all the proof I need.

We sleep that night under the trees, overlooking the silvery sand of the beach. It is strange to be on land again. I hadn't realized how familiar the sound of the sea had become, and the night birds sing differently here in the west. It is a long time before I drift off to sleep, and morning comes too soon. But we do not want to linger near the shore, and after a quick breakfast, we plunge deeper into the jungle.

The Tiger leads, slicing a path with his machete, and Le Trépas and Akra bring up the rear. The rest of us string out between them in single file along the river. Leo and I walk just behind Papa, ready to lend our strength when he needs it. The dog's soul makes the chair light enough to wrestle over the terrain at a fair speed. Still, the undergrowth clings to the spokes of the wheels, and ruts in the track threaten to tip Papa out if he moves too quickly. Despite our help, his shoulders are drenched with sweat by midmorning. And as gentle as we all try to be on the bumpy, pitted track, it can't be easy to jounce and judder through the brush.

Theodora suffers too, her blond curls limp in the weather, her face grim whenever she slaps a mosquito and has to wipe blood from her pale skin. But La Fleur doesn't complain, and whenever she slips, Camreon is beside her to catch her arm.

We move at a snail's pace, fighting the mud, the bugs, the slick and twisting paths. Sometimes there is a trail, other times it vanishes, and still other times I am certain we are retreading old ground but for the fact that the river is always to our left. We are drenched daily with sweat or rain. Every morning, we check our boots for centipedes; at night, we pull leeches from the backs of our legs and try to sleep to the symphony of croaking frogs. But there is comfort in returning to the jungle. I have missed the smell of the mud and the greenery, the soft quality of the humid air, the vibrant feeling of living things just out of sight.

The Kai Lin narrows as we walk, and the mountains of the Coffret draw sharply closer, until we reach a waterfall that tumbles from the crags overhead, diving straight down into a rock-rimmed pool. The cliffs are lined with moss like green velvet, and little ferns that brush the surface of the churning water. Boulders line the pool, and Tia plunks down on one of them, dunking her head into the pond and tossing it back like a mermaid. Then she rolls up the legs of her trousers and dips her toes into the water with a sigh.

I wade in too, till the water comes to my knees—it is bliss. But as I peer into the trees, I do not see the bright shine of souls. "How much farther?" I call to Cam, trying to keep the accusation out of my voice. His answering smile is almost apologetic.

"Less than a quarter mile," he says, and my heart leaps. "At least, as birds fly."

I narrow my eyes. "Up there?"

He nods. "Up there."

We all look skyward, into the silver clouds of mist that obscure the source of the falls. A flash of excitement shoots through me—the height is a dizzy thrill after the mind-numbing trek through the jungle. But Tia shakes her head so hard that water flies from her hair. "No," she says. "I live here now."

"How are we supposed to climb that?" Akra grimaces, but Cam points to what looks like a crack, zigzagging up the cliff face.

"There's an old stone stair cut into the rock."

"It looks too narrow for the chair."

"We might have to carry your father," Cam says.

Tia lifts her arms, pouting. "Who's carrying me?"

"There's a better way," I say, picking my way over to where the tabletop rests on a stone. Grabbing one end, I tip it sideways, dumping the remaining cans among the tumbled river rocks. Then I step aboard as though the platform is a stage, urging the soul up, up. The table teeters a bit, then rises into the air, and the looks I get from the others feel like a limelight. I half want to bow. "Who wants to go first?" I say instead, and suddenly everyone looks away.

All except for Theodora. "I'll do it," she whispers with a grin, but then Leo stands.

"Let me," he says. "We don't know what's at the top."

"Or if you'll even reach it, riding on that thing," says Tia. He makes a face at her, but he takes my hand. I pull him up beside me. The platform seesaws again, and I almost laugh aloud at the look on Leo's face. Instead, I check the satchel to make sure it's tightly shut against the drifting mist—the last grenade is inside, tucked beside the sealed jar. I do not want to ruin it in the damp. Then I whisper to the soul of the gull—steady, slow.

I keep hold of Leo's hand for balance, fighting the urge to tease him by going faster. The platform rises past the falls like a feather on a warm breeze. As we gain distance from Le Trépas, tiny souls drift nearer like old friends. Nearing the top, I look down, and then I do laugh—the height makes me giddy. But Leo grips my arms, pulling me toward the center of the platform, keeping us both steady till we reach the top.

Cresting the cliff, I gasp when I see the landscape laid out before us. The pool that feeds the waterfall is a crystal well, studded with a scattering of tiny islands; the edge is flat and stony, with tiny ferns tucked in among the rocks. The souls of minnows flash and shimmer in the water. But the beauty of the wide pool is not what catches my eye. Instead, I stare at the conflagration on the far shore. It takes me a moment to realize it is not firelight, but souls. It's been so long since I've seen so many. "The temple," I say, and Leo peers across the water.

"Where?"

I point at the cluster of spirits, but of course he cannot see them. Squinting, I try to make out the shape of the landscape behind the blaze of light. "Just inside the grove of trees, there. Don't worry," I say as he stares. "We'll see it soon enough. Stay here. I'll go back and get the others."

Leo grimaces as he steps off the platform onto the bank of the pool. "Hurry, will you? It's creepy up here by myself."

"You have your gun, right?"

"It won't be much use against a dragon," he says, only half teasing.

"Neither would the rest of us," I say.

"Yes, but at least I wouldn't die alone."

I step back onto the platform and give him a grin. "You wouldn't be alone. There'd be a dragon with you."

Leo narrows his eyes, but before he can retort, I whisper to the gull's soul. Quickly, the platform falls back down through the mist, and for one glorious moment, I am weightless. There is air beneath my feet. What would it feel like to fall? To step from the platform and feel the wind whistle by as I shot like a bullet toward the dark water below?

My hand goes to the flask at my waist as I tell the soul to go slow. I know better. I do.

Theodora comes up next, and she cannot hide her excitement as we rise. "I've dreamed of flying for years," she says softly. Then her smile deepens. "We should have traveled like this on our way up the river. Less chafing."

I can't help but laugh. "Next time."

"God forbid!" she says with a grin as she steps off onto the bluff.

The others come up one by one—Cam, Tia, Papa in his chair. What to do about Akra and Le Trépas? As I stare at them, I wish for a bigger platform. But there is nothing for it. I leave Akra at the edge of the pool and bring the monk with me first.

Holding him by the shoulders, I help him over the stones and onto the board. Under my breath, I pray to my ancestors that he will not speak, but they are not listening.

Or perhaps it is the wrong ones who intervene. "You don't come to talk to me anymore," he says as I take my place beside him.

"That's because you tricked me last time."

He raises his eyebrows. "I gave you exactly what you wanted."

"You didn't tell me what it would cost." I speak through my teeth, trying to stay calm. Gently, we lift off the rocks.

Le Trépas only looks amused. "This is blood magic, Jetta. It's fueled by pain and sacrifice."

"You think I haven't sacrificed?" My mouth twists, bitter. "You think I haven't killed?"

"Then why does it still bother you?" he says. "People die in this war every day. Mostly our people. If you could kill one person to save a hundred others, isn't their death the better choice?"

"That's not a choice I want to make."

"Alas." The monk shrugs. "That's the burden you and I bear."

"I'm nothing like you," I growl.

"Aren't you?" He gives me half a smile. "What if I told you I would kill your moitié boy unless you killed me right now?"

Underfoot, the transport wobbles, as though the soul inside heard the violence in my thoughts. I glance down at the crashing falls, the dark rocks below. All it would take to kill Le Trépas is a little push. Instead, I meet Akra's eyes— he's there at the edge of the pond, looking back up at me. His voice comes: a memory, this time. *You're not a monster.* I take a deep breath; the transport steadies. "You're very cocky for someone in a carcan," I say at last.

"You're very certain, for someone with so much to lose," the monk replies. "You must know that the Aquitans will die when the gods are whole again."

"The story says peace will come," I say with a wry look. "And what makes you think that will happen anytime soon?"

"They've brought us together, haven't they?" The monk sighs, almost wistful. "Life and Death, two halves of a whole."

"We'll be apart again soon enough," I mutter as we crest the cliff.

Le Trépas leans closer to whisper. "Not if you put my soul in your skin."

"What?" I stare at him, horrified as the transport bumps against the path. The monk takes a breath as though to say more, but I push him toward Camreon, who ushers the man to solid ground. Then the Tiger sees my expression.

"What is it?" he says, glancing from me to the monk and back. "What did he do?"

I open my mouth to answer, but the thought of repeating the monk's offer brings bile to my tongue. And it was just that—an offer. It is my blood, my power, my body. All Le Trépas can do is kill. "Nothing," I say firmly. "He can't do anything."

Still, Le Trépas stares at me until I disappear back down through the mists. Alone on the transport, I break out in goosebumps—as though the monk has already crept into my flesh. I run my hands over my arms, trying to slough off the residue of his words. By the time I reach the ground, my heart has slowed, but Akra frowns when he sees me. "Are you all right?"

"Just tired," I say as we lift off the ground. But I can't deny that his presence is a comfort, even though he presses so close to the center of the transport that he nearly shoves me off the edge. "Some space?"

He moves half a hair. It takes me another moment to remember how much he hates heights. So I take his hands, and he grips mine with white knuckles as we rise through the glittering mist. It feels good for a moment for him to need me as much as I need him.

ACT 3

ACT 3,

SCENE 26

Late night at the barracks, in one of many rooms reserved for the questioneurs. The walls are thick enough to muffle sound; the floor drains toward a gutter where a noxious stream of liquid flows.

The room is provided with a neat desk and a comfortable chair. These civilized furnishings are at odds with the crude board bed, built like a seesaw, so that one end can be tilted up and the other down. There is a scarred wooden bucket on the floor beside it, filled with dirty water.

A man sits at the desk, taking notes, and a young boy strapped to the board, wheezing through the wet cloth that still covers his face. The questioneur pays him no mind—the interview was a dead end.

He is finishing his notes when there is a knock at the door. The questioneur doesn't bother looking up.

QUESTIONEUR: I didn't call for the docteur!

The door opens, and JUNOT steps in.

JUNOT: I'm not the docteur.

Now the questioneur looks up, frowning.

QUESTIONEUR: Is my shift already over?
JUNOT: Yes.

In three steps, JUNOT closes the distance, his face sickly in the light of the room. The questioneur has no time to mention it before the revenant drives an awl into his ear. The questioneur's body convulses in his chair, limbs twitching as he dies. Under the wet cloth, the boy on the board starts to whimper.

JUNOT: Don't be afraid. You're almost free.

When the shocked akela steps free of the questioneur's body, the revenant withdraws the pick, sliding two fingers along the length of the iron, slick with gore. He uses the red jelly to make the mark of life on the questioneur's body, and the symbol of death on his own. The questioneur's soul is uninterested in the mark, but the disciple's soul is and steps inside its fresh skin. When the questioneur sits up again, he wipes the rest of the blood from his ear.

The next thing he does is strip JUNOT's stinking corpse and carry it to the cart in the hall outside. He lays it on the pile; it is not the only body leaving the barracks tonight. The uniform he keeps to dispose of later. Then he sets the chair aright and sits down at the desk.

Taking up the pen, he reviews the report. Name, KIET. Age, nine. Occupation, fouilleur. The boy's claim that he knew no one in the rebellion. Later, a claim that he could offer names of rebels if only the questioneur would stop. The revenent doesn't recognize any of the names—but neither would the rebels. The armée doesn't seem to care. And in the empty space left below, the revenant starts to write: The rebels have taken Le Trépas to the temple in the cliffs above Kai Lin.

The boy on the board is whimpering again, but the questioneur finishes his notes before he stands. At last he stands, pulling the wet cloth from the boy's face; the boy gasps as though he may never take a full breath again.

KIET (*shaking*): Please let me go.
QUESTIONEUR: I will.

The questioneur lets him take one more breath before he wraps his hand around the boy's slim throat. The last thing the fouilleur sees is the questioneur's blue eyes, and in them, something like pity.

CHAPTER
TWENTY-SEVEN

The day is fading, but the path around the pool shines in the reflected glow of the souls clustered in the trees on the other side. I take the lead, drawn to the brightness of the grove, so brilliant after the long walk in the soulless dim. But as we close in, the exodus starts.

At first, it is only a few souls—birds spiraling off into the dark night, or jungle cats prowling away into the mist. But the closer we get, the more souls flee their haven, a steady stream of bright lives running. The welcoming light fades like a dying coal. Behind me, I hear Le Trépas laugh. My lip curls; I bite back a sharp word. Then Akra speaks. "What is that?"

Catching movement out of the corner of my eye, I squint in the odd twilight of the shifting spirits. There is someone emerging from the trees—no, two people—and a strange creature cavorting in front of them. It takes me a moment to make sense of the play of light and shadow, but when I do, my heart leaps. Fashioned out of leather and paint, gold and gleaming copper, it is a long fantouche in the shape of a dragon, though she bounds toward me like the kitten spirit that animates her.

"Miu!" I kneel, holding out my arms as the fantouche leaps up, sending me sprawling. Stones prick my back as the cool mud seeps through the seat of my coveralls, but I don't mind. Miu is the most beautiful fantouche I ever made— and the only one I have left.

Leo laughs as I wrestle with the rambunctious creature. "I warned you about the dragons."

I push myself up to my feet—not easy, with Miu winding around my legs. She butts her nose against my palm as I stroke the smooth leather of her painted head. I catch Akra's appraising look; he was always a better leatherworker than I was. The approval in his nod makes me grin. Then I look up at the sound of running feet, and a high, joyful scream. "Look out," I say, and Leo turns just before the girl launches herself into his arms.

"Cheeky!" Leo staggers ankle-deep into the water as she wraps him in a full body hug. Regaining his balance, he spins her around as she buries her face in his neck. Then he yelps, tipping her out of his arms and into the lake. She screams again as she surfaces, shaking water out of her hair.

"You dropped me!"

"You bit me!"

"You're surprised?" She cocks a hip and turns to me; the way her dress clings makes me blush. "Jetta! Isn't there a shadow play about this? Something about a scorpion and a frog . . . ?"

"Crossing a river. Yes." I press my lips together as the memory surfaces—a performer's life feels like someone else's story. "She stings him because it's in her nature."

"You see?" Cheeky turns back to Leo, as though I've proven her point. Then she dabs carefully at the skin beneath her eyes, where the makeup is starting to run; even bedraggled, she is beautiful. "And now I'm all wet."

"That's also in your nature," Tia teases, coming in for a hug.

"Tia, ma belle. I missed you." Cheeky pats her cheek, then waves a hand at my coveralls—stained and torn. "But how could you let this happen? I sent her off in my second-best dress, and this is how she comes back to me?"

"Don't judge," I say, defensive. "We've just spent over a week in the bush."

Cheeky only gives me a sly grin, elbowing Leo in the ribs "You never told me it was that kind of rescue mission."

My cheeks grow hot, but the laughter eases something in me, and for a blissful moment, we are back in the glitter and smoke of the theater. "It's good to see you again," I murmur, and her look softens.

"You too, Jetta. All of you. If you want to follow me, I can show you to . . ." Her voice trails off—is it the sight of Le Trépas? No . . . Leo's sudden laugh reminds me: the old monk may or may not intimidate Cheeky, but my brother certainly does.

The silence stretches; the showgirl has forgotten her lines. Does Akra know why she's staring? His own expression is so severe—or perhaps it is only the shadows that make it seem that way. "The rest of us could use a bath too," he says at last, giving her a pointed look.

Her hand goes to her wet hair, flustered, but a new voice interrupts any answer she might have made. "Took you long enough!"

Despite the long shadows of evening, it is not difficult to recognize the Boy King coming down the path. Not least because he still wears a tailored Aquitan suit made of soft linen, and the ivory crown on his head. He grins at Camreon, clapping him on the back; in his other hand, he lifts a dark glass bottle. "Must have been a long walk. Thirsty?"

Cam pulls away, making a face. "Not for champagne."

"Bad luck to toast with water."

"So the Aquitans claim," the Tiger says drily. "What's the occasion?"

"Your successful escape!" Raik gestures at the rest of us with a grin. Their features are so very similar—it is their demeanors that set them apart. Where Cam is assured, Raik is cocky—but some of that confidence fades when Cam hands back the bottle, untasted.

"If we toasted every time we had to run, we'd be too drunk to stand and fight."

"The fight is almost over now that we have the nécromanciens." Raik glances at me, then back to Le Trépas, unable to hide the awe in his eyes. The look sours when he sees Theodora. "And La Fleur, of course. Looking much more wretched than last time I saw her."

I blink at him, taken aback. The hope of a marriage to

end the war suddenly seems like a child's idea. But La Fleur lifts her chin. Despite the fact that she is weary and travel worn, her expression is as haughty as a queen's. "I always try to dress for the occasion."

Raik's eyes narrow, but the Tiger steps between them. "In my letter, I asked you to come alone."

"To spare her feelings?" Raik asks, raising an eyebrow at Theodora. But Cam shakes his head.

"Because the last thing we need is gossip about Le Trépas."

"Too late for that," Raik says with a laugh. "I made the announcement the moment I got the letter. Besides, contrary to appearances, the girl can be discreet." The Boy King jerks his head at Cheeky, sliding his free hand around her waist. The gesture is either careless or cruel, and the showgirl is neither. She shifts on her feet, but Raik doesn't drop his arm.

Cam ignores the exchange, staring at his brother. "Announcement? Why?"

"To give them something to hope for," Raik says, defensive.

"Or something to fear." Cam presses his fingers to the bridge of his nose. "Have you prepared a place for him, at least? Somewhere secure. Away from the rest of the rebels."

"There are cells cut into the old mines," the Boy King replies. "The Aquitans used them for workers caught stealing. And it's where the weapons are being staged. I'll take him there myself."

"Is that wise?" Camreon says, glancing significantly at the bottle.

"The king's decisions are always wise," Raik says, and for a moment, everything seems too still. Then the Boy King pushes the champagne back into the Tiger's hands. "Oh, fine. Take this with you if you're worried."

"How about I take it and come with you?"

"Even better." Raik grins again, though the smile is strained. "And have a taste, for God's sake, it's imported! Cheeky, show the others to the temple!"

Without waiting for an answer, the Boy King turns on his heel. His brother follows, with Akra and Le Trépas after him. The four of them trudge downhill, the jungle closing around them, and my stomach tightens into knots. I have not liked traveling so close to Le Trépas, so why is it difficult to watch him depart? It cannot be that I want him near. No. It is only the uncertainty of not knowing where he is—not knowing what he's doing.

At least I don't have to worry about him creeping up

behind me. Almost as soon as he is out of sight, souls start to gleam again among the greenery at my feet. By the time I catch up with the others, the glow has returned to the grove ahead, and in the golden light, the tightness in my gut starts to ease. They are so bright, so beautiful. And so plentiful too. The temple must be close, though I struggle to see through the ropey vines of the tangle of banyan ahead. When Cheeky leads us between two twisted trunks like columns, I gasp— the grove did not hide the temple. It *is* the temple.

A network of living arches and arcades, balconies and balustrades . . . it must have taken centuries of daily tending to sculpt. Roots have been woven together in lacy screens: orchids and bromeliads stud the columns like jewels. Beside me, Papa sighs—the floor of the temple is black basalt. His chair moves so smoothly across it.

He rolls right toward the statue in the center of the sanctuary: the Maiden. As Cheeky leads the others down the hall, I linger too. The statue is almost untouched by the destruction ordered by the armée: a beautiful girl, fat and smiling, her rounded arms spilling over with a bounty of fruit and flowers. Gold leaf still glimmers on her brow. The only things missing are the jewels that must have been set in her eyes.

My own arms are thin and empty. Do I really serve such a bountiful god? We have so little in common.

"She reminds me of being young." Papa's voice is a whisper through his fingers. While the others have gone ahead, he has stayed at my side, and on his face is a look of peace.

I blink at the sound of his voice—unexpected, but welcome. "I've never seen a temple that the armée hadn't destroyed."

"I thought they only existed in my memory," he says softly—slowly. He wipes his lips with the back of his hand. "The monastery where I sp—" His voice trails off, and he looks pained. My mind races to fill in the gaps.

"Where you spent your summers?" It's a good guess—or so I thought. But if anything, the pain on his face deepens. I press my lips together, chastened.

"Yes," he says at last, still slurring the S. But he takes a deliberate breath, and the look on his face is now determination. I wait, tamping down the urge to speak for him—listening instead. "Where I spent my summers studying." He dabs his lips again, but his hands don't hide the satisfaction in his eyes. "It was dedicated to the Maiden too. It's where I learned to carve."

My eyebrows go up. He had never mentioned it, but I can see it now in the delicate scrollwork of our old roulotte—or of the fantouches he used to make: an echo of the lacy designs of the temple. I reach out, trailing my fingers along the altar, where stone fruit and flowers cover the Maiden's feet. Then I gasp, pulling my hand back. There among the verdure is the rounded curve of a stone skull—and another. And another. "I thought the Maiden represented life."

"One can't exist without the other."

I fold my arms, feeling betrayed. But Papa presses his palms together and bows to the statue. His face is so calm. Where do my fears come from? My ideas of death and life? Had they come from Chakran history, or from Aquitan propaganda? Then I frown—Papa's lips are moving. "What are you doing?"

It is a moment before he lowers his hands. "Praying."

The answer surprises me. Should I be doing the same? I have prayed to my brother's soul, to my ancestors, but never to the gods. "What did you ask her for?"

This time, the only answer he gives is a smile. In the silence, Cheeky's voice makes me turn.

"I'd wondered where we'd lost you." Her smile is soft,

all the teasing gone; she stands beneath the twisted roots of the archway like a forest spirit. "The baths are waiting. Do you need time?"

I glance at Papa, but he waves me off. Cheeky throws a half smile over her shoulder at him as she leads me down the hall. But once we're out of earshot, I lean in. "Is Maman here too?"

"Not in the temple," she says. "But Raik gave her a house in the valley."

"A house?"

"He can be very generous," she says, only a little defensive. "And you are rather important to the rebellion."

I turn the idea over in my head—somehow in all the time I spent in the spotlight, celebrated by Aquitan patrons, I never imagined the sort of importance that would earn Maman a house. "So . . ." I hesitate, needing the answer and dreading it all the same. "How is she doing?"

"Much better," Cheeky says. I sigh, relieved. But it's a strange feeling for Cheeky to know more about her than I do. "She was bereft, you know," the girl continues. "For weeks. For a while, I was afraid that . . . well."

Her tone stops me short. "Well, what?"

Cheeky stops too, toying with the thick leaves of a knot

of bromeliads; it is incongruous to see her so reluctant. "Leo told you how his mother died," she says at last. Is it a question?

I wet my lips, suddenly just as nervous as she looks. "Yes."

"I knew her for a few years," the girl says softly. "She was a diva in all the best ways. Sang like a nightingale when she was happy. Screamed like a hawk when she wasn't. She danced on tables and cursed her lovers and brought the house down with the songs she wrote. But for a month before she shot herself, it was like the spirit had gone out of her. She could barely get out of bed. Your maman was like that for a while. Raik hired a docteur for her too. Made sure someone was always watching her, just in case. But it makes sense, doesn't it?" she adds then. "She thought she'd lost you."

"It makes sense," I say quietly, but the thought is discomfiting: how close I had come to losing her. But I hadn't. I make a note to thank Raik for that.

Cheeky leads me through a long hall of living arches interspersed with curving stairwells spiraling upward. Overhead, old monk's cells are connected by crisscrossing bridges grown from woven roots. The place is huge—much bigger than Hell's Court—and every room seems full of people like me: Chakrans who had joined the revolution.

But hadn't Leo said the rebel ranks were growing? The mood here is high. Conversation drifts down around our heads, and laughter, and the bets of women playing cards. But as we pass, people peek out of doorways to peer after us, and why do they all look so young? The bustle ebbs, then blooms again behind us, whispers flitting down the hall like bats; I catch a few here and there, and none of them have anything to do with nécromancy or malheur. The word I hear over and over again is one from my childhood—from the village, from Le Verdu. From the places and times where there were fewer Aquitans about. "Ros parem," they say. Ros parem, ros parem. Old Chakran for shadow puppeteer.

My heart beats faster, like a drum. The murmur of voices sounds like distant applause. Is there time to put on a show for the rebels? Miu is my only fantouche, but with some bamboo and mulberry paper, I could make more. And perhaps we could borrow instruments. Akra could join us too . . . if he could somehow get a moment away from Le Trépas. The last time all of us had performed together was before he left for the armée.

By the time we reach the baths, there is a smile on my

face, old songs in my head. Tia and Theodora are already inside, and the air is thick with steam and the bright scent of herbs and soap. It is bliss to wash off the sweat and mud of the jungle trek, and when I finally pull myself away from the warm water, the selection of clothing Cheeky has provided is even more heavenly. Soft silk and light linen, richly dyed and delicately embroidered. "Where did you get all this?" I ask her, tying on a patterned sarong.

Tia chimes in as she towels dry. "Probably off her bedroom floor."

"Jealousy is beneath you," Cheeky says loftily.

"Everything's been beneath me at one time or another."

Their laughter rings like bells, but it fades when Theodora emerges from the bath. The soft rolls of her pale skin are dewy; the water smooths her blond curls. She stands with rounded shoulders, one knee cocked; could this famous beauty be shy? "You're very familiar with each other," she says at last, and is that judgment in her tone, or longing?

"We're old friends," Cheeky says, her own expression a mystery. What does she think, face-to-face with Raik's old fiancée, with Leo's sister? But as Tia said, Cheeky was never one for jealousy. "And there's always room for new ones. Here, this should set off the gold in your hair."

With that, she tugs another sarong out of the pile, this the color of a clear sky. Cheeky teaches her to wrap and tie it as Tia shaves. I return to the clothing, transferring my old things to my new belt: the elixir, the lighter, the tattered pages remaining from my book of souls.

But Theodora frowns at me as she adjusts the knot in her sarong. "If my math is correct, you must be nearly out of the treatment," she says. "Do you still have the jar of lytheum? I can mix the rest of it if you like."

"I do," I say, slipping the satchel over my shoulder. But I have not told La Fleur I am trying to stretch the doses. What would she say if she knew? Then again, we are no longer on her terrain—she doesn't set the rules here. "I actually still have at least a week's worth in the flask," I say. "I'll hold on to the lytheum till then. Just in case."

She gives me a look—not disapproval, but appraisal. "You've been taking less? For how long?"

"Since we made the grenades."

"And have you noticed any ill effects?"

I frown, thinking back. Have I? "I'm not sure. Maybe some strange thoughts at the falls."

"Mmm." She chews her lip. "If they get worse, tell me, will you?"

"Why?" I try to laugh; the sound echoes on the stone. "What can you do about it?"

"I can listen."

We head for the communal kitchen to find the leftovers from dinner are still warm. After weeks of tinned food and jungle forage, the bowl of congee they give me is a feast. We eat in a dining hall so large that the canopies of the trees do not meet in the middle. Above, the stars wink and twinkle, but none so bright as the souls that drift through the balmy air. I leave them the last bite of my congee as an offering. Just as Maman taught me when I was a child. Then I lean back, clean and full, as a gentle lassitude comes over me—something different than exhaustion. Something more like peace.

My eyes are closing; I'm half in a dream when Papa gasps. Blinking awake, I follow his gaze. There she is, hesitating in the archway, as if my thoughts had summoned her. "Meliss," Papa says, but I shout.

"Maman?"

I stand, uncertain. Her presence here shocks me— Maman, in a temple! Am I still dreaming? Her own eyes are wide. She looks like she wants to run, and I can't tell which direction. But she takes one step, then another, passing into the hall as golden souls swirl around her. Papa whirls in his chair, speeding across the stone, and I race after him. We meet in the center, the three of us, my arms around Maman, Papa's around us both. I can feel her shaking, but she holds me tight.

"You're safe," she murmurs, and the words have never felt more true. She pulls back looking into Papa's face, as though it's a marvel. "You're alive."

"You're here," I say in wonder. Maman was always terrified of the temples.

"I came the moment I heard. But where's Akra?" Her eyes dart around the room. Is she looking for my brother? No—by the fear in her face, I can tell she is looking for Le Trépas. She would have heard he was here too.

She'd known he was here and she'd come anyway.

"Akra's safe," I say carefully. "But he's . . . busy."

She bites her lip, peering at me—Maman is not easy to fool. "He's with Le Trépas, isn't he? The others told me he's acting as a guard."

"He is." I stare at her, taken aback. She never even liked hearing the old monk's nickname, but now, saying it aloud, her voice hardly shakes. "Maman . . ." How to put it? "You've changed."

"So have you, Jetta." She laughs a little—nervous—like

the flutter of a bird. "I heard about what you've been doing. What you can do. And if anyone should be afraid, it's *him*."

She pulls me close once more, my cheek against her ear—with a start, I realize she and I are the same height. And as we hold each other tight, I do not know which of us is comforting the other.

Still, I do not want to let her go—to step out of the warm cocoon of my parents' embrace. But I can't stay there forever, either. At last I pull away, and my parents fold in to each other like a love letter. Maman touches her husband's scarred cheek. She gathers up his crooked hand in her own. His eyes close and he sighs, as though her touch can heal. And maybe it does—at least, for him. But standing beside them, I feel even more alone than I did in Theodora's workshop. Somehow, in the past few months, I've gone from their daughter to their defender, and I don't know if I can ever go back.

ACT 3,

SCENE 28

At the mouth of the abandoned sapphire mine. Inside, AKRA guards LE TREPAS in a cell carved into the muddy stone walls of the tunnel. Here, on the rocky ledge overlooking the valley, RAIK and CAMREON share the bottle of champagne.

RAIK: I still can't believe you got him all the way here with no one dying. Do you think he's reformed?

CAMREON: I think there's death enough these days to keep him happy.

RAIK: Or maybe he just wants the Aquitans out. Like the rest of us.

CAMREON smiles a little.

CAMREON: I'm working on it.

RAIK: So am I.

RAIK's tone is defensive; CAMREON's smile fades.

CAMREON: I never said otherwise.

The Boy King narrows his eyes. Then he scrubs his hand down his face.

RAIK: Desolée, Camreon. It's getting to me. The pressure. The uncertainty. The godforsaken jungle!

He slaps a mosquito on the side of his neck and frowns at the blood on his hands.

We're in the middle of nowhere while those bastards sit comfortably in the capital. I wonder if they'd trade and call it even.

The Tiger raises an eyebrow.

CAMREON: You don't really mean that.
RAIK: No.

A pause.

Of course not.

Another pause. He takes a drink from the bottle.

But I wonder what they'd do if I went back.

CAMREON: To the Aquitans?

RAIK: To the throne. Their official story is that you've kidnapped me. If I claim I escaped, they'd be forced to welcome me with open arms.

CAMREON: And then they'd stab you in the back. Probably put it on my recherche too.

RAIK: Legarde would have. But as much as I dislike her, I don't believe Theodora wanted me dead. I think she and I can still marry, if she'll agree to my terms.

The Tiger's expression is careful.

CAMREON: It's Xavier I'm more worried about.

RAIK: The general would have to be shot for war crimes.

CAMREON: I don't think his men would let that happen so easily. Much less Theodora.

RAIK: They won't have much choice. The rebel ranks have doubled since I left the capital.

CAMREON: With people too young or old or injured to fight. Most of the new recruits are refugees from La Verdu.

RAIK: And armée ranks have been shrinking for months.

CAM: They still have better weapons.

RAIK: Not once Jetta starts her work. Or Le Trépas.

CAMREON raises an eyebrow. RAIK cocks his head, half teasing.

Come now, brother. I don't for a moment think you brought him here just to keep him locked away.

CAMREON sighs, then lifts the bottle to his lips, taking a sip before passing it to RAIK.

CAMREON: I won't lie—I've considered asking him for help. But it's too dangerous. We don't know enough. Not to mention that the country would never stand for it.

RAIK: Isn't that why the Tiger exists? To make the unpopular choices?

CAMREON makes a wry face.

CAMREON: So the king can take the throne with clean hands?

RAIK: Yes.

RAIK's reply is simple. But in the silence that follows, his eyes narrow.

We've talked about this, Camreon. You've seen how cleverly the Aquitans use propaganda. We can't give them more fodder. Don't tell me you're having second thoughts.

CAMREON: I'm not afraid of being unpopular, Raik. I'm afraid that if we give Le Trépas free reign, he'll kill more than just the Aquitans.

RAIK: Don't underestimate our people, Cam. Chakrans know there are things worth dying for.

The Boy King takes another drink from the bottle, then offers it to CAMREON. The Tiger takes it but doesn't drink.

CAMREON: That's very easy to say for those not tasked with dying.

CHAPTER

TWENTY-NINE

I wake late the next morning to the sound of whispering—Cheeky, at least, is already awake. The rest of us are sharing her room: a spacious atrium all to herself, the walls decorated with living braids and lacework dripping with orchids. Cheeky had been right about the Boy King: he clearly was generous when he wanted to be. There is a tray of fresh fruit on a wide vanity topped with a real silvered mirror, and the parts of the floor that aren't piled with pillows are covered with chests carved from sandalwood. When I crack my eyes to peek out from my makeshift nest, I see Tia admiring the contents.

Watered silk, gold thread, embroidered sleeves, cascading ruffles, a wealth of lace—so many clothes, and all much too fine to wear for fighting. But Cheeky looks less than pleased surveying her hoard.

Tia drapes a pomegranate silk dress against her body with a longing sigh. "Are you sure?"

"It's all yours," the girl replies firmly, chewing her thumbnail. "Take whatever you want. It's too much for me, anyway. I told him that, you know."

"You know what men like to hear," Tia teases, but Cheeky only folds her arms and looks away. The singer's face softens. "Come on, Cheeky. If there's one thing he knows, it's that a good time isn't always for a long time."

Curiosity spurs me out of my makeshift bed. I prop myself up on my elbow as Miu lifts her head from the scattered pillows, flicking her tail in irritation before burrowing back down in the silks. "Are you talking about my brother?"

"No!" Cheeky says, too fast and too loud. I would laugh if not for the panic on her face.

"Not directly," Tia adds. "It's the Playboy King. Pardon the term," she says then, glancing at Theodora, sitting up in her own nest of pillows. I hadn't realized she was awake too.

"You think I hadn't heard what sort of man I was supposed to marry?" A small smile tugs at the bow of La Fleur's lips. "It's the only reason I agreed to the match. I thought he'd be too busy to bother me in my workshop. I didn't realize that half of his clandestine meetings were held with rebels. It's a lovely dress," she adds. "Raik always had impeccable taste."

Cheeky's blush deepens to match the silk. "Help yourself to anything you like," she mumbles, but Tia rolls her eyes.

"Do you plan to woo Jetta's brother in the buff? Then again, if you can't bear to talk to him, it might be your best option."

I bite my lip, unsure whether to gasp or laugh. But Cheeky grits her teeth. "Do you like that wig, Tia? Because I'm about to feed it to you."

"There's an idea," Tia says mildly, nodding at the tray of fruit. "Bring him something to eat. I mean food. He's stuck in that mine with no one but Le Trépas to keep him company. I know I'd appreciate a soft smile and a good meal."

Cheeky's brow furrows as she thinks it over; in the silence, I open my mouth to correct her about the meal, then think better of it. Best not to throw Cheeky for a loop. And certainly my brother would appreciate the company, at least. "Why is she afraid to speak to him?"

Immediately, Cheeky shoots me a look. "I'm not afraid to speak to you, you know."

I throw my hands in the air. "Why, then?"

She seems to wilt, half exasperated, half helpless. "Because whenever I open my mouth—Tia, I am warning you," she adds, suddenly fierce. Tia mimes locking her lips with an imaginary key, and Cheeky sighs. "Whenever I open my mouth, something terrible comes out."

I could swear Tia snorts, but when Cheeky turns to glare at her, her face is carefully blank. "Tia's right," I say, echoing her expression. "Less chance of saying the wrong thing if your mouth is full."

Cheeky narrows her eyes, peering at me, but I am an actor—my face doesn't crack. After a moment, hers does, revealing a small smile beneath. "He probably *is* hungry, isn't he?"

"Not half as hungry as you are," Tia says under her breath, stepping into the pomegranate dress.

Cheeky ignores her; she's smiling now, shedding her misery like a garment. Dreamily, the girl sits down at her vanity, picking up a brush and some pins to freshen up her curls. I watch her for a while, mesmerized. How I envy her ability to hear the melody of love and beauty among the crash of the drums of war.

Beside me, La Fleur sighs. "I remember visiting Le Perl with my father," she says. "All the lovely girls with their pretty silks, when I was more used to playing with my brother in the barracks. Leo's maman was the one who gave me my first lipstick. I can see why our father loved her."

I cock my head, curious. "Did he?"

"Oh yes," she says, shooting me a look. "It's all over his journals."

My eyebrows go up—it's hard to believe. "Then . . . why did he leave her? Why did he pretend Leo wasn't his?"

"He loved his reputation more." Theodora smiles sadly, her eyes a little too bright. What does she love most? Before I can ask, she turns to call to the others. "Speaking of lipstick, I refuse to show my face outside this room until I've restored it to its former glory."

"I have a red bright enough to signal ships," Cheeky says, holding up a pot of rouge.

Theodora laughs. "Considering the rebel base is meant to be kept secret, maybe something a little more subdued?"

Cheeky waves her over to the vanity, and I watch as La Fleur puts on her colors: deepening her blue eyes, brightening her mouth. Is it art or armor? Both, perhaps. We spend the morning eating fruit and enjoying the clothing, the makeup, the conversation—all the little trappings of civilization. I hardly notice time passing until a knock comes at the door. Cheeky tosses her hair and sneaks a look in the mirror before she opens it. Her smile falls when she sees Raik just outside.

His own smile turns to confusion when he sees her look. "Didn't mean to startle you."

"You didn't," she says. When he reaches for her, she ducks back, out of reach. "It's not a good time, Raik."

Instantly, his brow furrows. He opens his mouth, but when he sees the rest of us in the room, he closes it again. "We came for Jetta, anyway," he mutters then, nodding back at Camreon just behind him in the hall. "I want to show you both the weapons we're assembling in the mine."

When I scramble to my feet, pillows tumble aside. This respite was too brief, but it is not like me to miss a cue. Slinging my satchel over my shoulder, I step past Cheeky to join the Tiger and his brother.

They lead me through the temple, past the statue of the Maiden and through the arched banyan entryway to take the path down from the ridge. The hillside is steep, the track gouged into it at sharp angles. The vegetation crowding us is newer than the growth along the river; when the mines were active, the area must have been stripped bare for fuel. I am grateful the mines had been abandoned before the Aquitans ordered the destruction of the temples—otherwise, the lovely banyan structure might have been so much kindling in a miner's cookfire.

As it is, the temple is impossible to see, even from just a short way down the hill. It had survived hidden from the armée, tended by the surviving monks—or even the nearby villagers. This far from the capital, people reclaim their heritage like the jungle reclaims the soil.

We duck beneath tangled masses of lianas that clamber over the stumps of old trees. Thick stands of fast-growing bamboo cluster along the path. This part of the jungle can't be much older than Papa. Leaves shiver and shush in the breeze; my nose wrinkles at the smell of something dead nearby. Or is that only the scent of ripening durian?

It is not long before we reach a rocky ledge at the opening of the mine. There is a notch in the brush here, and the valley is spread below us like an offering, complete with a village tucked into the basin, small and secret. The broken mirrors of the watery rice paddies reflect the steely sky, and little puffs of smoke rise from lunchtime cookfires. I can even see children splashing in the shallows of the river as their minders do the washing.

Is this where Maman has been living? It reminds me so much of Lak Na. Suddenly, I want to go down the hill. To find Papa and Maman in the house the Boy King has given them. To sweep the floor, build up the fire. To tempt friendly souls inside with offerings of rice. To be at home again. But Raik beckons us into the mouth of the mine. "The view in here is much more impressive."

He grins as he walks backward into the earth; I follow more slowly. Why is it so dark? I blink, waiting for my eyes to adjust; there are no souls to light my way. "Le Trépas is here."

"Farther down the hall," Cam confirms, pointing with his chin—indeed, there is a light ahead, dim or distant: the steady glow of a lamp. Is that where Akra is, stuck in the dark? The place is depressing. I make a mental note to tell Tia she was right—my brother could use some company. Then I swear, tripping on a branch.

No. It is too fine, too pale—and it rattles as it moves. I fumble with the fold of my belt—where is my lighter? But Raik has already pulled one from his own pockets; with it, he coaxes a flame from the oil lamp hung on one of the timbers bracing the tunnel. Too readily, I recognize the play of firelight on bone; what I had thought was a branch is a femur twice as long as a horse's.

It is bound with wire to the pebble bones of a joint; below those are a set of claws longer than my fingers. The skeletal limb is placed beside the arched bones of a long neck, each vertebrae the size of a man's fist. The rest of the skeleton snakes away down the tunnel; hidden in the shadows, it seems impossibly long. And at the other end . . .

Despite the improbable proportions of the creature before me, it is the skull that makes me gasp. Narrow and graceful, and antlered like a deer, with teeth like knives, large enough to tear a man in half. "A dragon," I breathe, and Raik grins.

"This one is the most complete." His voice is almost giddy. "But I have two others being assembled in the mine shafts downhill. Isn't it beautiful?"

"Where did you find them?" I say softly, running a finger over the curve of the ridged spine. I have seen apothecaries shilling what they claim is powdered dragon horn to the rich and gullible—and I have heard of the Aquitan craze for cigarette holders fashioned from their hollow bones. Indeed, there was a time when dragon parts rivaled sapphires for export, though no one has seen a dragon for ages—at least, not where I grew up in Lak Na.

"Collectors," Raik says proudly. "I still have connections at the palace, despite the distance."

"Connections?" The Tiger speaks as though handling each word carefully. "Are they trustworthy?"

Raik raises his eyebrows, gesturing at the bones. "They certainly delivered."

"And how much did this delivery cost?"

"Victory is priceless, Cam."

"So are bullets!"

The Boy King scoffs. "These are much better!"

I catch my breath as I understand his meaning. "These are the weapons you want me to ensoul."

"Can you imagine sending a dragon against our enemies?" Raik's expression is eager. "The legends say the teeth are sharper than steel."

"Sharper, perhaps," Cam says. "But not stronger. And the fire is the real problem."

"I didn't know about the avions until too late," Raik shoots back. "Besides, the dragon is the symbol of the country. Of the king. We need a symbolic victory as much as we need a material one."

The Tiger's own face is unreadable in the dim light, but the silence is heavy. To cover, I tug at the leather joining of the knucklebones. A little loose for my taste; if this were my work, Papa would purse his lips and make me do them over. But we may not have the time for perfection. Chewing my lip, I consider the framework before me. "If we wrap the bones in wet leather, it might prevent the fire from taking hold. At least long enough for them to bear the avions to the ground."

Cam shakes his head. "It might work against a handful of the things, but not a whole flock. Not with the way Theodora's fire burns."

"If we use a tiger's soul, the fantouche will hunt the armée from the shadows," I offer. "Maybe it would be best that way. Keep the bones out of sight."

"You won't use a dragon's soul?" Raik asks.

"No." I shake my head vehemently. "They've moved on."

"They have." Le Trépas's voice floats toward us down the tunnel. "But not beyond our reach."

"Don't listen to him," I say, but Raik puts up a hand.

"What does he mean?"

"I can fetch the dragon's soul for you," the old monk calls. "Cage it in its tattered skin. Send a creature like that against the invaders, and we will be unstoppable," he adds. "Give me the bones and a blade and I'll show you."

Camreon shakes his head. "I'm not giving you a toothpick," he says.

"You're not the one I'm trying to convince," Le Trépas replies. "Isn't it the king's decision?"

Tension coils under my skin. Le Trépas is pitting himself against me—and Raik against Camreon. But before he can reply, I hear shouting from outside the tunnel. "My king! My king!"

Both brothers turn as a rebel girl comes flying down the path and into the tunnel. Silhouetted against the bright sunlight outside, I can see her shoulders heaving.

"What is it?" Raik says as she catches her breath.

"Over the valley," she pants. "Avions!"

My heart sinks—how did they find us? We'd been watching the sky on our trek through the jungle; there's no way we were followed all the way inland. Cam swears under his breath. "How many?"

"Three so far," she says, and he swears again. It isn't as many as it could be—the village by the river is so small . . .

so defenseless. The selfish hope rises: are Maman and Papa still at the temple somehow? But no—there's no way she would have lingered with Le Trépas nearby.

The Tiger turns to his brother, speaking through his teeth. "Trustworthy connections, you say?"

Raik narrows his eyes. "It's far more likely they followed you from Nokhor Khat."

"Does it matter how they found us?" Le Trépas's question cuts through the tension; there is urgency in his voice. "You were always going to have to face the avions. Let me help you."

"No!" Is Camreon talking to his brother or the monk? "Akra, keep a close eye on him. Jetta, come with me. Raik, stay hidden. You too," he adds to the rebel girl as we pass.

Wide-eyed, she nods at him, ducking back into the mouth of the tunnel. Outside on the ledge, I blink up at the sky, my eyes adjusting to the light. There they are: three avions, coming straight up the valley. My heart hammers at the sight. I want to scream—run!—but the villagers are too far away to hear me. My hand goes to my satchel. Should I use the grenade? But there is no water here—none except what's inside my flask of elixir. And with three avions, one grenade is not much use.

My hands shaking, I slip the pin from my hem, casting about for a heavy stone. At least there are plenty of songbirds nearby. As I kneel to mark a chunk of rock, the Tiger crouches beside me. "We'll need more."

"Then find the next, will you?"

He goes to search as I send the stone up into the air. But as it picks up speed over the greenery, the avions pass right by the little village. Relief breaks over me like a sunrise— but what is their target? Do they see me standing on the hillside? Are they aiming for the mines? No—they skim the side of the mountain, swooping by overhead. Then, in formation, they bank to circle above the tangled banyans that shelter my friends.

When Cam returns and sees the avions, the stone falls from his hands. "How did they pick out the temple?"

I don't answer—I don't know. And I'm too busy urging my makeshift missile after the warbirds. The stone seems to creep through the air; any moment, I expect the fire to rain down. But as the avions swoop low over the treetops, what they release is paper.

It cascades in clouds from each bird, fluttering over the trees, slips of white like flyers for a show. The sight is so unexpected, it takes my breath away. The surprise of it all takes my mind off the stone until it smashes straight down into the trailing avion.

The wing twists; the craft spins in the air. The avion is so close to the treetops that the jungle seems to reach up and swallow it whole. Has it hit the temple? We are far enough away that I cannot tell, but close enough to hear the distant sound of screaming.

As the other two avions turn their noses back toward Nokhor Khat, I pelt up the path. The errant wind scatters the papers across the mountainside.

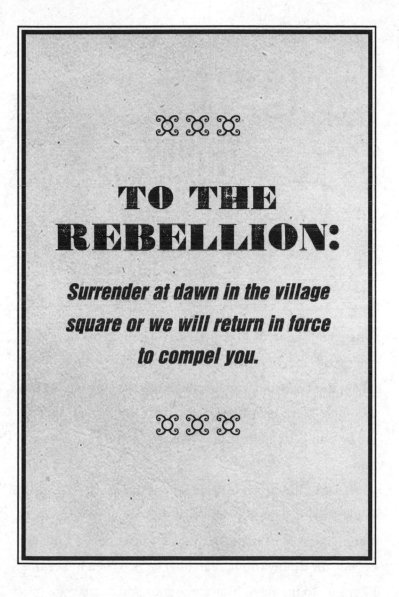

TO THE REBELLION:

Surrender at dawn in the village square or we will return in force to compel you.

CHAPTER THIRTY

There are hundreds of the flyers—tossed across the valley, caught in the branches, drifting on the surface of the lake—and every one carries the same threat printed neatly in simple black on white. But when I reach the ridge, the hubbub at the temple pushes the armée's message from my mind.

It isn't clear from outside where the avion fell, so we follow the distant din through the sanctuary, dodging scattered knots of panicked rebels in the hall. I find Leo outside the dining room, searching faces. When he sees me, he rushes to my side. "Thank the gods you're safe!"

"And the girls?" I say, still catching my breath.

"They're fine," he replies.

Over his shoulder, I peek into the dining hall. The once stately space is in shambles. Branches are strewn across broken tables; green leaves tumble down from the hole smashed in the canopy, and a bright groove has been scraped into the polished stone floor.

The avion is at the far end of it. One of the wings drags along the ground as the creature thrashes, struggling like the wounded bird she is. A handful of armed rebels hunker behind overturned tables, their guns trained on the metal beast, but their weapons won't do much to protect them. Nor will the tables, if the fire comes. Warily, I eye the twin barrels of the flamethrowers, but the soldat inside is slumped across the controls. There is blood on his brow. Have I killed him? I search the room for his soul among the others, but no—he is moaning faintly.

There are more wounded huddling in the corners: a woman with a gash on her back, a boy having trouble breathing from the panic. Still others with cuts from the splinters and debris that fell from the living ceiling.

Cam's voice cuts through the hubbub as he pushes through the crowd. "Clear the room! Take them to the docteur. You three, stay," he adds, pointing to the rebels covering the soldat. "Don't shoot if you can avoid it. We want the pilot alive. Jetta! Can you disable the avion?"

It is less a question than a command, but I hesitate. To make the symbol of death, I have to be close enough to touch the creature. Even without the flamethrowers, one sweep of a metal wing could cut me in half. But this is a chance to take one of the flying machines for the rebels. Am I fast enough on my feet to circle around to her tail? Cautiously, I enter the hall, stalking toward the creature, but Leo follows, shrugging off his jacket. "Let me."

"Leo—"

"Shhhh," he says. To me, or the avion? He lifts the jacket between his hands as though it is a net. But the cloth is barely enough to cover the creature's head. I frown—is that his goal? I have seen hawks calmed with a hood; would the avion respond the same way? The creature seems wary, shifting on metal claws as though tracking his movement. My own muscles tense as I wait for Leo to spring forward, to fling the jacket from a distance, but he moves slowly, steadily, till his own face is inches from the wicked curve of the steel beak. "Shhhhh."

Gently, he slips the cloth over the creature's head; in

the sudden darkness the bird goes still—calm. Suddenly, a memory surfaces: Leo back in Luda, as he stood before Lani, the water buffalo that used to pull our roulotte. "You were right," I say softly. "You are good with animals."

"They're only carrier pigeons, aren't they?" With a half smile, Leo strokes the metal neck. Can the soul feel his touch? The avion only shakes its massive wings, as though trying to fluff feathers. "All they want is a dark nest after a long flight. And to go home, of course."

"I don't care where the soul goes, as long as it leaves the avion." Cam gives me a pointed look. My hand is still bloody from marking the stone—it is almost simple to draw the symbol. The empty circle, the staring eye: death. The avion shudders again; a moment later, the pigeon's soul spirals up toward the canopy.

Leo pulls his jacket off the creature—now just a lump of steel—as Camreon waves the other rebels forward. They haul the soldier from his seat, his eyes fluttering open as they lay him out on a table, calling for the docteur. But I remain beside the avion, looking at the blood—my blood—drying on the wing. Suddenly, I feel so drained. And what about the soldier? "Will he live?" I call to Cam, wanting desperately not to have killed him too.

"For a while," Cam says, and the answer does not soothe me. He plucks one of the flyers off the floor as he follows the rebels and their prize. "I have questions."

Will he torture the man? I shouldn't ask—I know the answer. After all, this is war, this is the Tiger. I want more than anything to leave with Leo, to find somewhere quiet and close my eyes. But then, on the table, the soldat cries out.

The sound makes me jump—a wordless groan, pressed through clenched teeth. The boy's body starts to jerk uncontrollably, and the rebels lose hold of his limbs as they flail.

"Get his mouth open!" Camreon races to the soldier's side, but foam is already gathering at the corners of his lips as they turn blue.

"What is it?" I whisper, horrified.

"Poison." Leo's face is troubled. "The armée gives them capsules sometimes."

"Another invention from the scientist?" Leo clenches his jaw, but he doesn't defend his sister. The soldier's soul steps free, and Camreon swears as the body goes limp. Yanking down the soldier's collar, he presses two fingers under the boy's jaw, cursing again when he finds no pulse.

"Jetta!"

"What?"

"Don't let him escape!"

I glance at the body—at the wandering soul—then back to the Tiger as understanding dawns. "Cam—"

"We need to know what he's trying to hide," he growls. "Please."

I grit my teeth as I approach the soldier's body. For a moment, all I can see is Akra, lying too still on the stone floor of Hell's Court. So I turn away as I mark the soldier's clammy flesh. I don't want to see him drawn back to his skin. I hear it, though—oh, I hear it. The way his heels drum the table, the rattle of breath in empty lungs, the gasp of the rebels as they witness the soldier's rebirth.

And then—even worse—his voice in my head. "Kaveh vou fait?" he whispers, but when I turn back, I can see his jaw is still clenched—his blue lips do not move. "What have you done?"

Cam grabs the soldier's jaw and turns his head. "How did you find us?"

The soldier refuses to speak—at least, to the Tiger. But he is mine now, isn't he? "Answer his question."

"A report," the soldier spits, as though the words are being dragged up his throat on a hook. "From the questioneurs."

"The questioneurs?" Cam grits his teeth. "It must have been one of Raik's contacts."

"Does it matter?" Leo says softly. "They know where we are."

"Tell me about this, then." Cam holds up the flyer. "How many avions is the general sending?"

"All of them."

The soldier's claim makes my stomach drop. The Tiger looks at me. "Can he lie, Jetta?"

"Tell the truth," I order the soldier.

He curls his lip. "I have."

Leo's face goes pale; he puts one hand on the table, as though to steady himself. "How can we stop so many so soon?"

"I know what Le Trépas would say," Cam murmurs darkly. The monk's words come back to me too: kill the creator. I shift on my feet, wary—is the Tiger thinking about me, or the general? Leo takes my hand, protective, but Cam keeps his eyes on the soldier. "How far are they?"

"A few hours behind me," the soldier says.

"All in a group, or will they try to surround us?"

"How should I know?" the pilot says. "I had my orders. They have theirs."

"That's it, then." Cam frowns, considering. "You can release him, Jetta."

My laugh is bitter. "You make it sound kinder than it is."

"Would you rather we take him outside and shoot him?"

"That won't work," I say, but the Tiger shows his teeth.

"Take him outside and burn him, then."

At Camreon's order, the rebels pull the struggling soldat from the table, and his cries break my heart. Though he is the enemy, I can't help the tears that spring to my eyes. So I do it—I mark him, I pull out his soul and watch it flee.

How many have I already killed? Foolish things—the tears. The emotion. I dash them away, but not before Cam notices. He pulls a silk square from his pocket and tosses it to me. "It gets easier."

I toss the handkerchief back; it lands at his feet. "I wouldn't brag about that."

"You're still too soft," he says, though there is no mockery in his voice. "When the fields are burning, you can't mourn every grain of rice."

"I'm not made for war," I tell him.

"If you're at it long enough, war remakes you." His tone is gentle, but dread is a heavy weight in my gut. How many deaths till I stop counting? Leo puts his arm around me, reassuring, as the Tiger turns to the rebels. "Take care of the body. Leave the uniform, will you? You, organize a crew to get this place cleaned up. Jetta? Come with me."

"To the dragons?"

"To the avion. Leo, you too." The Tiger beckons us to follow as he strides across the floor. "We'll use it to scout the entire area. I want to know how their forces are positioned. The last thing we need is to evacuate right into the armée's claws."

I blink at him, nonplussed. Maybe he does want me dead. "You want me to go exploring in a flying machine when there might be dozens more at the end of the valley?"

"Of course not," Camreon says, cutting his eyes to Leo. "I want him to do it."

"What?" My voice has gone up an octave, but Leo cuts my protest short with a single word.

"Bien."

"I need you to be thorough, but fast," Camreon says to Leo, ignoring my shocked expression. "If they're as close as the soldat claims, it shouldn't take long."

"He's not going," I interject. "Send someone else."

"Who do you have in mind?" the Tiger replies, but he doesn't wait for an answer. "Leo and Akra are the only ones who have ever been up in the air. Aside from you and La Fleur, and you're both too important to risk."

"So is Leo," I shoot back.

"No more than anyone else." Leo's reproach is gentle.

"Then I'll go with you," I tell him. "Or I won't ensoul the bird."

"You're not a talisman," Cameron says. "You can't keep him safe just by being there."

I open my mouth, close it again. I cannot say what I am thinking: that I might not be able to keep him safe, but I can keep him alive. But would he want me to? Given the choice, would he rather live bound to me, or die his own man? "Akra, then," I suggest instead, ignoring the feeling that I am throwing my own brother into danger—after all, my brother is much harder to kill. "He can even report back while still on the wing."

Cam is already shaking his head. "We need him to watch Le Trépas," he says. "Especially now."

"I want to go, Jetta," Leo murmurs. But he hesitates. "Will you let me break my promise?"

My heart quails; my head floods with ways to stop him. Refusing. Demanding. Pulling Leo into the avion and escaping into the sky. But could I leave Maman and

Papa in the armée's path? And the girls—Leo would never leave them in harm's way. Neither would I, if it really came to it. And what about the other rebels?

I understand then why Camreon calls me soft. To me, the choice is impossible. Then again, it isn't mine to make. "I can't stop you," I say at last. "I never could."

"Find me as soon as you get back," Camreon says as he starts toward the hall. "I'm going to go tell Raik what we know so far."

"Wait!" Leo digs into his pocket for his gun as Cam turns back. "First tell me where to find the munitions. I'm out of bullets."

I try to laugh. "The avion has flamethrowers, Leo."

He does not smile. "I'd still feel better with a gun. Just in case."

Wordlessly, the Tiger pulls out his own weapon, the one with the silent barrel, and trades it for Leo's empty pistol. "I hope you don't find yourself in a situation where you have to use it," Cam says as Leo tucks the gun into his belt. Then, with a nod, he leaves us there in the vast and empty wreckage of the dining hall.

But the Tiger's parting words echo. The rebels don't have poison to help us keep our secrets. Nor do the Aquitans have nécromanciens to pry intelligence from the dead. But they do have questioneurs for the living.

It won't come to that. Will it? There is no reason for Leo to land in the armée camp—not unless they shoot down the avion. And why would they? Up in the sky, he'll be nearly indistinguishable from one of their own—especially if he's wearing the soldier's uniform. It's sitting there, folded, on the table. I shake it out, glancing at the costume with a practiced eye. "You can hardly notice the blood."

Leo snorts, shrugging out of his jacket. "I suppose it's not the worst outfit I've ever worn."

"Not even the worst outfit you've worn since we met," I say, wanting to see him smile. But the joke falls flat. In the back of my mind, all I can think of is the time we wasted.

Why hadn't we found more time to laugh together? Why hadn't I asked him for more music? Why hadn't I kissed him more? I hold out the jacket, helping him into it, trying to memorize the curve of his jaw. He starts doing up the buttons, turning to look at me over his shoulder. "Cam was wrong," he says at last. "You're not too soft, you know."

"And you're not a grain of rice," I say, and when he smiles I feel the tears creeping back. "I feel . . ." What? Anger? Fear?

Sorrow? It is impossible to pick one ending to the sentence. "Too much."

"Hold on to it," Leo says, suddenly serious as he gathers my hand in his. "The emotion. The softness. The feeling. Don't let war remake you. Remake the world instead."

"I can if you come back," I say, but he raises an eyebrow.

"You will, either way. And I will come back," he adds. "No matter what happens."

The claim should comfort me, but it leaves me cold instead. Deliberately, I focus on his face, and not on the souls clustered thick in the corners. "Nothing's going to happen," I say, as though it is a mantra. But I'm not a good enough actor to keep the fear out of my eyes.

To cover, I let go of his hand, pulling the pin from my hem and piercing the pad of my thumb. The blood wells up, and without hesitation, he presses his fingertip to mine. In the silence, I can hear my pulse in my ears, and the incongruous sounds of birds in the trees above. Then he turns toward the avion to make the mark, though only I can see the soul diving in. I frown. Is it the same carrier pigeon as before? It seems that way—but why would a soul I've only just freed be so eager to return to my command? Could it be that life is always better than the alternative?

The avion shakes, trying to flex her wings; together, Leo and I press with all our weight against the crooked hinge until the steel bends straight and the wing slides shut. The metal clangs and squeaks as she fluffs what she thinks are her feathers.

"Down," Leo says, tapping the bird's flank, and the metal beast crouches, waiting for him to climb aboard. But he hesitates, searching my face as though all the answers are there. "I keep wanting to kiss you," he says at last. "But I've seen too many shadow plays. If this is a tragedy, it will be the last kiss we ever share."

"It's not a play," I say, taking his hand again. "Or if it is, let it be a love story."

He gives me that crooked smile, leaning closer. When we kiss, it is not like a play, but a song, and it takes my breath away. And when he pulls away and steps into the avion, I do not say goodbye, but au revoir.

ACT 3,

SCENE 31

In the sanctuary. The docteur is at work, bandaging the wounded. Various rebels stand in groups, talking in hushed tones about the message from the Aquitans. Camreon winds through the crowds, moving fast toward the door. He meets RAIK coming in from outside, a flyer in the Boy King's shaking hand.

CAMREON: Raik! I was just coming to find you.

He nods at the paper in his brother's hand.

I see you found one of the love letters from the armée.

RAIK pulls his brother aside, into the far corner of the sanctuary, out of the range of hearing of the others.

RAIK: What are we going to do? The weapons aren't ready. I never expected the Aquitans to be here so fast.
CAMREON: We can still try to negotiate. We just don't have as much of an advantage as I would have liked. But in

case it goes wrong, I have someone scouting for evacuation routes by avion.

RAIK: Avion?

He frowns.

How did you get one?

CAMREON: Jetta brought it down. It isn't important, Raik.

RAIK: It is when you're making decisions that should involve me! What if we need it for the evacuation?

CAMREON: Exactly. We need to know what routes are open to the rebels—

RAIK: I meant for us! You, me, and the nécromanciens! We could take the capital while the armée is distracted!

The Tiger pulls back, staring at his brother.

CAMREON: And leave the rest of the rebels to fend for themselves?

RAIK: You said it yourself—most of them aren't fit for fighting. Best if they go back to their villages.

CAMREON: Most of the villages are gone, Raik! Besides, the avions only seat three.

RAIK: Me and the nécromanciens, then. You can lead the rebels to safety. Then again, with Le Trépas's help, perhaps we could go by dragon.

CAMREON: Stay away from Le Trépas.

RAIK (*shouting*): You're not the one in charge, Camreon!

Rebels turn to look as his voice echoes in the sanctuary. RAIK takes a breath, trying to calm down. The Tiger takes his brother's arm, pulling him close, speaking softly.

CAMREON: What's going on, brother? This isn't just about losing Nokhor Khat.

RAIK: Yes, it is.

RAIK pulls away, as though to leave. Then he turns back, his voice low.

No. You're right. It's about losing everything.

CAMREON: We haven't lost as long as we keep fighting—

RAIK: I lost it all the day you came home.

His whisper is harsh, ragged. CAMREON looks at him, not understanding.

CAMREON: You're afraid I'll betray you.

RAIK: You've made me a traitor myself!

CAMREON: What on earth do you mean?

RAIK: Don't toy with me, Camreon. I know what you see when you look at me.

CAMREON: I see my brother—

RAIK: You see an Aquitan!

The rebels are still staring, but RAIK no longer cares.

You think I'm useless. Or a burden. Or maybe even a pawn.

CAMREON: No—

RAIK: But the only thing I knew about being king was what the Aquitans taught me! And all of it was tainted the moment you told me what really happened the night our parents died!

CAMREON stares at him, overwhelmed.

CAMREON: Are you saying after all this you don't want the throne?

RAIK: Of course I do.

A pause. He takes a breath, breathing hard.

But I'm not proud of it. Not anymore.

Another pause. He gathers himself.

Come and find me the moment the avion returns.

Turning on his heel, the Boy King strides through the crowd as they part, uncertain, around him.

CHAPTER THIRTY-TWO

Hours pass. Leo does not come back.

Till We Meet Again

music and lyrics by
Mei Rath

Dark and ponderous ♩ = 84

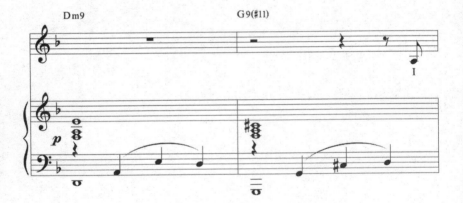

tell you___ not to go but I can't keep you. You

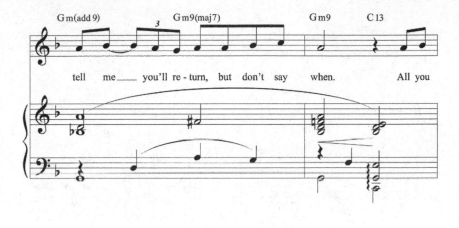

tell me___ you'll re - turn, but don't say when. All you

leave me hold - ing is your mem - 'ry. I hope it's

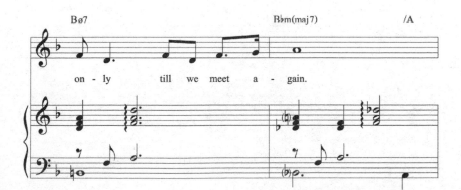

on - ly till we meet a - gain.

Till we ____ meet a - gain. ____ You

prom - ised me you'd nev - er leave me lone - ly, But

pro - mis - es are hard for you to keep. There's

one I must be - lieve, and that one on - ly. But

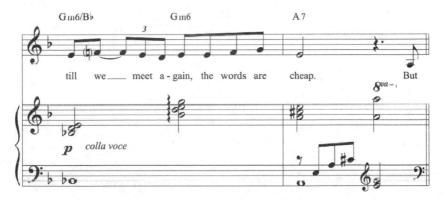

till we ___ meet a - gain, the words are cheap. But

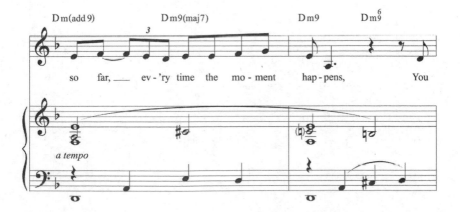

so far, ___ ev - 'ry time the mo - ment hap - pens, You

walk in____ through the door, and oh! But then, There will

be a next time you will whis-per: "Good-bye my love, un -

til we meet a - gain."_____

CHAPTER
THIRTY-THREE

Tia and Theodora find me in the dining hall. When I meet their eyes, my neck twinges—how long have I been staring up at the sky? The gray day has long since faded. Now the edges of the clouds are silvered in the moonlight, and from time to time the stars wink through. I rub my tired eyes as the girls approach. Then I notice their faces are red from crying, and Theodora is carrying a familiar violin case.

Instantly my heart sinks. I can only get out one word. "Leo?"

"No news yet." Tia's answer is an attempt at reassurance,

though I can see the truth in her eyes. No news isn't always good news. "But Cam sent us to find you."

I scrub my palms on my sarong; they are clammy with worry. "What for?"

"To tell you about the evacuation," Theodora says. "We couldn't wait any longer to get everyone out. That's why I brought this," she says, holding out his violin. "I think he'd want you to take care of it until he gets back."

I take the case, not trusting myself to speak. It's lighter than I expect it to be. How can it hold so many memories? I long to brush the strings, to hear the ghost of Leo's music— but I can't bring myself to open it. After all, it's still his, isn't it?

"The village in the valley was cleared this afternoon," Theodora adds. "Just before the armée arrived."

"They're here?" Blinking, I sit up straight. "Where are my parents?"

"They got away safely before the Aquitans set up camp," Theodora says, and relief floods through me. But why hadn't I spared them a thought till now? Had they been wondering where I was? Why I hadn't come to say goodbye?

But perhaps it was for the best. I don't know if I could have done it twice in one day. "Which way are they heading?"

"Toward La Verdu," Tia says.

I look at her askance. "La Verdu is occupied."

"They're going to travel at night," Theodora says. "And official reports say the armée forces are spread thin there."

"Besides, the only other choice is farther into the mountains, and they can't make a climb like that," Tia says. "Not with your papa's chair."

I frown. "But with his chair, they'll have to stick close to the main roads, won't they?"

Theodora hesitates, but after a while, she nods. "Possibly."

Fear twists my gut in knots—without me, my parents are just two more refugees. I have to hope the armée will focus on the rebels instead of chasing civilians through the jungle. And that Maman and Papa can find food and shelter on the run. "What about you two?" I say then, trying to distract myself. "Where is Cam sending you?"

"We're not going," Tia says, and La Fleur lifts her chin.

"I still think I can strike a bargain with Xavier," she says. "Cam agreed to go down to the village with me tomorrow morning."

"Oh?" I watch her face. Behind the brave facade, hope wars with doubt. If she's uncertain, how must Camreon feel?

But this is not the first time he's trusted her with his life. I hope it won't be the last. "Does the Tiger have a job for me?"

"You'll be up on the hillside to protect Raik and Le Trépas," she says promptly. "The mines will give you some cover if something goes wrong. The rest of the rebels are going down the falls toward the shore. They can forage along the river and hide in the trees until the Aquitans are gone."

"Is that where you and Cheeky will be?" I ask Tia, but she laughs, a little too loud.

"Cheeky and I agreed we'd rather face the avions than another jungle trek!" After a moment, her laughter fades into a sigh. "And it was hard being in the capital for so long, surrounded by the Aquitans. I don't want to evacuate to La Verdu, no matter how thin the armée's spread. She and I are staying here."

"I'll keep you safe," I tell her, hoping it's true. Then I look around the wide dining hall, empty so late at night, except for the souls that glow along the walls. "Where is Cheeky, anyway?"

"Visiting Akra," Tia says with a look. "She's not wasting any more time."

"Smart." I rest my hand on the violin case. "Neither should we."

"Oh?" Tia gives me a sly look. "Cheeky has some champagne in one of those trunks."

I raise my eyebrows, but what can it hurt? "Maybe just a glass." I stand, my knees are shaky from sitting so long. But my friends match my pace as we walk back to the room we've been sharing.

We pass rebels coming the other way—leaving the temple with bundles small enough to carry under one arm: everything they'd been able to bring with them from wherever they had come. How many times had I done the same? Despite the dread that approaches with dawn, I am strangely grateful I no longer have to run.

In the few moments of peace and stillness we have left, the girls and I settle down among the pillows and toast to old friends and new, to Leo and Eve, to Cheeky and Akra, to family and hope and most of all, to tomorrow.

ACT 3,
SCENE 34

The mine. CHEEKY picks her way down the tunnel, careful not to trip on the dragon bones. In one hand, she holds a lamp; in the other, a basket brimming with delicacies: lotus leaf packets of sticky rice, slices of sweet dried mango, roasted pork rich with fat and flavor, and a precious stick of real white sugar, boiled to crystals on a stick.

At first, she walks boldly into the dark, but as the cell gets closer, her steps grow smaller, till she creeps to the edge of the circle of light.

The ex-capitaine is sitting beside his lamp, his back against the iron bars, ignoring the old monk sleeping on the other side of the grate. When AKRA sees CHEEKY, his eyebrows go up. Then he frowns at the basket in her arms.

AKRA: What is that? Dinner?

Silently, she nods, passing it over. He looks inside, making a face.

If I'd known the rebellion ate so well, I would have left the armée sooner.

A smile flickers across CHEEKY's face, but it falls when he sets the basket down beside the bars.

I'm sure he'll enjoy it when he wakes. But you should tell the kitchen not to waste the good stuff on a murderous bastard like him.

AKRA pulls out the stick of sugar and holds it out to her. CHEEKY stares at it, dismayed.

What?

The silence stretches. Akra shifts on his feet, annoyed.

Why don't you talk?
CHEEKY: Why don't you eat?

AKRA stiffens, suddenly flustered.

AKRA: I'm not hungry.

CHEEKY: You could have the grace to pretend. I traded my favorite earrings for that candy!

AKRA looks down at the stick of sugar in his hand.

AKRA: Why?

Her exasperated sigh echoes in the tunnel.

CHEEKY: Because I find you fascinating, you absolute oaf! Gods, next time let it be a girl!

She spins on her heel and flees, but AKRA follows her halfway down the hall.

AKRA: Wait! Please.

CHEEKY slows, turning at last; AKRA stands before her, suddenly less sure.

I don't . . . I didn't . . . I wasn't expecting this.

She gives him a pointed look.

CHEEKY: Neither was I.

AKRA barks a laugh.

AKRA: I guess a girl as pretty as you is used to being seen.
CHEEKY: That depends on if you like to leave the lamp lit.

The sentence hangs in the air; the blush starts up her cheeks. But AKRA is delighted; he laughs so loud the sound rattles the bones in the tunnel.

AKRA: You are . . . I like you.

She rolls her eyes.

CHEEKY: Careful, flattery like that will go to my head.
AKRA: You expect me to put you into words?

CHEEKY catches her breath . . . the blush deepens . . . she is at a loss once more. Gently, AKRA reaches out, tugging on one of her pincurls, then tucking it behind her ear. He holds out the stick of sugar.

AKRA: You should go get your earrings back.

Her smile falls.

CHEEKY: Why?
AKRA: Because I don't need this.

He holds out the stick again, and she narrows her eyes.

CHEEKY: Me, or the sugar?
AKRA: Let's say the sugar.

The showgirl plucks it from his hand, then uses it to wave his claim away as though the words are only bad air.

CHEEKY: I didn't need earrings either, but they were nice while they lasted. Besides, everyone deserves a little sweetness.
AKRA: What if I don't?

His voice is soft; CHEEKY cocks her head.

CHEEKY: What could you have done that's so wrong?

AKRA's smile twists—bitter. The lamplight shines lurid on the scar on his chin.

AKRA: I was a Chakran in the armée. I made capitaine in three years. I served under Pique, for god's sake. You can guess at the rest.

His voice breaks; he goes silent. His eyes shine; are those tears? CHEEKY is taken aback.

CHEEKY: But you left.
AKRA: Not soon enough.
CHEEKY: Then use the time left to make it better.
AKRA: But how?

She lowers her voice, enticing.

CHEEKY: I'll think of something.

AKRA peers at her.

AKRA: Are we still talking about sugar?

CHEEKY laughs, holding out the candy. After a moment, he takes it, their hands brushing on the stick, each of them unwilling to let go of the soft touch, the hint of sweetness.

This is how RAIK finds them.

He looms out of the dark like a threat. AKRA startles; he is unused to being caught unawares. For a moment, he tenses, unsure, but RAIK's face is a tangled knot as he glares at the girl.

RAIK: Still a bad time, I take it.
CHEEKY: I'm sorry—
RAIK: Just go.

She hesitates, looking back down the hall toward AKRA. RAIK drops his hand to the gun at his waist, speaking through his teeth.

Get out! The both of you! That's an order from your king!

CHAPTER THIRTY-FIVE

"Jetta?" Akra's voice comes to me through the warm haze of half a glass of champagne.

"Mmm?" My answer is lazy. I look up from the violin case: it rests in my lap as I toy with the clasps, still unable to open it.

"There's a problem," he says, and my hand stills.

"Le Trépas?" I whisper the name through dry lips, soft enough the other girls can't hear me.

"Raik," my brother replies, almost primly. "He walked in on a private conversation."

I make a face. "That's very nearly as bad."

"We're fine," Akra says quickly. "But he was armed, and I didn't think it was wise to push him. And now the monk is unguarded, except by the king."

"Unguarded?" My voice edges up in both pitch and volume; hurriedly, I set the violin case aside. "I'll be right there."

Tia gives me a quizzical look as I grab my satchel. "What is it, Jetta?"

"Raik followed Cheeky to the mine," I say, slipping the strap over my head. "He ordered Akra out of the tunnel and went in with Le Trépas."

"This isn't about Cheeky," Theodora says, slowly. "Raik and Cam didn't see eye to eye on the plan for tomorrow. I have to let him know."

"Tell him to meet me down there," I tell her as we head for the door

Tia calls after me. "What if Le Trépas is out of his cell?"

"What if he kills Raik?" I shoot back over my shoulder. I do not relish the idea of walking into the dark tunnel, not knowing where Le Trépas is. Or of looking for the Boy King, dead or alive. But the rebels need him, and if he's gotten himself killed, I'm the only one who can bring him back.

Theodora and I part ways in the hall—her toward

Camreon's quarters, and I toward the sanctuary. The temple is nearly deserted now, the rebels fled to safer sanctuaries. But there is still life here—the wind in the green leaves, the souls lounging on the stone floor. Will it all be ash tomorrow? The thought is painful. As I pass the statue of the Maiden, I slow. Overhead, the light is shifting, and the shadows have turned strange.

Squinting, I peer up toward the canopy. The light has taken on an odd quality: cold, like moonlight cutting through the sunny glow of the souls. Have the clouds cleared? Then a shriek splits the air, like a spike in my skull. I bend double, covering my ears with my hands, but it does nothing to muffle the sound. Dread floods into the pit of my stomach. A sound that's only in my head . . . "Akra?" He doesn't answer. "Akra!"

His voice comes back then—not hurt, but scared. "Are you all right, Jetta?"

"Yes," I say over the pounding of my heart. "You?"

"I am," he mutters. "But I have a bad feeling."

"Me too," I say. It seems like an understatement. What was the sound, if not my brother? It comes again—a keening wail—as piercing as a hawk's, as heartbreaking as a child's. Wincing, I squint up at the cold light on the leaves, but the canopy is too thick to see the sky. I make my way across the sanctuary, ducking through the banyan archways and turning my face toward the heavens. Toward the source of the icy light, which is nothing like the moon.

In the sky winds a long ribbon of blue fire, incomprehensibly large. A soul—of course it is, though I have never heard one cry out like that. The spirit undulates through the clouds like a snake through water, but so much bigger. Still, more chilling than the size is the color: the sapphire blue of vengeful ghosts. As I watch, it cries out again, a sound to split heaven itself.

A hand falls on my shoulder; I jump, but it is only Cam. His brow is furrowed—he must see the look on my face, because I am the only one who can see the soul. Me . . . and Le Trépas. After all, it's one of his. "What's wrong?"

"The dragon's soul," I say, swallowing the lump in my throat. "Le Trépas must have summoned it back."

Cam's eyebrows shoot upward, but I do not wait for his response. Instead, I pelt down the hillside toward the mine. Dimly, I am aware of the Tiger calling after me as he follows. I am halfway down the mountain when the air shatters again. The ghost of the dragon gives one last aching cry—what life had it been living until Le Trépas called it back?

But the sound fades as the spirit dives toward the mine, disappearing among the greenery—the blue light flickers out as though it had never been. What is left is a sudden darkness, deeper than it should be. Where are the drifting vana, the little jungle spirits, the arvana of birds that chatter in the trees? Fled to the temple, it seems—are they wiser than me, or only more cowardly?

It is in the shadows of a soulless night that I come to the mouth of the tunnel, lit with unearthly blue. From the hole in the earth like an old grave, the skeleton of the dragon emerges.

The curved teeth lead, all limned in blue fire. Next come the dark hollows of the skull—the empty sockets stare right through me. Then a foreleg, the claws digging furrows in the trembling earth. The long horns shine silver in the sapphire glow of the vengeful soul, and there is Le Trépas, seated between them.

Gone is the demeanor of the old Chakran uncle, gone is the fatherly look in his eye. The carcan is gone too; his chest is bare and bleeding from a clean cut under his collarbone. And as I stand before the monk at the feet of the great beast, the dragon lowers its head until the teeth are inches from my face.

ACT 3,

SCENE 36

The officer's tent in the village square. The space is sparsely furnished; the avions have carried extra men from Nokhor Khat in lieu of supplies. Pique and the rest of the soldiers are bunked in the abandoned huts surrounding the square, but XAVIER prefers familiarity to comfort. He is asleep in the dark. Outside: a brief discussion . . . a short scuffle . . . a muffled cry. XAVIER's eyes snap open, his hand creeping up beneath his pillow. Then the canvas flap twitches, and a dark form slips in through the opening of the tent.

XAVIER: I'm armed.

LEO: That makes two of us.

XAVIER blinks at the sound of his voice. Slowly he sits up.

XAVIER: Leonin?

LEO nods, his expression grim as the gun he holds. Without compromising his aim, he digs in his pocket, pulling out a lighter and nodding at the glass lamp on the floor beside XAVIER's cot.

LEO: A little help?

XAVIER flips back the thin wool blanket with his free hand; the other is wrapped tightly around the grip of his own pistol. Together, the brothers light the lamp—XAVIER lifting the glass surround, LEO touching the flame to the wick. The flame sputters, struggling to take hold.

XAVIER: Is this to be a short meeting, or should I have my aide de camp bring more kerosene?
LEO: The boy outside? I'm afraid you'll be waiting a while for a response.
XAVIER: Too bad. He was just starting to get the hang of things.

The general makes a face, frowning at LEO's uniform.

Tell me you didn't steal that off a body.
LEO: Is it theft if the body doesn't need it?
XAVIER: Is that how you got past the perimeter?

LEO: The avion helped. The guards are looking for rebels in the jungle. Not soldiers on warbirds. And you've never put my name and description on a recherche.

XAVIER (*shaking his head*): That was always a mistake. I should have warned everyone how dirty you Chakrans can fight.

LEO: Can you blame us? This has never been your home. But the rest of us have nowhere else to go. You know we can't surrender tomorrow.

Quickly XAVIER stands, nose to nose with LEO, jabbing him in the chest with the pistol.

XAVIER: Is it the girl? The nécromancien? Is that why you chose their side?

LEO: You think it was my choice? Our father was the first to remind all of us that I'm something less than Aquitan.

XAVIER: But that doesn't make you Chakran, either. I've seen the way they look at you. Make no mistake, this is no more your home than it is mine.

LEO: That doesn't mean it's not worth saving. As for you— there's an entire country you love but have never really seen. Take the next ship back to Aquitan, and the armée with you.

Take the avions, if you want. But go, and leave us here to make our own choices.

XAVIER: I'm not going to disgrace our family name.

LEO: That was always my job, anyway.

At LEO's little smile, the general's facade cracks; for a moment, he is more brother than son.

XAVIER: Why couldn't you have stayed out of it? For the sake of the blood we share, I hoped it would be someone else who had to kill you.

LEO: It will be, Xavi. I have plans after this.

XAVIER: With your nécromancien?

The word hardens in his mouth; the general tightens his grip on the gun.

No. Desolée, Leonin. I'll send your regrets for you. Then again, who knows? She can't be far. And if your soul wanders back to her, you can give them yourself.

XAVIER pulls the trigger just as LEO does the same, but only one weapon fires, silent as a whisper. The general's eyes go wide, first in surprise, then in pain. Grunting, he curls over his stomach, pressing a fist to his ribs; it comes away bloody.

XAVIER: Salaud. You shot me.

LEO's impassive look breaks; air hisses through his teeth as though he feels the wound in his own flesh. Then he clenches his jaw, swallowing the rush of emotion.

Putain.

The general straightens up, taking aim again. The hammer clicks on the empty cartridge, once, twice, thrice.

What did you . . .

XAVIER paws at the gun, opening the chamber to find it empty. Groaning, he tosses the pistol aside—as his knees go weak, he reaches for the rail of the cot.

You stole my bullets.

LEO: I stole a move from the Tiger, really. You left the tent unoccupied at dinner, and I had a lot of time to kill. Did our father teach you and Theo both to keep guns under your pillows?

Heavily, XAVIER tries to sit, but he misses the edge of the bed. Instead, he falls to the floor beside it, a sharp grunt catching in his throat. The sound turns into a rueful chuckle. Then he leans back, resting his head on the bed. When he speaks next, his voice is much softer.

XAVIER: I can't believe you shot me. What would Father say?
LEO: He'd say I finally learned the lesson he tried to teach me.
XAVIER: I don't want to die here, Leonin. I don't want to die in this godforsaken country.

LEO presses his lips together; his hand trembles. At last he lowers the gun.

LEO: I'm sorry, Xavi.

XAVIER's hand creeps up to the medallion he wears; fumbling, he grasps it tight.

XAVIER: What will happen to me?

LEO: I . . . I'm not sure.

XAVIER: She said . . . the nécromancien said . . . souls live three days. Is that true? Three days to get to Aquitan. Do you think I'll make it to the cathedral at Lephare?

LEO swallows before he speaks.

LEO: I think so.

XAVIER: They say the trip is ten days by boat. How fast does a soul fly? Can you ask her for me, Leo? Can you . . .

CHAPTER THIRTY-SEVEN

All the world has narrowed to this moment—this time—to the inches between my face and the dragon's teeth. Memories fade, dreams wink out like snuffed candles as I wait for the final curtain. Le Trépas's voice breaks the spell. "Enjoy the show."

The old monk presses his palms together and gives me a mocking bow as the dragon leaps up to the heavens.

The next thing I know, I am staring at the dome of the predawn sky, amazed I am still here to see it. Was it the rush of wind that knocked me flat? Or did my knees simply give out? Either way, I am alive. How? Is it the Maiden who protected me, or the King who passed me by?

"War isn't like theater, you know," Akra says grimly as he arrives in my field of vision. "Front and center isn't the spot to covet."

I make a face, but I take the hand he offers. My head spins as he pulls me to my feet; I take hold of his shoulder while I regain my footing. "Where's Cheeky?"

"I sent her to hide in the next mine downhill," he says. "She's not exactly dressed for battle."

"You'd be surprised," I murmur, letting go of his arm at last. Then I catch a glimpse of the valley, lit by the first glimmer in the east, and the dizzy feeling returns. "What happened to the village?"

Akra follows my gaze, the scar on his chin twisting. "Pique always made a habit of destruction."

Below us the paddies have been churned to mud—the fields stripped, the livestock slaughtered, and the pastures replaced by a field of avions. And in the village square, beside the single tent—something too familiar, though I'd only seen them once before in the ruins of Dar Som. A row of crosses, each one leaning against a triangular structure instead of sunk into the unstable ground, all assembled from cut bamboo. The armée must be eager for prisoners.

Rage flares in my chest. I feel no pity for them as Le Trépas approaches the camp.

The men on patrol notice him first—or rather, they notice the dragon in the sky. I am too far away to hear the alarm they raise, but not far enough that I miss the ensuing panic. Can the Aquitans see by the light of the creature's soul? To my eyes, the encampment is lit in shades of blue and black; shadows turn and deepen in the rows between the tents as the beast approaches. Men scatter, stumbling as they flee toward the fields, to the jungle—and to the avions.

My heart quavers—the dragon is formidable, but fifty warbirds would take it down in short order. But there is something wrong. As soldiers clamber in, the avions stay on the ground. As the dragon passes overhead, the bone jaws gape, grabbing one of the avions and tossing it through the air.

The warbird tumbles like a child's toy, crashing through one of the huts on the green. A soul flares brightly against the destruction—a soldier, killed instantly. The distant sounds drift to my ears as more soldiers pour out of the huts—the shouting, the screaming. Guns pop like fireworks as the soldiers fire fruitlessly through the dragon's bones. Gouts of fire burst from the flamethrowers, but without the ability to aim the avions, the flame only licks along the fields and catches in the nearby thatch. The dragon's tail sends another of the avions rolling, but the rest of the warbirds are still.

All but one.

Where had it come from? The metal creature circles wide in the sky, bronze wings gleaming. The dragon banks again, returning to the village. The pop of gunfire makes me startle. Le Trépas is not impervious to bullets. The dragon pulls up higher, and the avion behind it closes in, like an arrow toward the creature's missing heart.

My own heart starts to pound. Can the old bones withstand the flame, or will Le Trépas drop out of the sky in a cloud of embers and ash? The beast turns, jaws opening, but the warbird dips like a swallow as the great teeth snap at empty air. Then the avion spirals upward in a gout of gold and scarlet.

The dragon screams as the avion shoots past, but most of the accelerant drips through the hollows between the bones. Still, there are patches of flame charring the creature's ribs, and spots burning brightly on the tail. And that was only the first volley from a single bird. I look back at the rows of avions, still inert on the ground. None of them are moving, not even a little. No rustle of wings, no shake of a head.

"Something happened to Xavier," I mutter as realization dawns, but the next thought strikes like lightning. Wide-eyed, I stare at the single avion still chasing Le Trépas. It is impossible to make out the pilot's face, but I recognize the color of his dark hair—the curve of his jaw. "Leo," I say softly. "That's Leo!"

As fast as my heart rises, it sinks again. Why is he attacking the monk? I turn to ask my brother, only to find him halfway down the path. "Where are you going?" I call after him.

"I'm supposed to guard Le Trépas, aren't I?" There is a threat in his voice, and his hand is on his gun. My breath falters in my throat.

"You can't hurt Leo."

"We can't lose Le Trépas, either," he says grimly. "It's hard enough watching over him when he's alive. What happens if his soul escapes?"

I blink at him. I don't want to find out. "I'm coming with you!"

Together, my brother and I race down the path to the valley. It switches back and forth down the steep hillside; I plunge through the knotted overgrowth of roots, tripping over tangles of vines, plowing through stands of elephant ears. My goal is the avions; I'll need one to get Leo and Le Trépas both to safety. But all of them are deep inside the armée perimeter.

Then the opening to the next mine looms down the path, and I slow to a halt. Hadn't Raik said there were more skeletons being assembled? "Akra, wait!"

"No time!"

"This will be faster!" I duck into the mine. The dragon bones gleam in the low light. This set is smaller than the first, and less complete. But it will have to serve.

On a nearby branch, the soul of an owl has settled in after a night playing at hunting; I mark the bones and draw the spirit inside. As the creature shudders to life, a string of curses drifts up from the back of the tunnel. I recognize the voice. "Cheeky?"

"Get that thing out of here!"

I don't bother to argue as I climb atop the bony shoulders; with a shake of her horned head, the dragon clambers out into the dim dawn. When we emerge, Akra stumbles back, and for a brief second the fear in his eyes breaks my heart.

But he grits his teeth and holds out his hand. Reaching down, I swing him up behind me. Together, we vault into the sky.

"Not this again." Did he speak aloud, or only in my head? Akra presses against me as we rise above the treetops, but I don't have the time to comfort him. There is Le Trépas's dragon, her blue soul flickering against the clouds. Leo is right behind her, the gold flame of his avion licking the dragon's tail.

Clinging to the bony vertebrae, I urge my mount faster. The trees pass by below us, the leaves shivering in the night breeze. I can see souls on the path beneath the canopy, heading toward the temple—some gold, some blue.

As we soar closer, smoke tickles my nostrils—the fire from the grounded avions is spreading in the village. Panic rises to my ears, like the songs of strange birds. In the haze, a group of armée men waves a white flag. Does Le Trépas see them? Yes . . . but he doesn't slow. My heart clenches as the dragon dives, shearing a man in half with her teeth. When the creature leaps skyward again, there is another soldier gripped tightly in one set of claws. In the other, the white flag streams.

Leo follows the dragon as it rises, a bright burst of flame unfurling toward the creature's tail. But as I watch, the tail flicks—the warbird falters in the sky. The avion's wings beat hard to regain balance. The old monk was right. I have so much to lose.

How will I stop them both? I press the soul of the owl higher, but behind me, Akra spits a name like a curse. "Pique."

"What?"

"There." He points toward the jungle, but it takes me a moment to make out a small group of men fleeing through the haze.

"How can you tell?"

"I can tell," Akra snaps. "We can't let him get away!"

"We can't lose Le Trépas either," I say. Ahead of us, Leo turns. Has he seen me? I raise my arm, and he returns the signal, then moves his hand in a circle to point at the fields below. His avion banks, circling, and I follow him down.

As soon as we splash down into the muddy ponds of the paddies, Akra leaps from the dragon's back and plunges toward the tree line. I climb down after him, calling for him to wait, but he doesn't even slow. My own little dragon tilts her head, peering after my brother as he vanishes through the haze. I can't follow, but she can. "Take care of Akra," I whisper to the soul, and the dragon leaps after him, half gliding, half bounding toward the trees.

Farther down the field, Leo lands his avion. I hurry through the mud to his side. He ekes out a smile as I approach, though his eyes are hollow. "Told you I'd be back."

"What the hell are you doing?" I demand, jerking my chin toward the sky. "Why are you taking on Le Trépas?"

"Because Xavier's dead, and so are the avions." Leo's voice is distant—shorn of emotion. "The soldiers will surrender if we let them."

I stare at him, taken aback. "What I mean is, why are you risking your life to save theirs?"

"I'm risking my life to do the right thing," he replies, with a look in his eyes like I've never seen. "And that's the only thing worth a damn right now."

His hand goes to a gold medallion at his neck. The one his brother used to wear. My heart sinks in my chest—all of a sudden, I want to wrap my arms around him. Instead, I climb aboard behind him. "Do you still have any bullets?"

"A few. Do you still have the grenade?" Leo glances back at my satchel as metal wings buffet the air. My eyebrows go up—I had forgotten about the explosive. But I shake my head.

"I have to be closer than that," I say as we climb. "If we have to kill him, I can't let his soul escape."

Leo narrows his eyes. "How close is close?"

I wet my lips. I don't want to think about it. "Just get me close enough to jump," I say then. "And be ready to catch me if I fall."

"Always," he says as we climb higher, but the wind pulls the words from his lips.

Leo is a natural pilot—or should I say handler? The bird responds almost eagerly to his touch, and the distance closes quickly. The monk is chasing down a group of soldiers, and he hasn't noticed us right behind him—not yet. Leo pushes the avion faster . . . faster . . . until we are soaring directly above the dragon's bony back. The earth shoots by beneath us, making my head spin, but I try to focus on the ridged spine: my target. Gripping my satchel in one hand and the side of the avion in the other, I crouch on the edge of the seat and jump.

For a breath, I am weightless. Floating. Gravity yanks me down a moment after. I fall, leaving my stomach somewhere in the clouds. It catches up and seems to go right past when I slam into the dragon's ribs.

With a grunt, I catch hold of one of the spines and pull myself desperately higher. The dragon is slower than the avion—the wind is not as bad here. But the open air beneath me seems to claw at my ankles, and the skeleton is not easy purchase, especially with my battered hands. Panting, I make it to the spiny ridge of the long backbone, swinging my leg over the creature like it is a horse. Glancing over my shoulder, I catch sight of Leo. He raises his eyebrow, but I shake my head. I am nowhere near close enough yet.

"Come to join me after all?" Le Trépas calls as I catch my breath.

"Bring the dragon back to the ground," I reply as I reach for the next vertebrae, climbing awkwardly closer. "The armée is in ruins. We've won."

"We haven't won till there is peace. And there's no peace until they're dead," he says softly, looking down at the scattered forces on the ground. "Including your moitié."

"Stay away from Leo," I growl, hooking one leg over the next rib. But the distance between us is much farther than it looked from above, and far more treacherous.

Le Trépas smiles, as though he can hear my thoughts. "I told you I would kill him if you don't kill me first."

I swing my left leg over the next ridge, crawling forward. "Are you so eager to meet the gods?"

"I don't fear death," he says. Then he drags one hand

across the blood that still drips from his chest. How had he gotten hold of a knife? I drop my eyes to the dagger at his belt. The hilt is jeweled and shaped like a dragon—a weapon fine enough for a king to carry. For the first time tonight, I spare a thought for Raik. He is almost certainly dead . . . but there is no time for mourning. Le Trépas lifts his hand, his fingers red and sticky. "Do you?"

"Not always," I admit, gauging the distance between me and the monk, between me and the blood on his outstretched hand. Then I take a deep breath and pull the satchel from my shoulder. In it, the heavy jar of kerosene still sloshes. "But I won't court it, either."

Clutching the bag in one hand, I push myself up with the other. Springing forward, I step from rib to rib, moving as delicately as if I were dancing, though the satchel swings with every step. Le Trépas reaches for me as I approach, his hand wet with his own blood, but before he can touch me, I swing the heavy bag around.

It connects with a meaty sound. The monk cries out, sliding sideways, gripping the bony spine with one blood-slicked hand. Growling, he takes a swipe at me with the other, but as I dance back out of reach, my foot slips on the thin rib.

I slide down the other side of the skeleton, catching myself one-handed as my feet dangle high above the jungle hillside. My satchel falls away, down down down, to the ground below. Grunting, I pull myself up much too slowly. Le Trépas does the same, grinning like a skull. And though his hands are slick, they are not half as battered as mine. He pulls himself back to kneel on the dragon's neck, reaching out for me. He is still smiling when the bullet hits his chest.

Le Trépas reels, slumping backward; Leo shouts at me to take his soul. Scrambling up, I regain my footing. Is the monk still breathing? I cast about for something to mark—something to contain the man's spirit. Will my belt do until I find something more permanent?

As I reach for the silk, Le Trépas lifts his head, fixing me with a deliberate smile. Before I can stop him, he plants a bloody palm on the dragon's skull and pushes, sliding off the bony neck and into the whistling wind.

I squeeze my eyes shut before he hits the ground, but I feel the impact in my gut—and in the way the dragon's bones go limp beneath me. A moment later, bright light pries through the cracks in my eyelids as the dragon's soul soars free: no longer cold blue, but brilliant gold. My mouth opens in awe; she is the most lovely soul I have ever seen.

But as she ascends, the body beneath me starts the long descent to the ground.

Leo pushes the avion faster, but he is not close enough. And though I do not fear my death, I do not wish for it either. So I make my own symbol next to the monk's bloody handprint—life, in red blood on the dragon's brow. Is it wishful thinking that her soul's return to this body is more joyful this time? Either way, the light flashes gold once more as the spirit dives into the bones, and together, we soar upward, circling above the temple as we search for a place to land.

ACT 3,

SCENE 38

The jungle at the edge of the paddies. The air is hazy with smoke as AKRA slips through the trees, following a hunter's track. He is almost certain PIQUE came this way, but signs are hard to find; the night lingers here in the dense greenery. All around him, the shadows are strangely quiet. The morning birds have fled from the armée men ahead of him—or are they hiding from the dragon just behind?

The creature glides from tree to tree, quiet as the owl that ensouls it, though much larger. Bark crunches under its claws every time the beast lands—not on branches, but on the trunks of the oldest trees. It peers into the greenery, swiveling its hollow skull on the end of the long neck. Nothing else moves aside from the wind in the leaves. Then the dragon leaps again, soaring toward the next trunk. As it lands, a gout of flame bursts from the thicket below.

The crackle of the fire hides AKRA's curses as he dives for cover in a patch of elephant ears; the dragon writhes as the fire engulfs the bones. It stops as quickly as it started, but it is too late. The blackened bones crash to the jungle floor in a heap; though AKRA cannot see it, the soul of the owl has fled. But up ahead, the sound of PIQUE's voice drifts back.

PIQUE: The dead are all around us. Keep an open eye.

Through the leaves, AKRA catches sight of the man. PIQUE has tubing looped over one shoulder and a tank of accelerant shoved into a makeshift backpack; he has pried the flamethrower from one of the grounded avions.

Move!

Ahead, the men return to the path, traveling single file. There are six of them, including PIQUE, and each of them has a gun. Even in the dim light, AKRA can tell the soldiers are on the edge of panic—they stand a bit too close, they look too sharply at shadows.

AKRA: You should be afraid.

His voice is so soft not even the birds hear him. Slowly, he nudges aside a broad leaf to take aim. Is he rusty with his first shot, or is PIQUE a lucky man? AKRA fires, but the bullet misses. Instantly, the lieutenant whirls.

PIQUE: Take cover!

He dives behind the closest tree as the other men scatter into the brush. AKRA can hear two of them crashing through the jungle without stopping.

AKRA (*a whisper*): That leaves four.

The sound fades into a silence that lasts so long the birds begin to call. AKRA wets his lips. Has the lieutenant slipped away? He can't let PIQUE escape. So he takes a deep breath and calls out.

Lieutenant?

Another silence. Then . . .

PIQUE: Who's there?
AKRA: Ex-Capitaine Chantray, sir. I served under you in La Sucrier, and through La Verdu.

PIQUE: Through part of La Verdu. You asked for a transfer before Dar Som.

AKRA: You were happy enough to see me go.

To his left, the brush rustles. Like lightning striking, AKRA fires. Deep in the shadows, a soldier cries out. Akra shoots again, and the scream cuts short. Three left, now.

J'étais un capitaine, putains! And a Chakran besides. I grew up in the jungle. You think you can sneak up on me?

He fires again, this time to the right; another soldier drops in the brush, but not before the man gets his own shot off. The bullet slams into AKRA's shoulder like a punch—he bites down on a curse as blood blooms on his right sleeve. But AKRA laughs, rueful, pitching his voice to carry.

Pique knows you can't. But he also knows my gun can't hold more than six bullets.

Silence again, though the quality of it has changed: there is only one soldier left aside from PIQUE, and neither man is willing to try sneaking through the leaves. But AKRA can't exactly sneak up on them either. His arm is throbbing, weak. Wincing, he transfers the gun to his left hand, but his aim is nowhere near as good. Chewing his cheek, AKRA takes another deep breath.

I have two shots left, Lieutenant, but I can take more ammunition from the men I just killed. I will follow you as far as you run. But I have nothing against your last soldier, poor bastard. What if we let him go while you and I both step onto the path?

Another silence. Is PIQUE weighing the options, or has he run while the others kept AKRA occupied? The ex-capitaine calls again, close to desperation.

Two bullets. How many do you have?

A long pause.

PIQUE: Six.

AKRA chuckles.

AKRA: Your kind of odds, ness pas?

Another agonizing moment. Then, with a rustle of the leaves, PIQUE steps out from his hiding place, his gun cocked in his hand.

PIQUE: What do you want?
AKRA: Peace.

AKRA takes a deep breath, steeling himself. Then he bursts from his hiding place, running toward the lieutenant. PIQUE fires in an instant. The bullet drills through AKRA's chest, right through the heart. He stumbles, doubled over with the pain. But he doesn't fall. After a moment, he straightens up and takes a step closer.

PIQUE fires again, this time hitting the ex-capitaine in the gut. Still, AKRA advances. Another shot, and another— AKRA's shoulder snaps back and his knee buckles. The fifth shot makes him wheeze as blood bubbles through his lips, but the sixth shot misses, whistling by his ear. PIQUE's eyes are wide with terror as he scrabbles for the nozzle of the flamethrower, but AKRA raises his own gun then; he is close enough to hit PIQUE twice between the eyes.

The lieutenant collapses on the jungle floor. AKRA sinks down beside him. Blood runs down his limbs, soaks his shirt, trails from the corners of his mouth as he smiles.

AKRA: Pique is dead, Jetta.

The words are a wheezy whisper, but the satisfaction in his voice is undeniable. JETTA's voice comes back almost immediately, but he can't make out her words over the struggling beat of his heart. Everything hurts. His eyes fall on the nozzle of the flamethrower, but on his tongue, life tastes less like blood than sugar. So he lies down beside PIQUE and closes his eyes for a while. His thoughts drift. Old songs play in his head—the memory of melodies he used to sing.

Does he sleep? If so, he wakes at a sound. The last soldier is standing over him, and for a moment, Akra wonders if the man has come to try to finish him off. But the soldier ignores him as he rifles through the lieutenant's pockets. When he straightens up, he doesn't hold bullets or the man's gun.

Instead, he carries a glass jar with a sludge of black liquid in the bottom.

As the soldier tucks the jar into his own pack, he notices AKRA's look. The soldier stares back frankly, his eyes a chilling blue. Then he disappears down the path. Relief washes over AKRA. He closes his eyes again and does not open them for some time.

CHAPTER THIRTY-NINE

It is the pool outside the temple that tempts the dragon down. When she sees it, she points her sinuous body toward the glassy water and dives. It is with some difficulty that I curb her instinct long enough to make her let me off on the shore, and once she is unencumbered by a passenger, she sinks comfortably into the silt to eat the ghosts of fish.

Back aground, my legs are oddly shaky—adrenaline? Exhaustion? Fear? Akra's words are still echoing in my head: Pique is dead. I am still waiting for the rest of the story. Then Leo lands, rushing to my side. Taking his arm makes the world more solid. We cast a single shadow in the orange glow of the rising sun. As we approach the temple, the rebels rush out to greet us.

There are more than I thought there would be—at least two dozen aside from Cheeky and Tia. Had they missed the evacuation or just refused to leave the Tiger's side? I have heard louder ovations, but none as heartfelt as this one. They cheer us like stars, they touch us like lucky stones.

Part of me wants to bow, to soak up the celebration. To enjoy the moment while it lasts. The rest of me feels like a fake—or a traitor. Leo had been the one to defeat the avions; I had only been the one to save Leo. If they knew that I had stopped Le Trépas from killing all the Aquitans and failed to capture his soul, would the rebels still sing my praises?

Then I see the look on Cheeky's face, the question in her eyes, and I push through the crowd to give her the best answer I have. "He went after Pique. Don't worry," I add, trying to follow my own instructions. "He won."

All around us, a murmur ripples through the crowd: Pique, dead. But Cheeky is scanning the area hopefully, as though she might have missed Akra the first time. "Where is he?"

"He's on his way," I say, wanting it to be true. Can she sense my uncertainty? She only nods, pasting on her best smile. Then Leo opens his arms, and she falls into them with a sob of relief. Her tears make my own eyes sting, but I take a deep breath, struggling for control. If I let it loose now, the emotion would overwhelm me.

Instead, I turn away, catching sight of the Tiger and Theodora. They stand side by side, their shoulders touching, their faces somber. "What happened down there?" Cam says as I approach.

"The armée was unprepared against the dragon," I say. "Especially with the avions grounded."

"And how did you manage that?" Theodora says, but by the look in her eyes, I can tell she fears the answer.

Still, I hesitate. Is it mine to give? But better me than Leo, especially now, while the pain is so raw for the both of them. "Xavier is dead," I say, and her breath catches like I'd punched her.

"I could have talked to him." Her voice shakes, and I can't tell if it's with grief or anger. "Why didn't you let me talk to him?"

"I tried that," Leo says, coming up behind me. "He wouldn't listen."

Theodora's eyes go wide as she turns to her brother. "*You* killed him?" Leo doesn't answer. He doesn't need to.

Her face goes blank, then pale. She takes a deep breath, and another, but the third hitches in her throat. "Excuse me," she says then, before turning on her heel and walking back into the sanctuary.

Beside me, Leo sags; this time, it's my turn to steady him. Camreon's jaw tightens. "What about Le Trépas?" he says.

"I had to stop him," I say, trying to explain. "He wanted all the Aquitans dead. Leo, La Fleur—"

"Not just the Aquitans," Cam says; when I frown, he elaborates. "I found Raik's body in the mine. We'll leave it there until we can hold a proper funeral. As for Le Trépas's corpse, the jungle can take care of it."

There is anger on his face, but it doesn't hide the pain. I am reluctant to add to the burden. "I'm more worried about his soul," I say carefully, glancing at the glow in the banyan grove behind him. Would Le Trépas's soul come to the temple? Would it come after me and try to creep into my skin? Will other souls warn me of its approach by fleeing as they did when he was alive? What will happen when it's finally reborn?

Camreon only gives me a grim look. "If you see it, feel free to raise the alarm. For now, I need your help."

I blink at him, more exhausted than surprised. "What for?"

"We need to send notes to the evacuees, telling them it's safe to return. Then we'll go down to the valley. I want those avions—"

"She needs to rest first," Leo says, though he looks even more tired than I feel. "Besides, there are still troops down there. It isn't safe until we have an official surrender."

The thought of a bed is enticing, but I shake my head. "My brother is in the valley."

Cam cocks his head. "As soon as we have people to spare, I'll organize the search."

With a sigh, I nod. "I'll help you with those letters."

Letting Leo go on without me, I follow Camreon into the temple. Under the dense green canopy, I find another audience, this one more somber. The souls of the dead from the valley—some gold, some blue. Thankfully, none of them follow as the Tiger leads me to the dining hall.

Here, a small group of rebels is already at work with pen and ink. I take a stack of letters and pluck the souls of songbirds from the branches overhead. But as the first few notes wing away through the canopy, the souls of the n'akela drift closer. I set the stack aside, half finished, and press my hands against a kerchief till the bleeding stops.

While I wait for the n'akela to lose interest, I beg a scrap of paper and a pen off a young rebel. They massage their hand while I write my own note addressed to Maman and Papa.

I am safe. He is dead. I'll see you soon.

Handing the pen back, I make one last mark and send the note off with a special prayer. Should I have sent another to find Akra? No . . . word will come faster if it travels directly. Cradling my battered hands, I walk back to Cheeky's room whispering his name. But the only answer is the gentle wind in the leaves.

I let myself into the room quietly. Leo is there, but he is not sleeping. He sits cross-legged on the floor, holding the medallion in his hands. I hesitate in the doorway, but he doesn't look up. So I close the door softly behind me and sit down beside him. "I'm sorry, Leo."

"Me too." The silence stretches. He rubs his thumb over the medallion. "Before Xavi died, he wondered where he would go. His soul, I mean. He wanted to know if he might make it all the way to the cathedral at Lephare."

I open my mouth to answer the question he didn't quite ask, but I hesitate. If it were Theodora, I know she'd want the truth—that the temple of the Maiden is full of akela after the fight, and most of those souls are Aquitans. Why would Xavier's soul be different? But for Leo, the story has always been more important. "I think you could at least bring something of the cathedral here."

Leo frowns. "What do you mean?"

Standing, I go to the nest of pillows where I'd been sleeping. His violin case is still beside them. "You played a hymn the other night," I say softly. "While we were on the ship. Isn't that an Aquitan song?"

"It is." Leo runs a hand over the case, but his eyes are on the temple walls—the braided roots, the shivering leaves where the souls hide. "Do you think the gods will be offended to hear it?"

"No," I say, but it takes him a moment to open the case. He tucks the medallion inside before he lifts out the violin. I lie down in the soft silk pillows beside him as he puts the instrument to his chin, and the souls and I listen while he plays.

The sky is dark when a knock wakes us both. I sit up beside Leo, my mouth dry, my head half in a dream. "Come in," Leo mumbles, but when the door opens, it's only Tia. I'm about to lie back down when I see the look on her face.

"They found Akra," she says, and I scramble to my feet.

"Take me to him."

Leo catches up to us halfway down the hall. Together, we follow Tia into a smaller room, and when I walk through the door, I gasp.

The pallet where my brother lies is red with blood—his clothes are stiff with the stuff. Memories burst through my mind: blood on the stone floor of Hell's Court . . . my brother's slack face. But he is not dead. Leo catches me as I sway, and Akra opens one bleary eye. "I told you I couldn't let him escape," he rasps.

"Shhh," Cheeky says. Kneeling beside him, she squeezes bloody water from a wet cloth, then dips it in a fresh bowl. Gently, she cleans his brow. Her fine dress is stained scarlet, but she doesn't seem to notice.

Someone taps me on the shoulder and I startle, but it is only Camreon. He jerks his chin toward the corner, and we step away from the others.

"My searchers found him and Pique," Cam says quietly. "The lieutenant is definitely dead. Akra will survive, of course. The docteur is on the way to remove the bullets. The problem is . . . he mentioned something strange."

The tone of his voice chills me—there is a warning in it. "What?"

"Pique was carrying what's left of the jar of your blood," Cam says. "But a soldier escaped with it after Pique was shot."

Air hisses through my teeth. "Can we track him down? Take it back?"

Beside me, Leo laughs darkly. "We're not that lucky, Jetta."

Camreon's look is confirmation. "One of my lookouts has just reported seeing an avion take flight," he says grimly. "I don't think the soldier is going by foot."

I swear softly . . . but not softly enough. Cheeky turns, glaring at me. Does she think a curse can hurt my brother? The thought makes me want to laugh—or is that only hysteria? I don't know; my thoughts are scattered. Cam's voice pulls me back to the present.

"I have men going back to guard the avions now," he says, glancing down at my hands, bruised and bloody. "It would help if you could ensoul them as soon as possible."

"Of course," I say, distracted, but Leo is frowning at me.

"How are you?" he says then, and by his tone, I know

what he's asking. My hand goes to my satchel—no. To the place where my satchel had been.

"I don't know," I say truthfully. "I don't remember when my last dose was."

"You're out of elixir?" The Tiger chews his lip. "We'll make it a priority right after the coronation."

"Coronation?" But of course; the Boy King is dead. "When is that?"

"After the funeral," he says tersely. He hides the pain well. Then something softens around his eyes. "And just before the wedding."

I try to smile—it should be a happy occasion. But Leo's pain is clear on his face . . . will his sister even want him there? As for me, it's hard to let go of the dread I feel. How much of my blood is left in that jar? I give my brother one last look as Cheeky dabs at his scarred face. "Let's go take care of the avions," I say to Camreon.

Rather than walk down the hillside, I lead the others out to the pond and whisper to my dragon. She rises from the water like mist, her long teeth shining in the thin moonlight. "In case there are still any soldiers around," I say, and the Tiger gives me his own toothy smile before we climb on.

But as we rise above the trees, his grin drops away. In the valley below, a fire rages. We don't have to get much closer before we can see it is the avions.

After the act of sabotage, the rebel camp is on alert, but the culprit is already halfway back to Nokhor Khat, or wherever the soldier is going. And the damage is already done: Theodora's accelerant is powerful stuff. By the time the fire burns out, the graceful avions have melted into ugly lumps of slag.

We don't have the manpower to move them. Instead, Camreon organizes groups to clear the village of bodies, stripping their weapons and stacking them for burning before the villagers return. For his brother, he orders a coffin built. The rebels look at him askance: burial is a city custom, imported from Aquitan. But Cam only shrugs. "Raik would have wanted it," he says.

The wooden coffin only takes two days to finish, but when the rebels carry it down to the mine, they discover the Boy King's body has gone missing.

When the news reaches me, I go straight to Camreon. He is at an ornate desk in his brother's old rooms, reviewing a list. "The avion," I say, out of breath, but not from running.

"The one that left. Did your lookouts notice how many people were in it?"

"No," he says grimly. "I already asked."

"Are there other bodies missing?" I ask him, and he tips the paper toward me with a grimace.

"I watched Pique burn myself," he says. "But the general's body is gone, too. I still have people searching for Le Trépas."

There is a knot in my belly. I don't bother offering to help search. When the message arrives that afternoon, it confirms my suspicions.

The note comes winging through the open ceiling of the dining hall, like the ones we'd sent off to the rebels just days before. But though this letter has my blood on the corner, I'm not the one who put it there.

No wonder Le Trépas did not fear death. He had another life waiting in the wings.

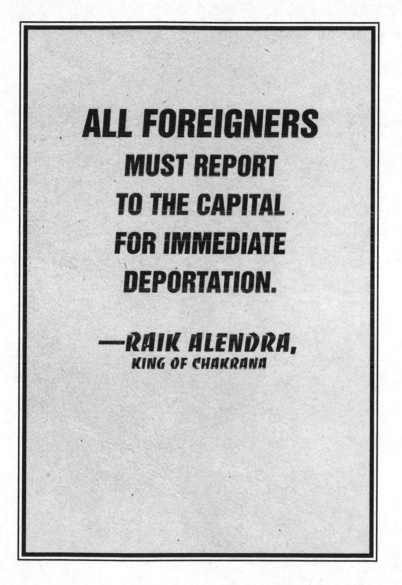

AUTHOR'S NOTE

I have taken liberties.

It seems like a strange confession. After all, this is obviously a work of fiction. But while fantasy is often set in opposition to reality, I have always seen history as the animus of any story I want to tell.

So while readers will see references to real-life things like French colonialism, bipolar disorder, and the chemical volatility of lithium, they will also note a fast and loose approach to specifics like language, the general dates of scientific discoveries, and the exact recipe for a jam-tin grenade. The book is also shot through with personal (and thus subjective) experience, including commentary on my own experience of being mixed-race, or the side effects of suddenly stopping mood-stabilizing drugs. There is also a heavy dose of pure fabrication in the culture, language, and religions referenced.

I'd like to claim there is a method to this madness, but it comes down to the speech from Shakespeare's *Henry V*, from which I found the titles for each book in this trilogy. I am invoking the muse of fire: the imagination. Because facts aside, we've all dreamed of using our art to strike back against a violent oppressor . . . haven't we?

ACKNOWLEDGMENTS

Writing a book—especially the second in a series—can be like taking an epic hike through a near-impenetrable jungle. My editor, Martha Mihalick, has always been an excellent path-breaker, though she wields her pencil much more delicately than a machete. Molly Ker Hawn, my agent, is the sort of companion you need on such a trek: one who keeps you from getting turned around or eaten alive by metaphorical mosquitoes.

My friend Mike Pettry, who wrote the music featured in the book, would be the one who brought his guitar to keep everyone's spirits up. Thank you, Mike.

After the hypothetical hike, designer Sylvie Le Floc'h is the one who makes it look so gorgeous that everyone else wishes they'd been along for the journey. Tim Smith's detailed editing always ensures that no one guesses how many bugs there were on the way. Of course, if Haley George or Sam Benson, master publicists, had organized this hike, it would have been a lot smoother and more fun in the first place (and we'd have stopped by a lot more bookstores).

Speaking of bookstores, a special thanks to the Indies—particularly East City Bookshop, One More Page Books, Oblong Books & Music, and Books of Wonder—you are beacons of civilization after a long time in the writing wilderness. Booksellers Cecilia Cackley, Nicole Brinkley, and Shauna Morgan, you have a special place in my heart. Thank you for your support.

To my boys—Bret, Felix, and Hansen—thank you for making the trek with me. It's always an adventure, wherever we go.